BLACK LIGHT: SUSPICION

MEASHA STONE

Black Light: Suspicion
by Measha Stone

Published by Black Collar Press
Don't miss a release! Sign-up for our newsletter here!

EBook ISBN: **978-1-947559-97-4**
Print ISBN: **978-1-947559-97-4**

Cover Art by Eris Adderly, http://erisadderly.com/

BLACK LIGHT: SUSPICION
BY
MEASHA STONE

BLURB

"I have my own suspicions about you, Sophie."

Sophie Nelson knows her kinky interests are no more than fantasy, definitely not something that'll ever happen in the real world. So the sexual playground Black Light is the best place to turn. A safe place to play. Until Scott.

Detective Scott Russo knows better than to get sexually involved with his partner. Mixing business with pleasure never ends well, but sometimes rules are meant to be broken. He can't avoid the temptation of giving Sophie exactly what she needs, even if that means a firm hand.

While Sophie and Scott find themselves mired in a high-stakes investigation, their off-duty kinky explorations intensify. With danger at the door, and complications that threaten to tear them apart, can they survive the tug of war.

CHAPTER 1

*F*ate could be a cruel fucking bitch.

Detective Scott Russo stared across his desk to where his newest partner sat clicking away on her computer. Her long hair was twisted into a high and tight bun, meant to keep it from being a danger when they worked cases on the street. To him, he could easily use it to grab in his fist and pull her head back and get her mouth lined up to meet his.

Or to get those pouty lips to start telling him why she hadn't taken a bite of the chicken sandwich she'd ordered from the takeout cart down the street.

"You gonna stare at me working, or you gonna actually jump in and help?" Sophie smiled at her computer screen.

They'd finished a case, thankfully rather easy and not too gruesome. Working homicide didn't exactly make for cheerful conversation most shifts, but Sophie's easy banter made the days less horrific. Since she'd started, he found himself less unwilling to get his ass to work every day.

"I finished mine already," he said, leaning back in his chair. "You can take a break you know. Your sandwich's been sitting there for a while. Probably cold by now."

She stopped typing and glanced at the unwrapped sandwich sitting center stage on her desk. Not once in the short time they'd been partnered up had she skipped a meal. Not even after working a crime scene that could have been taken right out of a Freddy Krueger flick.

Sophie had a few more curves than most female officers in the precinct, but unlike other women he knew, it didn't seem to bother her. So her staring at the sandwich, with her tongue running along her lower lip, and then shaking her head and going back to her report didn't sit well.

"I'm good. After I finish this," she said, her gaze sweeping over his face, but never landing on him.

He didn't push the issue, but he really wanted to. He wanted to yank her from her chair and demand full honesty, but this wasn't that sort of partnership. This was only work.

"Sophie, you seem distracted today? Got a new boyfriend causing trouble?" Okay, he was fishing, but he didn't care. The idea of her going home at night and meeting someone for dinner made his spine tingle. He had no right to lay claim to her. They were partners, friends, and he doubted she would submit to his type of relationship, yet he still needed to probe.

She reached over the desk for a file. "No, I don't have a boyfriend." She opened the file and flipped through until she found what she must have been looking for and pulled out the sheet of paper.

"Ah, hard to find Prince Charming in this city, right?" He pressed, pulling himself closer to the desk. His erection wouldn't be easy to miss if anyone walked past, and damned if he'd let her see how much of an effect she had on him.

"Not every girl wants Prince Charming," she muttered more to herself than to him and turned back to her computer.

"No, I suppose not." The last time he'd heard a girl say something along that line, she'd been negotiating a hard flogging scene with him at Black Light.

"But yeah, it's definitely hard to find what I want in this city-or any other city." She cast a short glance at him then straightened her back and dove into her report again.

Scott learned long ago not to play in the vanilla world. If a girl wasn't into submission, he wouldn't be the one to introduce the topic. But he couldn't get an accurate read on Sophie. One second she could look at him with the softness he loved in a sub, and the next it was gone.

Aside from the fact she had more beauty in her little toe than that last dozen women he'd taken out, she had the brains and the confidence to go along with it.

"Russo! I need you a second." Captain Peterson called from his office door.

He discreetly adjusted his hard on in his jeans and threw on his jacket to hopefully help hide it more before he stood up.

"Better go." Sophie smiled, peeking at him from around her screen. "Don't want to earn a spanking, "she teased. Her cheeks bloomed pink right before his eyes.

Fuck.

Yeah. Fate was a cruel bitch.

CHAPTER 2

*D*id people get food poisoning from bottled water?

Sophie Nelson rubbed her stomach as she inched her way through the crush of the crowd. She'd traded in her daily meals for large bottles of water in anticipation of the evening's events. Knowing nerves would finally show their ugly head at exactly the wrong moment, she wasn't taking any chances on getting sick because of them.

Except, her stomach still twisted and turned, though she was pretty sure she'd be able to hold it together. She had waited too long to finally go for it—no way she was letting a little nervousness get in her way.

A quarter of DC showed up at Black Light for the Valentine Roulette. Or rather it just felt that way with everyone crowding around, waiting for the event to begin.

She'd joined the club only a month ago, so it seemed like the perfect way to start down this new path of hers. Go to the party, get paired with someone, and fall to her knees in servitude. Of course, she knew it didn't really happen that way, but a girl could dream.

Even though she'd become a member, she hadn't actually set

foot in the club until the night of the roulette game. She considered the wasted money a down payment on her future bliss.

If this worked and she actually met someone.

She made her way to the bar and ordered another water. A bourbon straight sounded better, but on an empty stomach it was like lighting a match near an open gas line. She'd never make it back to work in the morning.

"Sophie?" a deep voice, a familiar voice, a spine-tingling familiar voice, called her name from behind her.

Placing the bottle of water back on the bar, she pushed on a smile and turned around.

Fuck.

"Scott! Hi." She forced lightness, while her toes scrunched up in her flats.

"What are you doing here?" He maneuvered through a small group of women and stopped right in front of her.

The odds of her new partner showing up at the same BDSM club, at the same event on the same night as her? Shouldn't it have been an impossibility?

Her face heated, but with the dark ambiance and the neon lighting, she could find some comfort in that he probably couldn't see how deep her blush burned.

"Same as you, probably." She gripped the end of the bar, pushing the edge into her palm.

"By yourself?" he asked, looking behind her and around.

"I didn't think this was really a plus one event." She tilted her head and bit down on her lower lip.

He took half a step back and ran his gaze over her. The ground could open up any time now to swallow her up. She'd gone with a pair of black leggings, a white tunic, and a thick black belt to accentuate her waist. His stare paused but didn't linger where she'd left the top two buttons of the low neckline unbuttoned, showcasing cleavage but more importantly the purple lace bralette she'd picked up for the evening.

"You're rolling?" he asked with a furrowed brow. He'd shaved. He must have gone home after their shift; his beard was trimmed, his hair neater, and styled. The sandy blond hair paired beautifully with his light brown eyes.

She cleared her throat to pull herself out of her trance. "Yes. Of course… Are you?" What could be more awkward?

He laughed. "Yeah. What are the odds, huh?" He leaned one elbow against the bar, regarding her with a relaxed smile that tore right through her.

After her move from the second district to the third within the Metropolitan Police Department, she'd been paired with Scott. As a partner, he was efficient, smart, and completely easy to work with. They'd already managed to get two closed cases under their belts. And while on duty, when she had the badge strapped to her belt, she could forget how handsome he was, how enticing his rock-hard body could be. She forced her libido to chill out. But now, with his casual smile distracting her and those tattoos of his she hadn't seen before peaking out at her from beneath his black t-shirt—she couldn't function.

"You okay?" he asked, placing his hand on hers.

"What? Yeah. Of course." She pulled away, his touch too warm, too tingling. Her head spun, a little tilt at first, but then it really took a nose dive, and she latched onto his arm to keep from falling over.

"You sure?" His eyebrows knitted together.

Blinking a few times and grabbing a few more sips of her water, she nodded. "Yep. Just got a little lightheaded. Must be all the people. It's really crowded in here tonight." She turned, pushing her back against the bar, wishing it had more of a bite. The rounded edges didn't do much for a distraction.

"How long have you been a member?" He angled his head. She knew that look. He'd given the same one to the suspect they'd questioned in an armed robbery case last week. Cool tone, but serious eyes. He was fishing.

"Recently enrolled. Really hoping for the free month though, right?" She laughed then cleared her throat again. When the hell were they going to get the party started?

"Uh, huh. So, you've been here, how many times exactly?" He took the water bottle from her hands when the plastic crinkled.

"What about you, new or veteran member?" Turn the questions on to him and maybe he'd drop it. She didn't need to explain her complete lack of experience. It was nerve-racking enough being a complete newb in the presence of so many people who appeared every bit like they belonged there. A neon light over her head alerting everyone how virginal she was in their realm would only make her nerves heighten.

Her stomach swirled, and she swallowed. The lightheadedness from a moment ago increased. The crowd moved forward, closer to the stage.

"Looks like they're starting." She pointed and moved along with the crowd. Scott followed, standing behind her.

Another couple appeared beside him, talking with each other. The low murmur in the room rose in volume. Chattering, laughing, a squeal from a microphone. She touched her forehead to steady her mind.

She was actually going to go through with it. She was going to be paired up with a man, who would spend the next three hours dominating her. Finally, she'd know what it was like. All the fantasizing, all the horrible attempts with previous boyfriends who placated her would finally be worth something. Those experiences brought her to where she stood.

What if she couldn't do it? What happened if she rolled the roulette wheel and landed on an activity that sounded perfectly hot when she'd filled out the application for the evening's game, but once in the middle of it, she needed to cry red? She wouldn't only be blowing her own chance at a free month's membership, but her partner's as well. It would be her fault. He'd hate her. He'd tell everyone in the club how much of a pussy she was, and she'd never find anyone. She'd be stuck in the vanilla world forever.

Her chest constricted. Air became harder to take in as the crowd moved again, closer. Too close to her. She tried to turn to her side, to give her chest more room to expand. Nothing. Maybe it was the bralette; maybe she had it too tight.

"This was a bad idea," she muttered to herself. Scott moved behind her. She could feel him shift from one foot to the other.

Again, her mind lurched, spinning off its axis. She needed air. She needed to get a grip.

"I have to go. I-I don't think I can do this," she said and turned to push her way out of the crowd. Instead of taking a step, she fell into darkness.

He glared at her.

When Sophie opened her eyes, the dim lighting didn't hide his hard stare. Scott sat beside the medical cot she lay on, leaning over her with a fierce frown planted on his face.

"You're awake," he said, although it sounded more like an accusation.

Of course, she was awake. Her eyes were open, weren't they?

"Hey." She smiled, pushing her hands against the cot and trying to get up.

"No." He shook his head and pushed against her shoulder, putting her right back down. "Not until Garreth examines you again and tells me you're okay."

"Can't I tell you I'm okay?" She pressed the heels of her palms to her eyes. She'd fainted. Fuck. She hadn't fainted since high school. Her head fogged up, and a headache wasn't too far off.

"No, but you can tell me what you ate today." No more lighthearted questions.

She sighed. "Nothing. I ate nothing. Which is probably what made my blood sugar drop and made me faint." No sense in lying. "Why are you here? You should be out there." She jerked a finger at the door. "They're going to start soon."

"They already did." He sat back in his chair, folding his arms over his chest.

"Oh." She closed her eyes again. She'd ruined her night, and his. No wonder he was pissed.

"You didn't need to stay with me. I'm fine."

"Hey, you're up. Good. How do you feel?" Garreth walked up to her with an open bottle of water and some sugar cookies.

"Like an idiot." She swung her legs over the side of the bed and sat up. Scott didn't move from his position, so she had to scoot down to make room for herself. "I'm really sorry."

"Not a problem. It happens. Nerves are normal when you're trying new kinks for the first time. And tonight is a big event." Garreth handed her the cookies. "As long as you're doing okay, I'm going back to the floor. There's a medical scene I want to be near tonight."

"Yeah. I'm fine. A few cookies, and I'll be good to go."

Garreth studied her. "Okay. If you need anything, Scott can come get me." He slapped Scott on his back.

"Will do," Scott answered, but continued to grind his glare into Sophie as she nibbled on her cookies.

"Okay, then," Garreth said and left.

"Don't look at me like that." She pointed a finger at him and shoved the last cookie into her mouth. The buttery, sugary crumbles melted on her tongue. Her stomach growled.

"Like what?"

"Like I'm the asshole sitting across the table from you in an interrogation room. So, I'm a new member, never been here before. I was nervous, so I didn't eat today. And now I've ruined my night, and yours. I'm sorrier about ruining yours." Her shoulders drooped. Humiliation could be handled but tanking someone else's fun just plain sucked.

She focused her attention on the bottle of water in her hands. He should be saying something. Anything would be good. The silence stretching out made her ears throb.

"Did you drive?" he asked after a heavy sigh.

"No. I cabbed it. Wasn't sure if I'd be—" She stopped herself from finishing her sentence. She wasn't about to tell her partner, her very hot partner, that she'd hoped to go home with someone that night.

Ugh. What a whore she'd sound like. She capped the water and placed it on a nearby table.

"I'll drive you." He stood from his chair and offered his hand to help her up.

"You don't have to do that," she argued. "Maybe you can still get a partner? Maybe they'll still let you roll? Or someone from the audience will want to join and take my place?"

He shook his head and wrapped his hand around hers when she didn't take his offer.

"I'm getting you a burger then taking you home and putting you to bed."

She didn't put up a fight when he pulled her to her feet. He didn't back up, either, making her breasts brush against his chest. She didn't match him in height, but he didn't dwarf her either. She stared at his chin in silence. He'd never been so close to her before, although they'd shared a car since being paired up.

Hell, he smelled good. Like musk and leather.

"A burger sounds perfect."

"Let's go." He laced his fingers with hers and pulled her along. "Before I change my mind and give you the ass whipping you deserve."

She heard him, but it had been said so soft, without a glance in her direction, she figured it hadn't been meant for her ears.

CHAPTER 3

*S*cott bit into his apple.

She was late.

Sophie was never late.

He checked his phone again to see if she'd left a message. Maybe she wasn't feeling well. She'd eaten her burger and appeared much better when he had dropped her at home afterward.

Better? No. She'd looked fucking angelic, all curled up in her bed, her comforter pulled up to her chin as though he hadn't already seen the voluptuous curves of her body with her outfit at Black Light. That purple lace thing she'd worn had his blood pressure up. Holy hell, she had a body that needed touching and pinching and licking, and biting and fucking.

He took another bite. Thoughts like that weren't going to help him through their shift. No matter how attracted he found himself, they were partners. They would solve whatever case came their way, do their paperwork, and head home to their own apartments.

At first, she hadn't wanted him to take her upstairs, but he wasn't leaving until he knew she'd eaten and was safe in bed. The deep-red blush that had crept onto her cheeks had proven what he already knew. She didn't mind being told what to do. At least when it came to being taken care of. He'd seen her in action in the field.

When a uniformed officer tried to step on her toes, or anyone got in the way of her getting the answers she wanted—she shouldn't be trifled with. It made being her partner all the more fun and satisfying. Being able to trust his partner had his back and took the job as seriously as he did made every case seem easy.

He took another bite. Where the fuck was she?

Even if she was a little embarrassed over the previous night, she wouldn't let that stop her from coming in. What if she'd fainted again? Or worse…and he'd left her all alone.

Tossing his apple core into the trash, he snagged his phone. If she wasn't going to return his text or answer his call, he'd just go to her apartment.

"Russo!" Captain Peterson called from the doorway of his office. "Got a call. A woman's been found dead in her apartment. Forensics is headed over there now. Sophie's on her way there, too."

"Do we know anything yet?"

"Only that she's dead. Single gunshot to the head. Here's the address."

Scott took the scrap of paper with the address scribbled on it and grabbed his jacket. The scene wasn't far, maybe a ten-minute drive. Easy to do in the middle of the morning.

Why hadn't she come straight to the precinct, though? He'd have his answers soon enough.

He parked behind her sedan in the parking lot of the apartment building. The forensic team arrived at the same time as him, and they all walked up to the apartment on the third floor together.

Inside was a gruesome sight. Unfortunately, one he'd seen too many times before. The victim was already being removed from the scene, and Scott stayed out of the way as they wheeled the body from the room. They'd have to meet with the medical examiner once he finished his evaluation.

Blood splatter and tissue covered the living room floor, just to the side of an overturned chair. Everything in the apartment appeared too expensive to touch. The chair was no different, other than it seemed to belong to the dining set, not from the living room furniture.

"Hey," Sophie greeted him with her usual smile and nod. With her pad in her hand and pen poised, ready to jot down her findings, she appeared as though this were any other day.

"Hi," he responded. The forensics team walked around them, cameras flashed from photographs being taken. It wasn't exactly the place to discuss the previous evening.

"So, from what the coroner, said, it appears at first sight to be a suicide. Gunshot to her temple. The gun was found here." She aimed the tip of her pen at the floor. "She was sitting there. And the splatter is on the other side."

He watched her examine the initial scene, her mind working, while she nibbled the inside of her right cheek. She'd pulled her thick, long, soft red hair back into a ponytail at the base of her neck and swapped out the white tunic with the low V-neck for her usual blue button-down blouse and black trousers, topped off with black and white running shoes. Everything appeared to be back to normal, but nothing was the same.

"You sound doubtful." Scott grabbed a pair of latex gloves and snapped them on.

"I think it's too early to call it that." She shrugged. "Look." She pointed at the video camera situated on a tripod and aimed at the chair. "She videotaped it?"

"Most people just leave a note," Scott said. "Do we have a time of death?" he asked, while she inspected the camera.

"No, not yet. I have a few units asking the neighbors if they heard anything. Most of the apartments are empty, though. It's late enough, they're probably at work." She turned the camera to the side.

"Who found her?" he asked

Sophie gestured toward the woman sitting at the dining room table in the next room. "The maid showed up and found her boss on the floor there, half her head blown out." Sophie sighed and went back to checking out the camera. "The battery's dead. I can't play the video. We'll have to watch it back at the precinct. Hopefully the battery didn't die before everything was captured." She waved a young guy from the forensics team over and bagged up the camera.

"I supposed in a building like this, there might be more privacy walls than in an ordinary building?" Scott evaluated the apartment. "I don't see pictures of a family, or any pictures at all."

"Yeah, you're right." She scanned the apartment. "We'll have to talk with the maid once they're done taking the initial statement."

Scott walked around the apartment, taking notes and considering what evidence he could find. Nothing appeared out of place or stolen. The front door hadn't been kicked in or tampered with. Other than the chair being tipped over, most likely from the force of the gunshot, no furniture was out of place.

"So, you sleep okay?" He eased into the conversation while jotting down an observation. Sophie, standing beside him, tensed with his question.

"Yeah. Why?"

"You were late this morning." He shrugged.

"I wasn't late. I was here."

He huffed a laugh. "You were late."

She paused in her surveillance of the scene and glanced up at him. Her dark brown eyes held him captive. Other than a thin layer of mascara on her lashes, she hadn't bothered with makeup. She never did. And she didn't need it.

"I overslept a little."

"So, you weren't trying to avoid me?" he asked, stepping over a spot of blood and heading to the windows. Shimmering gold window treatments kept out any sunlight. No chance of someone having seen anything from the neighboring buildings.

"Avoid you?" She laughed. It was forced. She swept her gaze away from him. "How would I do that when we're partners? Besides, there's no reason to hide from you. We saw each other at a club. No big deal." She took a large step away from him and focused on the coffee table.

"We're just not gonna talk about last night at all, then? Just two people running into each other?" He stuffed his notebook into the inside pocket of his jacket.

"What's there to talk about?" She shrugged.

He made his way to her side. The other cops in the room didn't need to hear what they had to say. "What? How about how you starved yourself all day yesterday? How about when I asked you if you were a new member you lied?" He kept his voice down, but he kept it firm.

Her throat worked as she swallowed whatever response she was working up to giving him. They were in too public a place to have this conversation.

"We can talk at lunch if you really think it's needed." She peered over his shoulder at the two uniformed officers watching them from the front door.

It was going to be a very interesting lunch. "I'll go talk with them. Why don't you try to get something out of the maid?"

"Got it." She paused for a moment, taking in a deep breath—like she needed to prepare herself for the conversation with the upset employee. Interviewing witnesses, and friends of the victim didn't usually unsettle her. Maybe it was him.

He waited until she'd introduced herself to the woman before engaging the officers at the door. The nervous, shocked-looking maid softened her expression after only a moment of talking with Sophie.

She had that way about her. Making everyone around her comfortable, like she'd known them forever.

Lunch was going to be difficult to navigate. She knew how to evade questions, and she seemed a little reluctant to admitting anything had transpired between them last night.

But he knew it had. He'd never felt such an intense compulsion to protect someone as he had with her. When her eyes had rolled back, and she'd fainted, his heart stopped. He'd gone into action without thinking about the roulette game or his friends who had been with him. All that mattered was making sure she was okay.

When he figured out her lack of eating had caused it, her neglect and her lie about being a new member to the club, his concern waned to irritation. If she were his, really his girl, he would have spanked her supple ass right there in the medic room then taken her home to finish the punishment with his belt.

But instead, she'd gotten a cheeseburger and a good-night kiss. On her forehead. Though she had been asleep by then and probably didn't even know he'd dropped the kiss there.

Lunch would be tricky, but she would answer his questions. They'd get to know each other a little more, and if he had any way of convincing her, maybe she'd agree to seeing him for dinner, too.

CHAPTER 4

*S*ophie pulled her car into the burger joint a few blocks from the precinct. Scott parked beside her.

He was going to have questions. He'd want answers. She took a deep breath. Why she'd gone to Black Light was none of his business. She'd just let him know they needed to keep their relationship professional, and anything he may have thought happened the night before didn't. And couldn't. And wouldn't.

A knuckle wrapping on her window startled her. She pushed the door open and gave him a glare. "You didn't need to scare me."

"Scare you?" he laughed. "What, seeing me park and walk over to you? Yep, I'm a real first-class ninja."

Point—Scott.

"Let's just get our food." She maneuvered around him and went for the door. He reached it first, pulling it open for her and letting her go first. She grumbled a thank you.

He picked an empty booth in the far corner of the diner. There would be no getting out of his questions. She would just need to be precise, direct, and truthful. Scott had the best nose for deceit she'd seen in a detective in a long time.

She shimmied into the booth across from him and pulled the

menu from behind the sugar container. There was no reason to even skim it. She was getting a burger. And a Coke. She'd go for a longer walk before bed tonight to make up for it.

Feeling watched, she peeked over the menu. Caramel-brown eyes stared at her. She put the menu down and folded her hands on top of it.

"Already know what you want?" she asked with forced levity. Lunch with him had never been awkward. He was making it weird.

"Yeah. I do," he answered. But not in the *yep, gonna have the mushroom burger* sort of way. This had a deep undertone. He hadn't smiled when he said it, either, and his eyes narrowed just a hair. No, he wasn't talking about lunch.

She fisted her right hand, digging her nails into her palm. Making more of things than what they were or what they could be would only end in heartache. For both of them. Or one of them. Her. She would be the heartbroken one, and he'd be bouncing off to the next woman. A hot woman. Like one of those women she saw at the club. The ones she couldn't go shopping at the same stores with because her hips were more generous in the curve and her tummy just as much.

Sophie didn't have a hang-up about her weight or her curvy body. It had taken a long time to love the body she was in, but she did. It was hers, and she wouldn't justify herself to anyone. That didn't mean she lived in a fantasy world, though.

"Hi. I'm Sandra, and I'll be your waitress this afternoon. Is there anything I can get you started with?" The usual beginning to a dining experience.

Scott turned his typical charming smile on the waitress, who couldn't have been a day younger than sixty-five. "I think we're ready." He gestured at Sophie to put her order in.

"I'll have the cheeseburger, medium rare, with a side salad, please. Oh, and a cherry Coke." She tucked the menu back in place while the waitress scribbled on her pad.

"Dressing?"

"Ranch." As though there were another dressing worthy of touching a salad.

"I'll have the same, except I'll have fries instead of the salad."

A few more scribbles and waitress Sandra was gone.

"I didn't get very far with the maid," Sophie said.

"No."

"What?" She met his eyes. He shook his head.

"No. Work stays at work. We're not working, now. It's just us, and we need to talk." He jammed a finger into the tabletop.

She grabbed a straw from the dispenser and peeled the wrapper off. "Fine. Talk." She slowly ripped the paper.

"How are you feeling, really?" He flattened his hands over one of hers.

"I'm fine, Scott. I told you it was just nerves."

"You didn't eat all day."

She sighed and pulled her hand from beneath his. Who could think with the electric current he sent up her arm?

"I was nervous about going to the party. And sometimes when I get nervous, I get an upset stomach. I was trying to avoid that, so I didn't eat. But I ate the burger you bought me, and I had breakfast this morning. I'm not a person who starves herself." She leaned back in the booth and waved a hand over her body. "As you can see."

He narrowed his eyes and stared at her silently, tapping the tabletop. As though his internal lie detector was calculating her response.

"Don't talk like that." He pointed a finger at her.

"Like what? I'm not being negative, I'm being honest. Telling a girl she's not curvy when she full on is—makes no damn sense. If there's no problem with a girl being a bit bigger than normal, then admitting it shouldn't be a problem, right?"

His eyes widened a fraction. "Yes. You're right, but that's not what I meant. I meant your tone."

"My tone?"

"Yes. You have a tone when you're about to get bitchy." He leaned back when Sandra brought their drinks, letting her slide their cherry Cokes in front of them and take her leave.

"I'm not getting bitchy." She stabbed her straw into her drink.

"No, not at all," he said with a sterner lilt to his voice. "Okay, so you were nervous."

"That's what I said, yes."

"Fair enough," he conceded and took a sip of his soda.

Tension left her muscles. Lifting her drink, she did the same.

"That takes us to the lying." He pushed his soda to the side and leaned over the table. "You told me you'd been a member for a little while. Which technically was true, but Garreth told me you haven't actually been to the club since your membership was approved."

"What happened to the whole confidentiality agreement thing?" Black Light was the most exclusive and most private club in the D.C. area, which was one of the reasons she sought a membership. No matter it was going to eat into her bank account every month.

"Garreth thought I already knew. Don't avoid the topic."

"I did sign up a few months ago, when I first moved to the neighborhood, but last night was the first time I actually went."

Sandra, thank her beautiful wrinkled face, arrived with their food. Sophie pushed the burger to the side and pulled her salad in front of her. The burger wouldn't have so much of an impact if she had her veggies first.

"Why?"

"Why what?" She pulled off the little paper wrapper holding her napkin and silverware hostage and pulled out the knife.

"Why were you so nervous? New to the scene or just here in D.C.?" He plucked a fry and tossed it in his mouth.

"You're not going to let me just eat my burger in peace, are you?" she asked.

"Nope."

"I'll tell you but then we can't talk about it anymore, okay?" Couldn't he see the land mines he was walking them toward with all his questions?

"Why not?"

She growled and put her knife down. "Scott. We work together. And not like have cubicles in the same department, but like depend on each other day in and day out during these cases. We can't mix what happened last night with what we do during the day."

He leaned back, studying her.

"So, us having this in common, the kink side of our personal lives, that will somehow mess up our work life?"

"So long as we keep our personal lives separate, then no."

"Separate." He grabbed another fry. "Yeah, that's not really going to work for me."

Her stomach fluttered, and it had nothing to do with hunger pangs. "Why not?"

"Because last night, when you fainted, I could have just carried you to the medic office and gone back to the game. But I didn't."

"And now you think I owe you something?" She fisted both hands.

"No. And really, you need to watch that tone with me." He lifted her fork and stabbed a tomato from her salad. "I didn't leave you there and go play because, after seeing you there, I didn't really want to play with some random girl. I wanted to play with you." He plucked the tomato from the fork with his teeth.

Her breath caught. It wouldn't come or go. She'd heard him wrong.

"And before you say more about us working together, I've already thought of that."

"Scott." She blinked a few times. "It would completely get in the way of our work." And she didn't want to move districts again. Starting over again in a new place, a new precinct. No, not again.

"How new are you to the scene. Really?" He took a bite of his burger.

"New." Maybe if she answered him, and he could see how impossible it was, he'd drop the matter entirely.

"And you were approved for Black Light membership and a spot at the roulette game?" He didn't bother masking his suspicion.

Her heart picked up speed. She'd never been good at out and out lying. Doing it on paper hadn't been hard, but with his focus acutely concentrated on her in that moment, her palms sweated.

"I wasn't exactly honest on that part of the application. I may have embellished my experience a bit."

"So, you lied," he said in a flat tone. No wiggle room on the subject apparently.

"Yes. But It's not like I haven't been around the BDSM world or learned as much as I could. I've just never been successful at it."

"Specifics."

"I brought the subject up with a few boyfriends over the years. A couple tried, but it didn't work for them or me, so we broke it off. I've read everything I can get my hands on, been to a few demonstrations, have a profile on a few kink sites. That's about it."

"Tell me about the boyfriends."

"I don't see—"

"Didn't ask you to, asked you to tell me about your boyfriends." His voice dipped. He wasn't giving her the playboy grin she'd gotten used to. Now, his jaw tensed as he talked.

She heaved a sigh but answered him. "Two of them gave it a try. But they weren't into making rules and stuff. They liked a little spanking during sex, but that was it. I didn't help matters by totally sucking at following any rule they set." She decided to dive into her lunch. If her mouth was full of hamburger, she couldn't answer him so easily.

"So, they didn't enforce the rules?"

She shook her head and took another bite. She'd already let

the conversation get completely derailed. Any further participation from her could only make it worse.

"But they liked the spanking for sexual purposes, so you have been spanked?"

Did he have to ask the question as if asking if she'd been to see a movie recently?

She nodded again and took a bite of her salad.

"And you joined Black Light but didn't have enough courage to go until last night because last night you would have been paired with someone. So, no threat of rejection, and you'd probably get to meet someone who was actually into the scene and not someone you'd have to convince."

"This is why you're such a good detective," she said, popping a cherry tomato into her mouth.

"So, say you got paired with someone, and his kinks didn't match yours. What then?"

"What do you mean?"

"I mean, what if you met a sadist who was only into pain play and had no interest in taking his domination out of the bedroom. There's a lot of people in the scene who really only like the dominant-submissive dynamic in a sexual sense. They don't bring it into other areas of their relationship."

"How can they do that? I mean, I get how. I just don't see how that works, though. I don't think I could submit in one area and not the others."

"Good. I'm the same way. Well, just swap the submissive for dominant."

Fuck.

"Scott, we can't."

"You haven't told me why." He pulled her plate away from her when she reached for her burger. "Answer me first."

She grabbed a napkin and wiped her fingertips. Delicious burger.

"I just said I don't think I'd be able to leave it in the bedroom.

And we are partners. How could I leave it at home if I'm with you all day long?"

He pushed the plate back to her, and she lifted her burger. Her appetite had waned pretty heavily during the conversation, but starting a new case meant long hours. She wouldn't get dinner until much later.

"Do you think a submissive is less intelligent than her dominant? Do you think the dominant can't let the submissive lead when the situation calls for it?"

She didn't answer, just took another bite of her burger.

"Subs aren't less intelligent—you wouldn't suddenly become less able to do your job. Dominants, smart ones, and ones who aren't assholes, can see when their subs have more experience or know-how in different situations, and give them the lead. I, as a dominant, expect my sub to be able to carry on an intelligent conversation. I expect my submissive to grow and achieve all of her goals. And I'm not the all-knowing and powerful Oz, just because I make the rules, and just because I enforce the rules doesn't mean I can't learn from my submissive."

"We've been working together for the past month. And never once during that time did you see me in a romantic light. Just because you saw me at that club last night doesn't really change that." She tossed her napkin onto the plate. Her stomach couldn't take anymore. Of the food or the conversation.

Women dreamed about men like Scott. Smart, funny, delicious to stare at—no way he was getting involved with her. It just didn't happen. And the last thing she needed was to blow what she had. A good job in a good district.

"Actually, Sophie, it changed everything," he said. "You don't know what I was thinking before. I'm not blind. I can see how beautiful you are. But I learned a long time ago not to waste my time on a vanilla woman. I don't want to change them to fit my needs any more than I want to change to fit theirs. When I saw you at the club, it was like getting the green light."

"It won't work. It's a bad idea."

"So, says you. And who has all the experience here, me or you?"

"That's not a fair card to play." She pointed at him.

"You're right, it's not. Look, we'll go slow. Real slow. As slow as you need. Dinner. Let's have dinner tomorrow night."

"The case—"

"During the day, we talk about the case. At night, at lunch, we only talk about us. Personal lives happen during off hours. "

He was crazy.

But she was worse because she wanted to believe him.

"Fine. Dinner tomorrow night. It's just dinner, right?"

"Yes. After dinner I'll have you kneel and suck me off all night, maybe throw some hot wax on you, you know, the usual."

She felt her face contort before she could stop it. He laughed and slapped the table.

"Just dinner. I was kidding."

"I knew you were kidding. It just wasn't funny." She grabbed the check which Sandra had dropped off during their talk. Sophie had been so distracted, she hadn't noticed. Had the old woman heard what they were saying?

Sophie grabbed her jacket and coat from beside her and scooted out of the booth. He followed right behind her.

"What's funny is you thinking I'm letting you pay for lunch." He reached over her and snatched the bill from her hand just as they arrived at the cash register. Sandra appeared to handle the exchange of cash with Scott.

"See, I can't even let you pay for lunch," she barbed.

He smiled, took his change from Sandra after leaving her with a healthy tip, and gestured to the door.

"Don't worry about any of that. Right now, just worry about getting to my place for dinner tomorrow night and figuring out if we are ruling Mrs. Moneybucks' death a murder or a suicide."

"You have doubts, too?"

"Yeah. Something felt wrong there. We should be able to watch the video this afternoon."

"Good. I have a feeling there's something in it that will give us what we need to decide," Sophie said and got in her car. She hadn't even realized they'd walked outside and to her car. He'd distracted her with work.

Point—Scott.

Damn.

CHAPTER 5

*I*t took until the next afternoon to be able to see the video or get any information from the evidence taken from the scene. Tentatively, the case was ruled a suicide, but it hadn't been formally filed.

"Okay, it's ready." Sophie patted his shoulder and headed toward the AV room. She'd been successful avoiding any sort of personal conversation since their lunch. Which was fine. It gave him time to sort out what he really wanted with her. She may appear and act tough, but there was something gentle beneath all that exterior. And taking things too fast, forcing things would only break her.

While he'd been in half a dozen relationships that had dominance and submission as the foundation, Sophie had none. At least none that were handled successfully. First thing he needed her to see was she didn't suck at submission. Of course, she hadn't seen it, but he had. How easily she'd followed his lead at the club, at her apartment. Hell, even at lunch, with all her resistance, she'd answered his questions honestly and didn't outright tell him to shove off.

Scott followed her into the darkened room and took a seat beside her in front of the computer monitor. Craig the tech guru brought up the footage.

The dark screen sputtered to life with bright lighting. The camera focused on the victim's face. Tears welled in the crystal blue eyes of the victim, her salon-gifted blonde hair pulled back into a bun, showcasing the single-pearl drop earrings that matched the string of pearls around her neck.

"Who gets dolled up for a suicide?" Scott asked.

"I...I don't think—" The victim shook her head. "Please. I—"

The camera shook. "I can't. I'm just so sorry. Please for—I just can't," she pleaded with the camera, tears streaking her face. Mascara ran freely, marring her porcelain face.

"I'm so sorry," she sobbed as the barrel of a pistol came into view at her right temple. "Please," she cried out, just before the shot rang and she was thrown from the view of the camera lens.

Sophie moved closer to the screen, her head tilted to the right. She'd spotted something. Scott let her examine the footage without question.

"How long does this video run?" she asked, sitting back from the monitor.

"An hour and a half," Craig said.

"And the battery?"

"It was dead when it came in but depending on how much was already left on it, it wouldn't really tell us much anyway."

"Can you tell if the video cut off before the battery died?" Scott asked, seeing where Sophie was headed.

"No. The camera she used has a thirteen-hour consecutive-record function. So as long as the battery was working and it was recording, I don't think it would have stopped."

"Unless someone else turned it off," Sophie said, turning back the video. "Play it again." She scooted her chair a little closer.

Scott watched the screen, the victim, the crying, the gunshot.

"Again," she said.

"What are you looking for?" Scott asked, examining the images flashing before him more closely.

"Like you said, who gets dolled up for a suicide? If it was an on-the-fly decision, she wouldn't have taken the time to set up the camera and make a show of it. See how perfectly center she is in the screen? If it was calculated and well thought out, would she be so distraught right before?" Sophie touched the screen where streaks of tears appeared on the woman's face.

"Stop here." Scott reached across Sophie to pause the video. He tapped on the victim's expression. "She's not looking at the camera, here. She's focused just to the right of it."

"Think she was talking to someone, not the camera?" Sophie asked. She wore perfume or had changed her body wash. She normally had a fresh-towel sort of scent, but he could definitely pick up traces of lavender.

"Scott, see?" she said, when he didn't answer right away.

"Yeah. Turn it back on." He cleared his throat. If he was going to prove to her they could work together and still have something in their personal lives, he needed to keep his head in the game and his dick in his pants.

"You guys got this," Craig said. "Just turn it off when you're done." And he left.

Sophie hit the button, and they returned to watching the scene unfold.

"Wait. Let's go back," she said during the sixth viewing then worked the video backward. "Watch." She pointed the to the screen.

"Please for—I can't," the victim said.

"There!" Sophie jammed her finger into the monitor.

"What? I didn't see anything." Scott leaned in.

"Right after she says she can't." Sophie rewound again. "There. The wiggle."

"Play it again," Scott said.

And there it was. Right after the vic said she couldn't, the video glitched.

"It's like the recording stopped and started again, right?" Sophie said with a triumphant smile on her face.

"Yeah. Rewind once more, a little further back this time," he said. "Where does the gun come from? We can't see her hands, but her body never shifts. Her shoulders don't move, but she raised a gun to her head?"

Sophie wound back to the beginning. "Fuck, you're right. This was no suicide."

"Nope. This was murder."

"Does the ME have anything for us yet?" Sophie asked, still grinning.

"Let's go over there and see. The sooner we have the time and cause of death, the better." He clicked the monitor off and pulled her chair out for her. She paused at his action but didn't comment on it.

He'd pulled her chair out for her before; this wasn't the first time. But, this time, she seemed to notice.

DR. DAN GREENE, THE MEDICAL EXAMINER ON THEIR CASE, MET them at the door.

"I just called up for you. They said you were headed down." He shook Scott's hand then Sophie's.

"Do you have anything for us?" Sophie asked, pointing at the victim lying on the middle metal table in the room. The other two tables were empty.

"Well, cause of death was gunshot to the head, obviously." Dr. Greene flashed a grimacing smile and led them to the table. A white sheet covered the body to her neck, exposing only her head.

Dan took a pencil from his lab coat and pointed to the wound on her right temple.

"These burn marks caught my attention, though." He pointed at the dark tissue surrounding the wound. "In a suicide, usually the barrel is pushed against the temple. Which leaves a bruise along with the burn from the shot itself. But there's no bruise here, and the burn isn't just around the wound but spread out from it. Like the gun wasn't pressed to the head." Dr. Greene mimicked the action, forming a gun with his hand and showing them where it would be placed on his head.

"Like someone else held the gun?" Scott asked. "There's footage of the shot," he pointed out.

"Yeah, and it wasn't pressed against her head. Just like he's saying," Sophie pointed out.

"We don't think it was suicide, but we need your official ruling before we investigate further," Scott said.

Dr. Greene pulled the sheet up to cover the body completely. No matter how many times he saw it, seeing what a gunshot does to the human body still sent shivers through his body. Between his tours in Afghanistan and years on the force, he'd seen it too often.

"This wasn't suicide. There are no hesitation marks, no other bruising, I don't think she even pulled the trigger. I know you say it's on tape, but—" He sucked in a long breath and shook his head.

"Yeah, but no hand. The video was zoomed in on her face. There's no hand in the screen," Sophie pointed out.

"We should look at it again, make sure we don't see something. A finger or something. Maybe it can tell us if the shooter was even female. Thanks, Dr. Green." Scott shook his hand again and placed his palm on the small of Sophie's back.

"Can you send your formal report directly to me? I'll read over it tonight," Sophie said.

Scott put pressure on her back, guiding her toward the door. "Don't you have plans tonight?" he asked, trying to sound casual but putting his authoritative spin on his tone.

"I'm sure I'll have time," she said.

"I'm sure you won't," he whispered for her ears only and opened the door for her.

She gave him a side glance and walked through, giving him, another look over her shoulder as she climbed the stairs.

CHAPTER 6

*S*ophie gripped the bottle of wine with two hand and stared at the doorbell to his condo. Not an apartment. A condo. In one of the most upscale buildings in Alexandria.

She really shouldn't be surprised. He was a member of Black Light, after all, and that membership didn't come cheap.

Her mind flip-flopped the entire drive over on her decision to keep the date she planned with Scott. During the five minutes she'd spent applying a thin layer of mascara, she'd checked off all the reasons going would be good for her. An evening out wouldn't kill her, he might be able to help her with becoming a better submissive, and, worst-case scenario they could work on the case.

She'd spent her afternoon digging into the victim's past. Susan James didn't have a record. Not that Sophie would have expected one, with such a posh background. Susan appeared to have the sort of money that could buy her way out of any trouble she found herself in.

Ugh, focus.

Before she could talk herself out of it, she pressed the doorbell and waited.

The door swung open, and there he stood. Her mouth dried.

He wore another black shirt, button-down, this time. The material stretched over his shoulders and arms. She doubted there were shirts made to accommodate his particular physique. If he arched his back, would the seams pop and give her a full view of his muscular build? His sleeves rolled to his elbows showed off the tats on both of his forearms. How had she not noticed those before?

It took a moment, but she finally found her mind again and realized he'd greeted her.

"Hi." She threw on a smile and shoved the bottle of wine at him. "I brought this." *Excellent. Very smooth.*

"Thanks." He stepped aside, letting her into his condo.

She cased the joint, keeping her mind busy so she'd stop trying to visualize him naked. Clean. Organized. Casual. Just about what she'd expected from him.

"Décor by Bed Bath & Beyond?" She laughed softly and pointed at the canvas print of a city skyline. It could be any city but definitely wasn't D.C. Chicago maybe?

"Yeah. Not much of an interior designer. Just shopped from the catalogue," he admitted and helped her out of her coat.

"Easy way of doing it," she said. This was awful. Small talk? Horrible.

"Come on, I have dinner all ready." He grinned and placed his hand on the small of her back again. That gesture, so simple, so light, sent her body into a tailspin of desire.

She'd had boyfriends before. A few had done the same; it wasn't some secret move. But it had never felt like his hand. Maybe his was bigger. Maybe he had a higher body temperature and that made her feel so damn warm every time he did it.

"You cooked?" she asked, following him into the living room.

"If by cooked you mean dialed the phone, then yes. Hope you like pizza." He placed the bottle of wine on the coffee table beside the pizza box and paper plates.

She peeked inside the box. "Cheese?"

"Didn't know what you liked, so I figured cheese would be safe." He handed her a plate. "Grab some. I'll get this wine opened and poured."

"Actually…" She stopped him. "Any chance you have beer?" Wine wasn't a pizza drink.

His lips spread into a wide grin. Hell, he was sexy when he smiled like that—like she'd just pleased him. "Yep, be right back."

She grabbed a slice of pizza. Sliding it onto a plate, she sat on the couch, pushing her back into the corner. He returned with two bottles of beer and placed one on the end of the coffee table nearest her.

"So, how was the rest of your day?" he asked, snagging a slice for himself.

"Good. The usual. Research. Digging into her history, but I didn't—" She stopped talking when he shook his head at her.

"No. We aren't talking about the case. Tonight, we are just two people having pizza." He took a large bite of his. Cheese strung out and dropped onto his chin as he pulled the slice away. Even sloppy, he was hot.

"Okay. Right." She bit into her pizza. It probably tasted delicious, but he moved over to sit closer to her, and all parts of her brain were redirected to deal with the tingling sensation only he seemed to bring to the party.

Sitting in the living room instead of at his dining room table, or out on the patio should have put her more at ease. Casual dining. Not so much date dining, but just having him so close fogged her brain.

"Did you have an activity you were hoping to spin the other night?" he asked, as if he needed to derail her further from any sort of work talk. He wasn't wrong. If left to her own devices, she'd be bringing them right back to the case. It was what she knew, what she could talk about with confidence.

"No, well, not really." She bit into the thick crust. Noting he'd already eaten his entire piece, she gave him bonus points for not skipping the crust. Why anyone would do that made no sense to her whatsoever. Ruined a perfectly good piece of pizza.

"Which means you did, so what were you hoping to roll?" He slid his paper plate onto the table and grabbed his beer.

"What about you?" She stuffed the last bite of crust into her mouth.

He shook his head again and arched a brow. "I asked you a question, and I expect an answer." He took a sip of beer.

She swallowed back the sarcastic retort tingling in her mouth. Would he spank her if she didn't answer him? Tempting.

"I guess something light. Impact play, maybe?" She tossed her paper plate onto the table. Getting the one piece down had been hard enough with the nerves firing off in her brain, trying to eat a second while he wanted to talk play activities wouldn't end well.

He smiled. "Impact play can be light or heavy. Almost any of the activities they had listed could go either way."

"Breath play can be light?" She really didn't know much about it, other than what'd she'd read, and seen in the multitude of videos she'd watched over the years. But nothing about it looked lighthearted in the least.

"It can be. Everything can be done with a varying degree of intensity. Even knife play, although the light play might be heavy play to someone." He pushed his bottle onto the coffee table.

No one was coming at her with a knife.

"Knife play, hard limit?" He grinned. He must have seen the concern on her face.

"I don't like them." She swallowed hard. Did he like them? Did he play like that? Drawing blood for fun?

"Good. I'm not much of a fan, either. Though watching a knife scene can be exciting."

"I guess I'll have to take your word for it." She shrugged.

"Maybe not. I'm sure there'll be some play at the club we can watch." He rested his hand on her knee. "So, impact play is what you were hoping for, or you thought that would be the least intense?"

How the hell could she think with him touching her? "I figured it would be the safest starting point."

He rubbed her knee. "You said your boyfriends have spanked you before?" He used his settling tone, the one he used when he wanted the suspect to feel at ease in hopes he would spill usable information, if not a full confession.

She wasn't so easily played.

"I have a list for you." She hopped off the couch. How could she have forgotten? She'd made the list knowing this exact thing would happen. He'd touch her or look at her, and she'd stop thinking coherently. Good thing she planned ahead.

"A list?" He stood from the couch but didn't follow her to the front hallway where she'd left her purse.

She returned, holding it, and waved it in the air. "This way we don't have to have this long drawn-out conversation. These are the things I'd like to do, learn about." She thrust the folded loose-leaf paper at him.

He arched both eyebrows and took it from her, held eye contact while unfolding it then glanced down. His lips formed a straight line, his pulled-down eyebrows almost matching them.

"Like a limits list?" It sounded like he was trying to lead her to the right answer.

"Well, no, not exactly. I think that list would be longer? I don't know. But these are things I want you to do." She watched his expression, and her stomach dropped again. Obviously, she didn't give him the right answer.

"Was there a particular order you wanted me to do these for you?" he asked, still reading the list. It wasn't very long, only ten items. Maybe he didn't know what some of them were.

"No, I don't think that's necessary." She leaned over to see the paper. She'd written it, but since he still hadn't glanced up at her, she wondered if something else was holding his attention.

"Get down on your knees." He folded the paper, first in half and then again. His voice dipped. A new tone. Darker. It matched the firm line of his jaw, and the shadowed look in his eyes when he tilted his head and found her gaze.

"What?"

"Get on your knees, Sophie. Right now. Fold your hands behind her back and grip your wrists. Do not say another word until I give you permission, and don't get up." He stuffed her list into the back pocket of his jeans and pushed the coffee table toward the entertainment center, putting more space in front of the couch.

He didn't sound mad, just firm, but he seemed upset. Like she'd just cut his manhood off or something. Maybe the list was too long?

"I was just giving you some ideas."

"Knees," he simply said and stood with spread legs and his arms crossed.

Did he practice that scary expression in the mirror? How did he know how much to narrow his eyes and tense his muscles in order to get her body moving without terrifying her into running away? Although, she supposed a woman who didn't know him might see this expression and hightail it for the door instead of sinking into a soft submissive state.

She sank to her knees, unable to keep her eyes on him while she did so. The soft area rug cushioned her knees, where her leggings failed. Maybe changing into the leggings and sweater outfit had been a mistake.

When he didn't say a word or move, she realized she'd forgotten her hands, and quickly rectified that by grabbing her wrists behind her. Her stomach rolled with nerves, her chest constricted with concern, but when he approached her and squatted, bringing his eyes level with hers, she melted.

He reached out and fisted her hair, tugging from the scalp and pulling her head back. "Hair pulling was on your list," he reminded her when she opened her mouth. She wasn't going to argue; she was just surprised. It hurt more than she thought it would. Her scalp burned from the pull, but it seemed minor when compared to the heated glare he gave her.

She'd done something wrong, obviously. Within ten minutes of starting, she'd ruined everything.

Scott ran the back of his hand along her jawline, keeping their gazes locked as moments ticked by. The comfort of his touch mingled with the burn of his possession slowly ebbed away her tension.

"Ah, there you are." His stern expression softened, his lips pulled back into his casual smile. "How does this feel? Me taking control of the moment?"

She licked her lips. He'd said she couldn't talk. Was the ban lifted because he asked a question? Taking chances didn't always pan out for her, but when he didn't continue, she figured the odds were in her favor.

"It feels warm," she said. His brows pulled together, so she went on to clarify. "Like, inside, everything just got warm and easy. Not so cold and tense. Does that even make sense?" She sounded like a fool.

"Total sense." He slowly uncurled his fingers from her hair and cupped her chin. "You don't want to be in control, but you've never really given it up either. I'm guessing your boyfriends weren't really into the lifestyle to begin with, and you probably made the list of rules and told them what the consequences should be. Am I right?"

Exactly right.

"I suppose," she said, turning her gaze from his. Obviously, he could see too much from her expression. And she didn't need to be giving up all her secrets on their first date.

He tilted her chin. "Eyes on me when I'm talking to you, Sophie."

She conceded, seeing as his grip tightened and he probably wouldn't let up until she did so.

"I'm happy to go over the list with you. They are things you'd like to experience, are interested in, and I should know them. But you can't hand me a honey-do list when it comes to this, when it comes to us. We learn from each other what each other likes and doesn't like. But I ultimately decide if you'll get a spanking, or your hair pulled, or if I take my belt off and wrap it around your neck and face fuck you until you either orgasm or pass out."

Wow. He'd already memorized most of the list.

"I'd prefer you not pass out, though." He winked and patted her cheek. "You can sit on the couch." He stood at his full height and helped her up from her knees.

Once she perched on the edge of the couch, she pushed her hair back behind her ears and forced herself to look up at him. He pulled the list back out of his pocket and handed it to her.

"I want you to rank these. The most desired to the least desired." He walked over to the entertainment center and grabbed a pen from a drawer.

"It wasn't easy making the list," she said, taking the pen from him. The first items hadn't even needed thought—spanking, a little rope bondage—but when it came to the harsher stuff, like the belt scenario, she'd only written them because she had planned to hand it over and let things play out.

What a fool she'd been. Who just hands over a list of things to be done to them as though Scott were some robot?

"It'll be even harder talking about them, but don't worry. I think I can get us through it." He patted her knee and sat beside her. "Go on." He tapped the paper then grabbed his beer.

She nibbled on her lip while contemplating the series of activities before her. Maybe making the list after watching a few videos on Pornhub had been a bad decision. She crossed off suspension bondage, remembering her motion sickness issue. She doubted anyone would find a sub vomiting while hanging upside down to be sexy. Then again, who was she to judge anyone's kink?

Silence surrounded her while she worked. Even Scott remained completely quiet. Maybe he would start with the first item tonight. Just the prospect of having her bottom bared and spanked by his large hands made her squirm with arousal.

"What was that little thought?" he asked lightly.

She glanced up at him. Were her thoughts so transparent to him?

"Just thinking about these things." She waved the paper.

He wouldn't let it go. "Which one?" He moved closer and peered over the edge of the paper. She'd already finished marking them but needed another moment before they discussed them.

"Spanking." She thrust the paper at him. Her face didn't just heat, it was a damn inferno, but she was never one to back down. She'd written it—it's not like it would shock him.

Though, the silence stretching between them after she answered didn't exactly bolster her confidence in the situation.

"Do you want me to spank you tonight?" he asked, as if he were giving her the option of what movie to see. Could it be that easy? Just ask and ye shall receive?

"Well, I mean, if you'd like that." She tucked her feet under her. Aloof. Good, disconnect, just a little. Enough to get her breath back under control with the way he was now staring at her.

Like he'd like to eat her for dinner instead of the pizza getting cold on the table.

He let out a breath and grinned. "It's one of the things I'd like to do to you tonight." He dragged his hand through his hair, ruffling the short blond curls.

"I mean, we can rent a movie or something if you'd rather. We don't have to— I mean we did say it was just dinner." She was rambling. She didn't ramble. Damn him for making her so unsettled.

He clamped a hand over her mouth and grinned. "Here's what

I want from you tonight. Keep your mind on following what I say, answer any questions I ask, and just let yourself feel. No dissecting everything. Just go with what feels good."

She'd heard that line before. Go with what feels good. Except most of the guys preaching such knowledge didn't have any idea on how to make her feel good. But when his grin stretched into something a bit more menacing, her insides fluttered. He was already making her feel good, and he he'd barely touched her.

Since he still had his hand over her mouth, she answered the only way she could.

She nodded.

CHAPTER 7

*E*very reaction she had played so freely in her eyes. If she was trying to hide from him, he would only have to keep her eyes locked with his. She could force her body to relax, shove a plastic smile on her lips, but in her eyes, he would see everything. And this woman, this strong, independent, fully capable woman was melting in his hands.

The submission had a sweeter taste when it came willingly and from a woman who easily stood on her own two feet. He wasn't the rescuer type. Women who needed hand holding and strict rules in order to make them adult in an orderly fashion didn't appeal to him, and they rarely lasted very long.

But Sophie didn't need to be reminded to pay her cable bill. He didn't need to text her to make sure she'd set her alarm for the morning. Hell, she probably had a to-do list with checkmarks next to her bed.

And here she was in his hands, wanting him to spank her. No not just wanting. The hunger displayed in her eyes wasn't playing around. She needed it. He'd set her mind at ease, but now her body needed the same assurance.

Whatever fool had tried to dominate her in the past really had no idea what sort of jewel he had been holding. No matter. Their stupidity was his gain.

He released her mouth, enjoying the little red imprints of his fingers fading away on her cheeks.

"You've played a little bit. Have you been spanked with a brush or belt?" He ran his thumb along her jaw. She softened when he touched her like that, as though the connection with him made it easier. And given how hard his cock was, making it harder on her would only make his pants more constrictive. He'd save his fantasies for later. Right now, he had a bottom to spank.

"No, just the hand. Well, unless you count the time I got smacked with a belt when I was in high school. But he was just screwing around; he didn't mean it." She tilted her head with a gentle smile. She was cute when she rambled.

"Ah, and is that when you realized you might like to be really spanked?"

"I wanted him to do it again, if that's what you mean. But seeing as he was my track coach, it would have been really inappropriate."

He sat straight. "Why the hell would your track coach spank you?" He would hunt down the pervert first thing in the morning.

She started laughing. "It wasn't like that. It was a strap used to bundle the equipment bags together. He'd been walking past us swinging it, and it accidentally hit my ass. He nearly fainted when he realized what happened."

Scott sat back and waited for his heart to stop jackhammering in his chest. "You did that on purpose." He pointed a finger at her.

Her smile widened. Little brat.

"For that you've definitely earned a spanking. I had thought we'd wait until we could go through the checklist, but since you were so organized as to give me your list of wants, I think we can proceed." He moved to the next cushion and patted his thigh. "C'mon, over you go."

"Over I go?" she asked with wide eyes. Was she expecting some romantic gesture? A rose stuck in her teeth first?

"You're overthinking and planning this all out in your head," he accused and tapped her temple. "I don't have the script you've written, and even if I did, I wouldn't use it. Now, do as I said and lie over my lap or this playful spanking can become a punishment very quickly."

Her lips parted as she took a surprised breath. Did she really think he would just follow her lead in all of this? Even when she gave over, she still tried to hold the reins. He couldn't fault her. She'd never been able to hand over control to someone who knew what to do with the power before. But she needed to learn quick that he wasn't her puppet, and she would get a lot more out of submission if she actually submitted.

Settling back on the couch, he patted his thigh once more. If she was going to bolt, this would be the moment. But she was made of tougher stuff. She unfolded her legs from beneath her and crawled over the cushions until her belly rested on his left thigh and her ass was positioned perfectly over his right.

No way she couldn't feel his erection pushing against his pants and now her body, but that didn't matter. Let her know how hard she made him; it wasn't something he would be able to hide anyway.

"I'm going to pull down your leggings and your panties unless you have objections?" He pushed her gray knit sweater up to get to the elastic band of the leggings.

"Uh. I guess not." She peered at him over her shoulder. Uncertainty. Would this hurt her, and would she like it?

"If it's too much, and you want to slow down or pause, you say yellow. If you need me to stop completely, you say red. Both of those are your safewords. You do have control here, Sophie. I won't do more than you can stand, and I won't do more than you think you can stand. But at some point, I will push that boundary." It was his job to push the limits, but never would he break them.

"Okay. Yeah. I know." She'd turned forward again. He could imagine her squeezing her eyes closed, waiting for the first strike to land. Silly girl.

He peeled her leggings down first, letting her panties stay in position. His little gift to himself, seeing the blush of a woman's ass cheeks grow beneath the panty lines just before he removed the barrier altogether and got down to serious business.

She'd worn a pair of light-purple cotton panties. Hanes, if he read the elastic band correctly.

"Shit," she cursed softly.

"Cotton panties are just as sexy as silk, Sophie. When worn on the right woman." He slid a finger beneath the elastic on her ass cheek and traced it along her flesh. "Fuck your ass is beautiful." He meant it, too.

She grumbled something, but he didn't hear it. Probably nothing positive, and definitely something he'd want to really spank her for.

"What was that?" he asked, running his hand in circles over her round.

"I said my ass is big, not beautiful. And I've come to terms with that so-*ow*!" She was cut off by the sharp slap of his hand directly to her thigh. "I wasn't being negative, just realistic."

"If I say your ass is beautiful to me—it is. Are you questioning my taste or my opinions?" He rested his hand once more on her ass, readying to deliver another stinging smack if she got cheeky.

She was right that her body had curves, more curves than society felt would make a woman beautiful. But she had a lot more to her than that, and everything wrapped up together created beauty.

"No, I was just stating a fact."

"You've never come across as self-conscious. It's one of the things I really like about you. Don't start proving me wrong on that front. I don't like being proved wrong. And, if you keep it up, I have a fraternity paddle in my closet that will help me show you how much I don't like it." He squeezed her ass, loving the feel of her squirming in his lap.

"I'm not. I just—well, call a spade a spade." She rested her forehead on the couch cushion.

"Your ass is perfect for what I'm about to do to you. Now, if we could get back to your earlier naughtiness of trying to freak me the fuck out with a that track coach bit, it would make things easier."

"For you," she mumbled. He couldn't help but smile, and since she wasn't looking at him to notice, he gave himself permission to enjoy the bit of sass.

"Feel free to cry out as much as you'd like. My neighbor's away on vacation," he said and lifted his hand.

Fucking beautiful. She said nothing at first, as he lightly spanked her bottom. Just the edges around her panty lines. Once the pink blush began, he intensified the swats, getting a little squeal from her. Maybe he was more of a sadist than he could proclaim, but when he smacked her right cheek in the same spot repeatedly and got a groan and squeak from her, his cock pulsated.

He paused the spanking and rubbed the pink flesh while watching her breathe. She wasn't gasping for air, not like she would be by the time he was finished with her, but she had definitely begun to feel the effects. She rose on her elbows and took several deep breaths.

Without warning, because where would the fun be in that, he grabbed the elastic of her panties and yanked them down to her knees where her leggings were already trapping her legs quite nicely.

"So, do you still think it's funny to try and get a rise out of me?" he asked, hand poised and ready.

She giggled. Most likely out of nerves, but still, he couldn't let it go unchecked.

"Oh, I see."

"No!" She tried to push up. "I didn't mean to laugh, really!"

"Mmhhm..." He took no pity.

He laid into her ass, leaving no inch of flesh behind. After the first dozen strokes she wiggled as though her ass were on fire, and from the delicious bounce and deep reddening of her cheeks as he continued, it most likely felt like it was.

"Scott," she breathed, throwing her hand back.

He snatched it and continued to pepper her ass, though he lightened the swats. This was her first spanking, he reminded himself. He paused only a moment to shove her panties and leggings farther down, past her knees.

"Spread your legs a little," he instructed, rubbing her thighs. He'd left them mostly out of the spanking, but there was a tint of crimson he decided to rub away.

Her thighs parted, and her ass lifted from the new positioning. "Perfect. How do you feel?" he asked, running his tingling hand over the warm flesh of her bottom.

She sniffled. "Hot."

He chuckled. "I'm not very chilly myself." He ran his hand to her crease, skimming his fingers just inside the little canal her ass cheeks made until he found her sex. Plump and wet. Perfect.

"How about here. How does this feel?" he asked, lightly tapping her pussy.

"Needy," she answered with her face buried in her hands. She parted her thighs another half inch and put her ass higher in the air.

"Would you like me to take care of it for you?" he asked, moving his fingers lower and finding her clit.

She loosed a loud moan and wiggled her bottom.

"Sorry, I don't speak ass wiggle. Can you verbalize?" He pinched her clit, delighting in her hiss.

"Yes. Yes, Scott, please help me." She still focused her attention ahead of her, not sparing him a glance.

He grazed her clit then moved to her entrance, rimming it

with the tip of his middle finger. He'd planned pizza. Talk about kink. Ease into things, maybe a deep soul ripping kiss that would leave them both wanting more. That's what he planned for them. But there they were, her ass bent over his lap, and his cock bursting at the seam.

He couldn't wait to taste her. Now that he saw her, really saw what was inside, what could be between them, he didn't want to waste time beating around the bush. He wanted to dive right in, consume her completely.

He released her hand from the back, and she twisted so she could face him with some ease. "Is it bad if I tell you I want you to fuck me? Or do I have to wait until your cock actually breaks through your jeans to mention it?" She reached between them and ran her hand over the length of his erection.

He sucked in a breath. "I always want to know what you want, but you may not always get it." He moved her from his lap to kneeling beside him.

"You want my cock?" He moved to stand in front of her and unzipped his jeans. He pulled his dick out and wrapped his hand around the shaft. Just that little bit of pressure was almost too much with her licking her lips and looking at him through lowered lashes.

"Yes, sir." She ran her tongue over her bottom lip. "Please."

He shoved his jeans down and fisted his cock, bringing it level with her mouth. Keeping her eyes on him, she licked the tip of his dick. He groaned and grabbed a fistful of her hair. "Open that mouth of yours," he ordered. Nice Dom would be taking a break, gentle wouldn't get either of them where they wanted.

Her response couldn't have been more perfect.

"Yes, sir." She parted her lips wide and pushed her tongue out, inviting his cock to enter.

Not that he needed an invitation. He ran the head of his cock back and forth over her tongue, teasing her and sensing the tension building in her body. She wanted him inside her, her mouth her pussy, and he wasn't just handing it to her. No, she'd have to earn it.

"Wrap your lips around me." He pushed into her mouth. She didn't just accept his cock, she pushed toward him, taking him deep. He touched the back of her throat. She swallowed, stuck her tongue out again, and licked the underside of his dick.

He yanked out of her mouth, closing his eyes briefly and taking a breath. "Yeah, fuck. Holy shit," he panted. "Stand and lie on the couch." He shoved his jeans down farther and kicked them away. If she wanted him to slow down, she didn't show it. She bounded into action, doing exactly as he directed.

Once she was standing, he dropped to his knees, grabbed her leggings, and yanked them down to her ankles. He lifted one foot then the other, taking each of her flats and tossing them aside so he could get her leggings off.

"I could have done that," she said, which he responded to with a sound smack to her ass.

"You can do what I told you to do." He pointed to the couch.

She climbed onto the couch, parting her legs for him. He unbuttoned the top buttons of his shirt and pulled it over his head, tossing it to the floor with his jeans.

He slapped the inside of her thigh until she parted her legs more. "Holy fuck," he said again and grabbed her hips, shifting her ass to the edge.

"Scott, wait, oh, fuck." He silenced her well enough with a flick of his tongue over her sex. Using his thumbs, he pried her lips open and suckled on her clit.

He slid two fingers into her passage, groaning when her body squeezed them. She panted over him as he began to fuck her with his fingers and continued to lick and nip at her clit. He couldn't get enough of her. She made the cutest sounds of pleasure that quickly morphed into deep satisfying moans of desire.

Her thighs trembled, and her pussy clenched.

He pulled back, resting his chin just above her clit but still plowing his fingers into her tight pussy. Curling his fingers into a come-here motion, he strove to drive her as wild as she'd driven him.

"No coming yet, Sophie. Not until my cock is buried inside you."

"Please. Scott. I can't wait. Please." She reached down and tried to pull him up by his shoulders, but he laughed and swatted her hands away.

"Patience." To accentuate his statement, he dragged his fingers out and slowly pushed them back in, licking her clit in the same leisurely fashion.

Her hands fisted on her thighs, and he could hear the frustration in her moans. Her hips lifted from the couch. His girl had been good enough; he should really give her what she was hoping for.

But what was another moment or two?

"I can't wait. You're being mean," she moaned, and he chuckled.

"You haven't seen mean yet, sweetheart," he mumbled and sucked her clit hard, removing his fingers from her. She arched her back, and just as he could feel her body getting ready to burst, he sat back on his heels.

She glared down at him, her breath huffing so hard her hair moved from it.

"Oh, are you getting pissed with me?" he asked, not at all worried about it.

"You said you'd help," she pointed out.

"I am helping," he promised, readjusting her on the couch to make room for him. "I'm helping teach you that you'll get rewarded when you obey and be completely disappointed when you try to force me to give you something."

He lined the tip of his dick up with her pussy. Keeping his gaze linked with hers, he slowly began to push forward. Her mouth opened, her hands unfisted and he gripped his shoulders. She looked ready to punch him, he tormented her so well. He almost hoped she would lose her patience, and he could plow into her and take what he wanted. Leaving her unfulfilled would be a perfect punishment for trying to rush him.

But this was their first time, and as happy the sadistic side of him would be to see her pout from being denied, he wanted to hear his name on her lips more. He wanted her yelling and cursing and writhing from the force of her orgasm.

He fit inside of her perfectly, like her pussy had been molded for him. A shiver ran through her body, coursing through to him.

Gripping her hips, he leaned forward, crushing her mouth with his. The first kiss usually happened before the first fucking, but nothing with Sophie went according to his plans so far. She melted beneath him as he rocked forward, fucking her slowly at first then picking up speed and force as she wrapped her hands around his neck and intensified the kiss.

"Fuck," he breathed when he pulled back from their kiss. Her nails dug into his shoulders.

Nothing felt better. Breathing was not what kept him alive at that moment. It was her body, it was her.

"I can't. Please. Scott, I can't wait." She begged, pulling her legs back farther.

"Oh fuck, baby." He threw his head back. "Fucking come."

Her first scream of release drowned out his grunting as he thrust forward again and again, until his body clenched and released hard. Her hands were still on his shoulders, her nails biting into him. Her pussy squeezed him, milking every last drop of his release from his body.

Once his chest stopped heaving, and the heated air between their bodies began to cool down, he pressed his forehead to hers.

"Holy fuck," he whispered.

"You say that a lot," she whispered back.

"I blame you." He pressed a kiss to her forehead and eased

himself off her then reached for his shirt on the floor and cleaned her best he could.

"Your shirt." She tried to pull it away from him.

"It's just a shirt, Sophie," he assured her. Once he was satisfied, he picked up her panties-and-legging combo and separated the items before handing them to her.

He pulled on his jeans and shoved his shoes under the coffee table, before sitting back on the couch and wrapping her in his arms. She'd barely gotten her pants back on, and he was kissing her again. She tasted perfect. A little like salt and honey.

"Scott." She pulled away, pushing her hair behind her ears. "You're ringing." She gestured to the vibrating phone on the coffee table.

He smiled. "You just can't relax, can you?"

"Oh, I'm very relaxed, right now. Too relaxed, really." She pressed her head to his chest. "But it could be the precinct, and my phone is all the way in the hallway in my purse." She waved a hand in that general direction with obvious feigned exhaustion.

He laughed. How could he not?

"Okay." She shifted off him, and he went for his phone. The call had rolled to voice mail already, so he clicked on the icon to bring up the message.

"Scott. I left a message for Sophie, too. We've got a guy down here confessing to the James murder. Call me back."

He shoved the phone into his back pocket. A confession?

"That was Captain Peterson. Someone has been kind enough to confess to Susan James's murder."

She scrambled off the couch. "What? Who? We need to get down there." She shoved her feet into her flats and combed her fingers through her hair.

"Let me just grab a shirt, and we'll go. My car's in the garage downstairs."

"What? No. I'll go, you wait five minutes then go. We can't walk in together," she said, speed walking around the couch. "Do I have that freshly fucked look?" she asked, pausing at the mirror on the wall to check.

He laughed. "No, but if you don't slow down, you'll have that freshly spanked look."

"You can't joke like that. We're on the clock." She grabbed her purse. "Remember, wait five minutes then go." She threw her purse over her shoulder, fisted her coat, and was out the door before he could grab his shoes.

Two steps forward, one tiny one back. Still. It was progress.

CHAPTER 8

"*A*t least you waited for me to get here." Scott trekked up to Sophie. She eyed him as he stalked toward her from across the station. Being close to ten in the evening, the desks were empty.

She stood from the desk she sat at with her cup of coffee. She had stopped in the bathroom as soon as she arrived to brush out her hair and pull it back into a tight bun, making sure there weren't any physical tells that she'd just been fucked.

Thoroughly and satisfyingly fucked, but still, not the most professional appearance to have when beginning an interrogation.

"Of course, I did," she said.

His jaw was set as he made his way around the empty station toward her. He'd put on a clean shirt. Long-sleeved button-down dark blue, tucked neatly into his jeans, with a wide black leather belt secured just below his navel. Of course, he'd seem even more spectacular after a roll on the couch. She probably looked like she'd been tossed around, but he still emerged as well put-together as ever.

She pushed away the memory of his hard chest when he'd

pulled his shirt off barely over an hour before. She hadn't seen anything like him before. Fit, but not overwhelmingly rock hard. Tattoos covering his shoulders and down both arms, and one just below his right pec. Had she not been spreading her legs and mentally begging him to fuck her senseless, she might have taken the time to read the words inscribed there. Next time. She'd look next time.

If there was a next time.

Scott's eyes darkened as he drew closer to her.

"He's in room one." She handed him the cup of coffee she'd made him and walked toward the interrogation room.

"Wait." The single word could have boomed in the empty room.

"What?" She turned to face him.

"Tomorrow morning I'm picking you up at your place." He took a long swallow of the coffee. "Okay, now. Who is this guy, and what's his story?"

Just like that, he turned off the deep dominant baritone, and the Scott she'd been working with over the past month returned. How could he switch that on and off so easily? She'd spent the entire ride to the station house trying to bring her mind down from the high he'd given her.

"Sophie, who's the guy?"

"Oh. His name is Michael Carmichael—I know, who names their son that. Anyway, he walked in, told the front desk he wanted to confess, and said he's the one who killed Susan James." She nodded to the officer standing outside the room to open the door for them.

"Any idea other than that?"

"He's a co-worker of the victim's at McAnistor and Associates. Accountants, top in their firm from what I can see so far. We don't have much yet on her background. Or his."

"Okay, let's get his story and then we can check out the backstories." Scott gestured for her to walk ahead of him.

Michael Carmichael was a puny little thing. With his cropped black hair, thick plastic-framed glasses, and a white button-down shirt, he fit the stereotype of every nerd joke in the world.

"Mr. Carmichael. I'm Detective Russo, and this is my partner Detective Nelson. I understand you have some information regarding the death of Susan James." Scott took a seat at the table across from the suspect while Sophie stood off in the corner. They had a routine. He warmed them, and she finished them off if needed.

"Yes. I want to confess. I told the officers that already, but they insisted I had to wait for you." Michael flattened his hands on the table.

"Well we're here now, so why don't you start at the beginning. How did you know the victim?"

"We work together. She has-had—the office next to mine. I hated her, so I killed her."

Scott sat back in his chair and folded his arms.

"I can understand that. I hate a few of my co-workers, but I wouldn't go so far as to murder them. What made you do that?"

"She was just a horrible person. Horrible." Michael Carmichael shook his head as though he was disgusted with her still, even after death.

"How so?" Sophie asked.

"She stole accounts, for one thing. She'd visit clients and sweet talk them onto her list. I'm sure she even—even—" He swallowed. "Even had sex to get them."

The show of mortification on Michael's face at his own statement made Sophie want to laugh. He could barely say the words; how could he have acted on them.

"So, what happened? You went to her apartment, then what?" Sophie asked.

Michael glanced at her then Scott. "I shot her."

Scott drummed his fingertips on the table. He was a casual

guy, but he hated having his time wasted. And Michael Carmichael was wasting their time.

"You shot her. Okay. Where, when, what happened? We need all of the details, or we can't really know you actually did it," Scott said, sliding the yellow pad toward him.

"Well, I—I mean, I went to her apartment. We talked for a bit, and then when she wasn't looking, I shot her." He pointed to his left temple.

"Hmm. On the left side?" Scott asked.

"Or was it the right side? How far from her did you stand?" Sophie added.

"Right. I was on the right side. Uh, close, but not close enough she could take the gun away," Michael Carmichael lied.

"I just have one more question. Why would you come to the police station late at night and confess to a murder you didn't commit?"

"Yes, that's the real question here, isn't it?" Sophie added, pressing her hands to the table. Scott kept his focus on Michael.

"I-I-I didn't. I mean why would I make this up?" Michael pulled at the top button of his shirt.

"That's a good question. How about you think about it, and we'll be back after breakfast to get your answer." Scott stood and grabbed the legal pad.

"Wait," Michael called out as they reached the door. "Okay, I didn't. I mean... I wanted to, she really was horrible, but I didn't." The tension evaporated from his features.

"Why would you confess? You know you go to jail for murder, right?" Sophie asked, walking back to the table.

"My family. I did it for my family," he said simply. She noticed the silver band on his ring finger.

"What does that mean?" Scott asked.

"She stole a lot of clients from me. Some really big accounts."

"That doesn't really answer the question, though, does it?"

Sophie pushed. "Why would you confess to a murder that hasn't been officially filed as murder yet?"

Michael turned to her, surprise in his eyes.

"It hasn't?" His fingers stilled on the button. "I heard her body had been found with a gunshot to her head. Why wouldn't it be murder?"

"So, you heard your co-worker was dead, and you assumed murder and then decided to cop to it? Why?" Scott asked.

"I-uh." Color drained from Michael's face, and he bowed his head. "There's a price on her head." Sophie walked around Michael, coming to stand behind him.

"Like a bounty?" Scott asked with narrowed eyes.

"Yeah. A million dollars." Michael turned around in his chair to plead his case to Sophie. "My wife just delivered our little girl two weeks ago. She was born with a small hole in her heart. Do you know what heart surgery costs? My insurance doesn't pay enough. Between my deductible and out of pocket costs, it's close to three hundred thousand dollars."

Sophie's heart pulled for the guy.

"So you thought you'd claim the bounty because she's dead."

"Yeah." He nodded. "That's why I came tonight. I wanted to get in before the real killer claims it."

"Wait. Are you telling me the killer is going to waltz through the door and just confess?" Scott asked. His lips pulled back into grin and he started laughing. "This might be the easiest case we've ever had." His eyes met Sophie's.

"Am... am I in trouble for lying to the police? Giving a false statement?" Michael wrung his hands and alternated his look of panic from Sophie to Scott.

Sophie shook her head. "We need to know how you know about this bounty and how to get in touch with the person paying out the cash."

"Oh. I don't know any of that." Michael shook his head and wiped his hand across his forehead again.

"How can you not know?" Scott pushed.

"I read an email about the bounty, but it wasn't sent to me. It was open on a laptop in the break room."

Sophie rolled her eyes. This guy was completely useless. "Someone just left it open for anyone to see?"

"I don't know. I read it, but before I could get any information, the door to the bathroom started to open. I didn't want to be seen, so I ran out of the room."

Scott didn't even try to hide his disgust at him. "Fine. Write up what you do know, and if we have questions, we'll call you." He tossed the legal pad onto the table and knocked on the door.

"Thanks for coming in, Michael Carmichael. It's been a real treat." Sophie decided against flicking him in the back of his head before ditching him to write his statement. She and Scott headed out.

"So, that was a waste of fucking time," Scott fumed.

"If what he's saying is true, we could have more people coming in to confess."

"Right. So instead of investigating the fucking murder, we'll be sorting out these assholes? Who would put a bounty on her head? Because of some accounts?" Scott pulled out his chair and threw himself into it. "And is a million dollars really worth prison time?"

His head was in the game, fully focused on the case, but she couldn't help but feel some of his abrasiveness, some of his irritation was directed at her.

"Let's talk with her boss. Find out to what extent she actually stole accounts. Get a list of those she affected the most and talk with them," Sophie suggested.

He nodded. "Let's go. I'll drive you home."

"I have my car," she reminded him.

"Don't care," he said and swung his keys around his finger. She followed him out of the station house and to his car.

"I drove my car here. You don't have to drive me home. I've been driving myself to and from work my entire life. You don't get to just step in and start dictating where I go and how. It won't work that way."

Scott stopped walking and turned to her. "I'm well aware that you are capable of driving yourself where ever you want to go—when you want to go. You made that abundantly clear at my apartment. Me wanting to drive you home has nothing to do with your capabilities."

Was that it? He was sore because she'd left him behind at his place and made her own way to the precinct without him?

"Scott, if you're mad at me because I—"

He put his finger to his lips, signaling her to be quiet. "We're not talking about *that* right now. I just want to go over some of your thoughts on this case on the ride home. We'll talk about *that* tomorrow, like I told you earlier."

A beep of the car signaled the locks had disengaged, and she opened her door. Was he making her wait to talk because his anger was that great, or because he was fully invested in the case at the moment?

For now, she'd just follow the flow. In the morning, she'd deal with the blowback from fucking him. Because obviously, that had been a big fucking mistake.

CHAPTER 9

*T*he next morning Scott walked up to Sophie's apartment door and knocked. He may have knocked harder than needed, but it was still the far cry from the full-fist banging he wanted to actually do.

He'd thought waiting until morning to talk about her blowing out of his apartment would have given him the time he needed to smooth out his edges, but it only gave him time to simmer in his annoyance. If she wanted to keep them quiet at work, he could understand that, but for her to just run off the way she did, completely unacceptable.

Obviously, communication needed to be worked on. Relationships like this didn't work without communication.

The chain lock on her door, a flip of the dead bolt, and the door opened. Fuck she took his breath away.

Her hair lay around her shoulders, wet. She wore a deep-purple cotton robe, tied around her middle.

"You're early," she accused.

"How can I be early when I didn't specify what time I was coming?" He raised the box of pastries he held. "I brought breakfast."

She eyed the white box. "A little cliché, don't you think? Cops having donuts for breakfast?"

He laughed. "Not just donuts, Danishes. Cream cheese and raspberry." He gestured to the door. "You gonna let me in?"

"I suppose." She stepped back to allow him inside.

It wasn't the first time he'd been in her apartment, so he brought the pastries to the kitchen. "Don't let me get in your way. We can talk once you're dressed." He smiled.

Her eyes dropped, like he'd disappointed her somehow. Maybe she was hoping he'd rip the robe from her body, bend her over the kitchen table, and sink his cock into her hot, tight pussy. Not that he hadn't imagined doing that exact thing the second she opened the door, but they needed to talk. And talking worked better with both parties clothed. At least, for him.

He heard her bedroom door close softly down the hall. Whatever misconceptions she had would be worked out in the next hour before they headed into their day.

When she came back to the kitchen a short time later, she was fully dressed in her usual button-down shirt and black trousers. He frowned at her coiled braid.

"What?" she asked after too much time went by without him speaking. She touched the bun. "You don't like my hair? It would have taken longer to dry it and iron it out."

He shrugged. "I like it down is all."

A little glimmer shone in her eyes. "Because hair pulling was on my list?"

He let out a low laugh. "Sweetheart, I can pull your hair in a bun, out of a bun, French twisted, French braided. It wouldn't stop me." Her cheeks tinted the sweetest shade of pink. "I like your hair down because it gives you a softer look. Not so stone-hard serious."

"We're detectives. Aren't we supposed to be serious?" she asked, fumbling with the hem of her shirt.

"When it calls for it, sure." He leaned against the counter where he'd and had gotten a pot of coffee brewing.

"You made coffee?"

"Yeah. Figured we'd have a chat before we go in to work."

"You figured you'd lecture me before we leave." She nodded. "You were upset with me last night." She walked around the kitchen table, retrieved two coffee cups, and placing them on the counter just beside his hip. "I know I sort of bolted, but we had to get back to the precinct. And it's not really a good idea to let this slip out yet." She motioned a finger between them.

The coffee pot brewed behind him.

"And that's why we need to have a talk. We probably should have done this before I spanked you or we became intimate, but we didn't, so we'll take the time now." He turned around and poured coffee into the two mugs, handing her one and taking his to the table.

She kept her back to him while she poured a spoonful of sugar and cream into her coffee. He waited while she stirred it, set the spoon in the sink, and put away the carton of creamer.

"Okay, go ahead." She gestured once she was settled in her chair across from him. The Danishes remained untouched.

"You ran off, but I don't think it had everything to do with work. We've had witnesses sitting and waiting on us, and you've never hightailed it like that before." He gripped his mug. "Did you regret what happened? Were you maybe grateful for the reason to escape so quickly?"

"No." She let go of her cup and flattened her hands on the table, like she needed the stabilization. "Did you?"

He laughed. "Regret spanking your delicious ass and then taking your body on my couch? Uh. No. No regrets from me." He continued when it didn't seem like she was going to speak. "Why would I regret it? I mean, maybe we should have gone a little slower, but no, Sophie, I do not regret anything last night. Except that I didn't stop you from running out."

"We had work," she argued again, but her eyes didn't quite meet his, and her fingers curled on the tabletop.

"Gonna call bullshit on that, and if you lie to me one more time, you're going to experience your first punishment spanking. Seeing as we have a really long day ahead of us, you're going to want to avoid that this morning."

She sucked in her bottom lip and turned away.

"Sophie, this doesn't work if you can't be honest with me. If you hide shit and run off, then this breaks down. So, if you don't think you can engage in honest communication with me, then we have to stop now, before one of us gets hurt." Namely him, because he was already starting to fall for her. He'd been falling for her since meeting her, and after seeing her desire to be submissive, and experiencing how naturally she fell into that role it would only be a matter of time before he sank too deeply into her.

She stared at him silently as a soft blush deepened and rose to the tips of her ears. "You're right." After pushing the coffee away from her, she rubbed her temples. "I'm just not used to a guy being the one to talk about honesty and communication."

"I'm not like most guys," he interjected. "So, tell me why you bolted."

"It really was because of the call, but I'll admit I was a little freaked out. I mean, we're partners, Scott. We work with each other every day, and we had just had sex—like amazing sex, and that changes things doesn't it? I mean it's different now, right?"

He reached over the table and grabbed her hands with his. "It changes things outside of work. It changes nothing while we're on the clock. You're intense. I think you feel everything so much more than a lot of people. That's why when you were nervous at the club, it got to the point it did, and last night, the little worry you had blew up into a huge deal—right? That phone rang and you couldn't get out of my place fast enough. I was surprised you even put on your pants first."

She gave a little laugh. "Okay, so no more running off."

"No more running off. If work calls, we handle it together. You don't run away, and you sure as hell don't tell me to wait five minutes before following you. You don't ever give me orders outside of work, got that?" He squeezed her hands.

"I get it." She nodded.

"Good. Then you've been completely warned." He rose from his chair and walked around her, cupping his hands around her chin and pulling her head back until she her eyes met his. He wrapped one hand around her throat, not hard, no squeeze, but left it there until he saw the hard edges of her eyes soften. "There won't be another warning. If you snap orders at me, if you try to pull control away from me when we both know you don't really want that, I will punish you. And it won't be pleasant. For either of us."

Her throat constricted beneath his hand.

"I get it. Really, I do."

"You said you suck at being submissive, but I think you've never had someone you could completely trust to be the dominant one. You always waited for him to stop trying, to threaten but not follow through, you couldn't really rely on him to stay in control so you always had a soft grip on it. Am I right?"

She didn't need to answer him. The well of tears in her eyes told him everything. He'd hit the nail on the head.

"You can trust me, Sophie. I won't let you steal the control, and I won't let you give up on yourself, either." Leaning down, he kept this hand on her throat and crushed her mouth with his.

Kissing Sophie was like taking his first breath.

He'd meant it to be a soft kiss. One to seal his promise, but once his lips touched hers, he couldn't help but dive deeper until he heard the soft moan of a woman losing herself in him. He broke the kiss, pressing his lips softly to hers one more time before releasing his grip and stepping back.

"Shit, Scott," she whispered. "You can't kiss a girl like that then make her go to work."

He laughed and tapped the pastry box. "Grab a Danish. I'll get your shoes for you. Where are they?"

"Gym shoes by the front door, but I need socks." She started to stand but he gave her a gentle push to stay put. "I'll get those, too. Just eat something."

She gaped as he walked down the hall to her bedroom.

He expected to find a categorized room. Color-coded closet and all. What he found was chaos. Her closet door was open, and a mound of clothes, presumably her unwashed laundry, kept the door from closing. The bed hadn't been made, and wet towels from her shower were tossed at the foot of the bed. He grabbed them and found a pair of socks among a pile of rolled up socks on the top of her dresser.

Stopping in the bathroom, he hung up the towels and was relieved to see more of the usual Sophie. Orderly, clean.

"Here's your socks." He tossed the rolled-up ball to her as he passed the kitchen and went to the front door to grab her sneakers.

"My room's a little messy." She blushed when he came back with her shoes.

"I noticed." He winked.

"Behind on the laundry," she defended while pulling the black socks on over her purple manicured toes.

"I saw that, too. Maybe instead of taking you to Black Light tonight like I was hoping, we should hang here and wash clothes?"

She shot up from her seat with a wide-eyed expression. "Black Light?"

"Yeah. I thought maybe we could go tonight. Play a little, relax. Nothing serious. Just unwind after work." He'd found a solid play session after a rough day of dealing with assholes much more efficient than downing a bunch of beers at the local bar. "But if you have chores to do, we can put it off."

"I don't mind delaying the laundry for one more day." She sat back down and slipped into her shoes.

"Good, then. We'll go." He brought the coffee cups to the sink and flipped off the coffee pot. "Bring the Danishes. Something tells me it's going to be a long day."

CHAPTER 10

*T*he day dragged. Maybe because getting Susan James's boss to cooperate had taken over an hour, or maybe because every moment he wasn't talking to her, looking at her, or anywhere near her, Sophie was thinking about what would happen when they went to the club after work.

The spanking he'd given her the night before had awoken a part of her she'd thought she would have to ignore forever, and his words that morning had dragged desires and hopes out of the shadows she'd shoved them into.

Scott had insisted on doing all the driving for the day. Not unusual, and she didn't worry about anyone at the station house suspecting anything, but it seemed different today. Every move he made or word he said now came with a soft sense of authority behind it she hadn't felt before. She doubted anyone other than her even noticed it…or that he did it on purpose

Maybe she was playing it all in her head, and it wasn't real?

"Scott, Sophie, come here please." The captain called them into his office the moment they walked in.

When they entered his office, he tossed a folder down on the desk near them. "That's the listing of every account your vic took from her co-workers. Her boss finally sent it over a few minutes ago. Seems he was watching her behavior, but seeing as she was bringing in big clients, he didn't really care."

"Yeah, that was the impression we got, too," Scott said, opening the folder. "Claimed not to know anything about the bounty or any sort of bad feelings between her and anyone else in the firm."

"Said it was normal for some jealousy. She was up for becoming partner in the spring." Sophie added.

"Did you talk to any of the other employees while you were over there?" The captain asked, sitting back in his chair.

"A few. Most of them weren't all that sad to hear of her passing, but I didn't get a feeling they had much to do with it. None of them admitted to knowing anything about a bounty, though. I believed them," Sophie said.

"Me too. One of the other associates up for partner wasn't in the office. We'll go back on Monday and talk with him then." Scott closed the folder.

"Well, you may be in luck with another confession." The captain smiled at them. "She's waiting for you." His grin told them, the captain didn't think the confession was legit.

"Great. Another pocket protector who heard there's a price on her head and wants the cash? Don't these idiots understand what jailtime means?" Sophie asked.

"Mrs. Nancy Singleton. Room two." The captain gestured toward the door.

With a sigh, Sophie left the room and headed toward the interrogation rooms.

"Let's just let her talk and make her statement. It'll be easier to find the holes in her story and get rid of her." Scott grabbed his legal pad from his desk and clicked the pen in his hand.

"Mrs. Singleton," Sophie addressed the confessor as soon as they walked in. Sophie could have folded the woman up and put her in her pocket, she was so small. The captain hadn't told them this woman was on the verge of retirement.

"Hello. Yes. That's my name." She smiled softly. The bit of lipstick still in place cracked with the movement.

"I'm detective Russo, and this is my partner, Detective Nelson. We understand you have some information for us regarding the death of Susan James." He placed the pad on the table and slid it to her, dropping his pen on top.

Sophie took the chair this time, letting him walk around the room.

"Yes. Susan worked with me at the McAnistor firm for a time. I left the firm six months ago, after she managed to finagle my last big client." She fingered the edges of the legal pad. "A Senator," she added.

"Okay, go on," Scott prompted when dead air followed.

"Well, she found the firm I moved to and started working on my clients there. See, Susan can't get clients of her own. She sneaks in acting like she's filling in, or following up on a detail or something small and innocent enough, but then she worms inside. She finds an error, or she makes one up and wedges her way in. Well, she went after the biggest client I had again. This time I fought for the account. But she won in the end—she had found an error on a tax document."

"So, she fixed what other people messed up. That made you mad enough to kill?" Sophie leaned back in her chair. The vic may not have been completely ethical in her approach, but if she was fixing issues and could offer better work, then didn't she deserve the bigger clients?

"She didn't stop at accounts. She had—well, she—she tried to steal my husband, too. Flirted with him like crazy at the office parties, always asking me about him."

"Did your husband have an affair with Susan?" Scott stopped pacing to ask.

"Well, no, but only because he's a wonderful, devoted man." Mrs. Singleton teared up. "A wonderful man," she said again, only softer.

"Mrs. Singleton, you've obviously heard about the bounty. What do you need a million dollars for? What's making you come in here and tell us you killed someone when you obviously didn't?" Sophie leaned across the table. The woman's hand shook when she flicked away a tear.

"I-didn't know about any sort of…what did you call it? Bounty?"

"Mrs. Singleton, answer me one question and then we'll go from there. Okay?" Scott came around the table and faced her from behind Sophie.

"Okay, yes. Of course."

"Do you know how to record a video with a digital camcorder?"

The older woman's eyes widened and refilled with fresh tears. She had no clue. Sophie doubted she could operate a smart phone well enough to record anything let alone work the video camera they'd found on the scene.

"I'm so sorry," Mrs. Singleton sobbed, pressing her hands to her face.

Scott moved to sit on the table beside the crying woman. "You can help us, though. We need to know how you found out about the money."

"My husband—he's so ill. He's diabetic and has gone into kidney failure, and just recently was diagnosed with Alzheimer's. It's moving fast. That horrible woman! She said she'd-" She started sobbing again. "I knew it wouldn't work." Another sniffle.

"I think I can see why you need the money, but if you aren't working at her firm any longer, how'd you find out?" Scott placed a hand on the woman's shaking shoulder. With so few words and such an easy touch, he could heal frazzled nerves.

She wiped her eyes and took a deep breath. A sense of clarity seemed to fall over her, like she had lost her place but found it again. "I received an email?" She wiped her cheeks again.

Sophie tapped her fingers on the table. "You're not sure if you received an email?"

"I did." The woman gave a firm nod and thrust her chin upward.

"Do you still have it? Does it say how to collect the money afterward?" Scott continued to speak slowly and in a calm voice. Sophie gave him the floor, letting him make the connection and get the information they needed.

"No. I deleted it. I didn't even consider it, but then I heard she'd been killed. I heard on the news this morning. And I just, well, since the news report said there weren't any suspects, I figured, well. Here I am."

"And how do you collect the bounty?" Sophie asked.

Mrs. Singleton straightened, frowning at Sophie. "I don't know. It said once the arrest and confession were recorded, the money would be awarded. I assumed that meant whoever was posting it would contact me?"

Any hope Sophie harbored they'd be getting anything useful out of the distraught woman faded. Of course, it would continue to be illusive.

"Mrs. Singleton, I'm sure the financial strain is making the emotional side of all this even worse. I know of a few great groups who can help with the home health and financial sides. Just sit tight, and I'll get the list for you, okay?" Sophie patted the woman's hand.

"Can we get you some coffee or water in the meantime?" Scott offered, sliding off the table

"No, thank you. I'm so sorry. Will I be in trouble now?" She asked Scott.

Sophie had to suppress a giggle at the question. If she only knew what that question could lead to with Scott, she doubted Mrs. Singleton would be asking with such innocence.

"You've actually helped us, so no, no trouble." Scott smiled down at her, that casual smile Sophie enjoyed so damn much.

"Oh, but one more question. Susan wasn't really going after your husband, was she?"

Mrs. Singleton slowly shook her head with a sigh. "No, I just thought that would be a good reason, you know…if I did it."

Scott touched her shoulder lightly. "I get that. Okay, just sit tight and we'll get you out of here as quick as we can."

"I'll get that list together for her," Sophie said once they were outside the room.

"You have a soft heart, Sophie." Scott leaned closer to her ear to say. She couldn't fight the silly grin that crept across her lips. "Get her list, and I'm going to see if Craig would be able to get into the email server at McAnistor's and track down that email. When you go back in there, see if she remembers the subject line of the email."

"Sure thing." Sophie nodded and started to walk off, only to be stopped by his big hand grabbing her arm and pulling her back.

"Oh, and we're leaving here in one hour." His words came out in a growl. Like the very prospect of getting her out of the precinct and into the dungeon drew out the animal in him.

Which was good for her. She liked his beast.

THE CLUB BUSTLED BY THE TIME THEY WALKED IN TOGETHER. Sophie held tight to her bag with the non-street-legal outfit she'd brought to change into. When Scott had picked her back up after dropping off for a shower and some dinner, he didn't mention the bag. Probably because he'd texted her and told her to bring something to change into at the club.

With the music playing, the dark ambiance with the neon lighting, the nerves she'd been fighting on the drive over sent electric tingles all through her.

Scott placed his hand on her back. "It's okay, Sophie. I'm right here. I'm with you," he said into her ear and led her toward the bar.

"Why do you call me Sophie when everyone else calls me Sophie?" Focal points helped when her stomach twisted with nerves.

He found them a seat at the bar, ordered two sodas, and pushed a bowel of pretzels toward Sophie.

"Have a few of these. I know you didn't eat dinner." He grabbed one and tossed it into his mouth. Completely avoiding her question, he plucked a pretzel and handed it to her.

"You don't know that, you just assume that." She gave him a smile and grabbed the pretzel.

"Did you?" he asked with the right corner of his lips turned up.

"No, but you didn't know it." She threw another pretzel in her mouth while he chuckled.

"You're nervous about being here, and you said you don't eat when you're nervous so you don't get a stomach ache." He thanked the bartender when she brought their drinks over.

"Do you have to remember everything I say?" She focused on getting her straw into her mouth. She hated that the threat of getting sick when her nerves got out of control could get in her way of having a good time, but now that he knew it, too, it just embarrassed her.

"Did you bring a change of clothes?" He popped another pretzel into his mouth and touched the strap of the bag crossing her chest.

"Yeah. I just need stop in the bathroom and change." She remembered the general layout of the club but surveyed around to find exactly where the changing rooms were.

"You're going to change now?" he asked, confused.

"Yeah. You wanted me to bring club gear, right?" Obviously, she'd been wrong.

"I meant for after we played, like a comfy sweater or something." He leaned closer so she could hear him better.

"Sophie?" A familiar voice called from a short distance away.

She closed her eyes at the sound. The odds really liked stacking up against her.

"It is you. Hey!"

She spun around on her stool to greet Tate.

"Hey, Tate. Good to see you, again." Good thing society had a set of predetermined greetings that fit pretty much every situation.

He hadn't changed since the last time she'd seen him. Large and in charge. Scott slid off his stool and moved closer to her. Two Neanderthals hovering. Great.

"Tate, this is my-uh-well, this is Scott." She gestured to her side where he stood. "Scott, this is Tate. We used to work together." The dark lighting of the room hid his features pretty well, but she could definitely see the tick in Scott's jaw. Could he be jealous? Of Tate? The thought was laughable. Tate had eyes for one person and one person only.

"Isn't Sydney with you?" She leaned over to see if she was hiding behind the hulking man.

"Washroom." Tate didn't even hide sizing up Scott.

"Good to meet you." Scott held his hand out first.

"Yeah, same here. So, you and Sophie are together?" Tate asked, relaxing after the handshake. How much did men actually learn about each other from a simple handshake?

Scott nodded. "You were her partner before?"

"No. We worked a few cases together here and there, but we weren't really partners," Sophie interjected.

"You two partners?" Tate waggled a finger between them.

"There you are. I thought you were going to wait by the water section." Sydney bounced into the conversation. "Sophie! Wow." Her face lit up with her smile. No wonder Tate adored the ground she walked on. She was gorgeous. Inside and out.

"Hi." Sophie gave a little wave. How could Scott think to play tonight with these two in the room? They'd have to cancel.

"I didn't expect to see you, well, here, or really anywhere. I thought you were heading off on some big excursion, to see the world?" Tate hauled Sydney to his side.

"See the world?" Scott asked, sounding puzzled. Leave it to them to say the wrong thing at the wrong time. She didn't want to have to relive it all over again.

"I just changed districts," Sophie said, hoping Tate and Sydney could read her eyes because she was trying to make them say, *drop it*.

Tate turned back to Scott. "So, you're partners then?"

"Yeah." Scott gave Sophie one more side glance then focused his attention on Tate.

"Is that why you're here? You working a case?" Sydney asked, sliding toward Sophie. "I'll get him away in just a minute," she whispered so the guys didn't hear.

"No. Well, we do have a case, but that's not why we're here." Sophie's face heated, and it had nothing to do with the crowded dungeon.

"Ah." Tate reached between Scott and Sophie to grab a pretzel. "Not going to say I'm surprised, but, well, maybe a little."

"Maybe we should go." Sophie turned to Scott. No way she was playing now, not with witnesses from her previous life hanging around. She didn't need the critique or the judgment. She'd gotten her fill of that before leaving District One.

Scott shot her a worried look.

"No, absolutely not." Tate put a hand out. "I didn't mean to make you uncomfortable, Sophie. I know better. Straightlaced Type A women can be just as into the lifestyle as anyone else."

"How do you know he's not the submissive?" Sophie asked, jerking a thumb at Scott.

Tate's lips quirked. "I suppose that could be, but I've seen him here before. Never seen him on the bottom of the dynamic."

"Maybe we should go find the cross you promised we could play on tonight." Sydney gave Tate a playful shove.

"It was nice meeting you two. Maybe we can catch you guys for drinks sometime." Scott offered his hand again to Tate.

"That sounds good. You didn't change your cell, did you, Sophie?" Tate asked. She hadn't. But maybe it would have been better if she had.

"No." She shuffled her feet.

"Great. Then we'll plan something."

"It really was nice seeing you again, Sophie." Sydney wrapped her arms around her for a quick hug.

"Thanks, same here."

Scott laced his fingers with hers as they watched Tate sink his fist into Sydney's hair and lead her into the dungeon.

"He can switch gears pretty quick," Sophie said, swinging her hand—along with his.

"So, you want to explain what all that was about?" Scott pulled her to a stop and tugged her until her chest pressed against his body.

How long could she keep from clarifying the mystery Tate had just unveiled. Hopefully, Sydney would give him a run for his money tonight.

"What's that?" She sugared up her smile.

"Why would he think you were off seeing the world? Somethings not right, something you haven't told me. You said you switched districts because you moved and wanted to be closer to home."

"I did move." It was only a few miles over, but it put her an entirely different area from her old district. Not that running into anyone would destroy her world, but she'd had enough questions and assumptions, she just wanted to move on with her life.

"What is it?"

"Can't I have my own past without having to explain it and dissect it with you?" She tried to pull her hand free, but he wouldn't allow it.

"Fair enough. How about this. I was thinking we would just

have a little impact play tonight, some spanking over the bench, maybe I'd introduce you to the flogger, but I think maybe another sort of play will get us both what we want. You'll get a deeper sense of your submissive side, play with your limits a little, and I'll get the answers to all my questions."

He pulled her chin up and pressed a kiss to her lips. He wasn't so scary.

"And how is that going to happen?" She eyed his mouth. He tasted like arousal, was that even a flavor? She wanted more of it.

"Well, how tough do you think you are? Think you'll crack right away, or do you think it'll take some doing?" He gave her hand a tug and started walking her through the lounge and into the main floor of the club.

"What do you mean?"

They walked through the dungeon, past several stations. Moans of pain and groans of ecstasy came at her from all sides. A paddle raised here, a whip cracked over there, and between the sharp sounds and the arousing sights he brought her over to the washrooms.

"What do you have in that bag? Like how sexy is it?" He took the bag from her arms and opened it.

"Why ask if you're going to paw through it anyway?" she asked. "It's just a shirt with a skirt. I didn't have time to get real fetish gear."

He closed the bag and threw it over his shoulder with to his own bag of tricks. "Okay, well, I think I prefer you nude anyway."

Without explanation, he pulled her back through the busy club. The sounds and sights were less of a distraction this time as he headed toward the semi-private rooms.

"Are you sure? You seem a little indecisive," she teased when he threw back the curtain and propelled her into the room. "First, you drag me to the changing area then here. I mean, if you want to take a moment to think this through—" He clapped his hand over her mouth, stilling the next smart remark dancing on her tongue.

He pushed her head back, exposing her neck. She pressed her palms against his chest but didn't push. The heat in the room kicked up a notch, or maybe it was having him so close, the confidence rolling off of him, his control seeping into her body.

She didn't make a sound.

Until he ran his tongue up the length of her neck and bit into her jaw.

She moaned. Closing her eyes, she let out an aroused groan when he did it again—this time licking her cheek and biting her earlobe.

"Do you remember what yellow and red stand for?" he asked, kissing his way down her neck.

Her mouth still hid behind his palm, so she nodded.

"I'm trusting you to use them if you need them. If you don't, I'll punish you until you'll wish you had. Now, do you think you can trust me to take us where we both want to go tonight?"

He peeled his hand off her mouth. She licked at her dry lips.

"Yes. I trust you." She did. With her life. The job called for it, but this wasn't work. This was deeper, more intimate.

"Good." He removed all touch and stepped back three paces. "Strip down."

"What are you going to do to me?" she asked, gripping the hem of her sweater. The curtains between the room and the main space were closed, if someone stood in the right spot they'd see everything going on. And it sure as hell wasn't soundproof.

"That depends on you, sweetheart. If you answer my questions honestly, then you'll get a lot of rewards. But if you start being evasive and lying, well, things won't be so pleasant." He turned away from her and went to the table and hoisted his bag onto it.

He pulled an array of implements from his bag. Rope, crop, paddles made of leather and wood were the ones she could see before he shifted his body and blocked her view completely.

"You aren't undressing. That's not a good sign of your future cooperation," he said without turning.

"Are you going to use all those things?" she asked, still not peeling off her clothing.

He walked away from the table, giving her full view of the arsenal. She'd seen a lot of gruesome shit in her line of work, and she'd handled every one of those scenes with an iron stomach and steel spine. But seeing all the paddles, and belts and things she couldn't name made her tummy lurch and her knees wobble.

"Get undressed, and examine everything on the table. If I come back and you have so much as a sock on, you'll have your first punishment spanking before we begin."

The curtain swayed after he disappeared. She swallowed his name, wanting to call him back at first. Taking a deep breath, she realized the reprieve he'd given her. She could obey him and settle her nerves by familiarizing herself with the implements before he came back.

She peeled her clothes off quickly and folded them in a pile on a chair in the corner and hightailed it over to the table where she picked up a few of the toys and fondled them.

"Ah, the vibrator. Only if you're good will you get that, Sophie. Now come here. Exploration time is over," Scott said. A man with a similar build helped him carry in a chair of some sort. She wrapped her arm over her breasts and moved to the end of the table, anything to put some distance between her and the stranger.

Why take her to a private area if he was just going to traipse in with some strange man?

"Thanks. I got it from here." Scott maneuvered the contraption more into the center of the room.

The chair seemed like an inquisitor's tool. The legs and arms were moveable—straight out to the sides or vertical for the arms. The legs could bend and open wide or come together. Metal clasps would keep the wooden limbs of the chair positioned, and leather straps would keep the victim restrained. At least she wouldn't be sitting on bare wood. The seat and headrest were cushioned.

Scott worked the hinges and limbs until it resembled an actual chair, aside from the arms sticking straight out to the sides. He stood to his full height and wiped his hands on his jeans. As though he finally remembered there was a sub nearby, he looked up and found her still hiding behind the table.

"I said come here, Sophie." He gestured, no more urgent than beckoning a small child over for a piece of candy.

"What are you going to do?" she asked with a tentative step. She hadn't noticed the chill in the room before, but her nipples were budding and a shiver building in her spine.

"I'm going to ask you a few questions, that's all." A nonchalant grin settled on his lips. She'd seen that one before.

"Why don't you just ask now?" She let loose a soft laugh at the end. Dammit, she would be giggling like an idiot soon if he kept teasing her with his darkened stare.

"Okay. One chance." He folded his arms over his chest. "Full truth. Why did you switch districts, and why would Tate and Sydney think you'd be traveling the world?"

She could get it over with and move on. But she wasn't ready to go through all the bullshit again.

"I wanted a change of scene." As a lie, it could have been better. Moving three districts over wasn't exactly a big change.

Scott laughed and dropped his hands to his sides. "Well, then. I suppose you'll need to sit down so we can get started." With two strides, he was at her side and gripping her elbow, pulling her to the chair.

She plunked down on the seat and gave him a solid glare while he took each wrist and shackled her to the device. As he moved from her right side to her left, he paused to wink at her. She huffed and turned away, refusing to watch him buckle the strap on her left wrist, or admit she found the situation even remotely arousing. Hell, all he'd have to do was check between her legs to know for himself.

With each ankle strapped down, and her thighs bound to the chair as well, he stepped away and looked down at her. His fingertips drummed against his chin.

She avoided his eyes, his inquisitive eyes that would see right through her bravado. Watching him question a suspect enthralled her. No matter how defiant, how stubborn the suspect came off, Scott bided his time, wiggling through the holes in their stories until he got to the truth. He remained in complete control, never once wavering in his confidence he would get the answer or backing down in the dominance he displayed.

But now, those eyes were focused on her. And he wanted answers. Could she really hold out from him?

"Tits first," he announced and walked behind her where lay the table with his instruments of doom. Twisting her neck, she tried to see what he picked up, but he held it behind him until he stood in front of her again.

"What do you have?" She leaned to the right, not getting anywhere with the restraints on her arms.

"Here's the rules." He tucked the implement into the back of his pants and stepped up to her, straddling her legs and sitting down on her lap. He fisted her hair and gave a quick pull, and she was looking at him down the length of her nose. "Rule one, I'm asking the questions—not you. Rule two, you will answer me honestly or you'll be punished. Rule three. You will use your safewords if you need them, no brave hero shit tonight."

His lips closed in on hers, nearly touching. The jackhammering of her heart had to be echoing in the room. How could everyone not hear it? Just as she closed her eyes to accept his kiss, he released her and stood.

"Now that we have the rules straight, let's get to it."

She opened her eyes just in time to see him smirk on his face and pull out a short flogger from his pants. Her lips tingled.

"I wonder how long you can last—what do you think? Fifteen lashes?" He flicked his wrist, maneuvering the flogger in a crossover pattern, bringing the tips of the falls close enough for her to feel the cool breeze.

"Sure. I can do fifteen." She nodded. Fifteen smacks and she'd win. "But wait. What do I get if you can't get me to crack?"

His lips quirked with a laugh. "Have I ever not gotten the guilty to talk?" he asked then held up his hand. "Don't answer. We aren't bringing work here. Fine. Just so you can have a glimmer of hope, if you can hold out, if you don't give me the answers I want, I'll pay for a month of your membership dues. Since you didn't get a chance to win it at the game, make it through this scene with your secret still hidden, and you'll get a free month."

He couldn't be serious, but then again, she would admit, she had not seen a reluctant suspect who didn't crack beneath him. She knew how he worked, though. She could get through it.

"Fine." She nodded.

"Good." He sealed the deal by pulling his arm back and unleashing the first lash across her exposed breasts.

The wind from the flogger blew her hair. Her breasts jostled from the impact, but all in all, not bad. Fourteen more to go —bring it.

She straightened her back and brought her gaze to meet his. He shook his head, still wearing that damn grin of his, and brought his hand back again, this time landing a hard smack to her thighs. She bit back a cry, clenching her jaw instead. The third and fourth lashes came hard and quick, one to her chest, the next to her thighs.

He moved around her to her right side and brought his hand back again.

By the tenth stroke, her breath came in ragged bursts. Her nipples budded in pained arousal, but the lashes to her thighs throbbed more.

"Doing good, sweetheart," he said as he ran his palm over her aching thighs. "Do you think you'd like to answer me now?"

"I already told you." She lifted her chin and avoiding his stare.

He wiped a strand of hair from her heated face. "That's my girl. I'd almost be disappointed if you made this easy on me." He kissed her forehead and stepped back into place. The flogger came quickly across her breasts, one way then the next. Her chest became his canvas, his flogger the brush.

She cried out, no longer able to bite back the sound of her torture.

Hanging her head, she gasped for breath. A droplet of sweat rolled down her cheek and dripped onto her stomach.

He touched her, fingers running through her hair and tucking it behind her. He placed kisses on her forehead. She'd taken it down from the tight bun she wore for work, much to his pleasure.

"Why did you change districts?" he asked, moving his fingers along her jaw and down her chest to her breast. Using his knuckles, he soothed her heated flesh.

She raised her head, finding his eyes and pushed a smile on her lips. "I didn't like the coffee."

He grinned back at her, and his fingertips—the ones soothing her breasts, dug into her. Grabbing her breast, he dragged his nails along her skin until he reached her nipple. She sucked in her breath through gritted teeth. Not yet. She wouldn't cave to him so easily. She could hold out longer.

"Did you want to say something?"

"No!" She clenched her eyes closed when he moved to her other breast and dug his nails into her skin. "Fuck," she yelled, jerking her legs with the need to kick out.

"If you would cooperate, we could get to that." He placed a soft kiss on the tip of her nose and walked away again. When he returned, he bent over, unlatched the hooks keeping her legs closed, and spread them apart wide.

Every inch of her body, every tender spot that could be licked, kissed, or smacked became exposed to him. She scooted her butt back, noting the wetness of the leather beneath her. Through the bite and burn, her body hummed and came alive. She took a deep breath, readying herself for whatever he came to her with next.

A vibrator appeared before her eyes.

She'd won! That hadn't been as hard as she thought it would be; maybe he took it easy on her because she was so new to the game.

"You like this?" he asked, flicking the switch to start the bulbous head of the toy vibrating.

"Hell yeah." She laughed.

"Well. We'll see." He squatted between her legs. Not really the visual she liked to display to anyone, but least of all a man she found so intoxicating. It was somewhat easier to smooth out the curves when she was standing but sitting resulted in poor results. Scott didn't so much as blink at the imperfections of her body as he pushed against her belly and gave himself better access to her clit.

"Why did you change districts?" he asked again, looking up at her.

"You're like a parrot, you know that?" She grinned. She would win this. No problem.

Holding her gaze, he flicked on the vibe and pressed it against her clit. Not just above the hood where the vibrations could sink into her sex and rev her arousal. Or just below where the extra pressure could result in a quicker release, but directly onto the swollen nub.

She screamed and tried to wiggle back, but she had no retreat option. Jerking her hips didn't do anything other than meet the damn vibrator head on.

"Oh fuck. Oh fuck." A hard orgasm built, painfully quick. "Fuck." She threw her head back, waiting for the explosion, welcoming the release from the vibrator. The first wave began to peak, and the vibrator was taken away.

She was left with a slow ache, a deep throb that brought no satisfaction.

"No!" Quickly matching his glare, she pulled against her restraints, not entirely sure of what her plan would be should she get free. But it definitely had something to do with getting that vibrator away from him and back on her clit.

"Why?" he asked again, readjusting his body, probably for his own comfort.

"No." She refused more on principal now than actual need of hiding. He would not break her. She would keep it from him, no matter what.

"Got it." He flicked it back on, the speed increased, and once again he placed it directly on her clit, this time twisting it, grinding it into the overstimulated bundle of nerves.

"Oh fuck. Fuck." She wiggled again. The higher speed dragged her to the edge straightaway. She bit down on her lip, determined not to let him see how close she was, but she should have known better. He could read expressions better than any partner she'd ever had.

The flip of a switch, and the sensations were gone, along with her impending orgasm.

"Dammit." She jerked against her binds, wanting to cry for her loss.

"All you have to do is tell me why. Is it so bad?" He waved the vibrator in front of her face.

"No, it's not bad at all." She put her head back and took a long breath. "But I'm not telling you."

She didn't even get to finished with a snide remark before he spread her pussy lips wide and jammed the vibrator between her pussy and the chair. She tried to wiggle, but it only seemed to wedge the bullet shaped toy farther.

"Go ahead and come," he told her, waving his hand at her dilemma.

Not one to look a gift horse in the mouth, she moved against the vibrator until she found a sweet spot. "Oh fuck." She breathed, clenching her eyes closed, fisting her hands and gyrating her hips until the sweet peak swept her away. Another scream unleashed from her, full of pleasure.

She really did win.

CHAPTER 11

$\mathcal{T}$he victorious grin spreading across Sophie's lips was almost too delicious to wipe away.

Almost.

The adorable little sub thought they were finished—that she'd gotten her way.

Not at all.

"Did you enjoy that?" he asked. Turning the vibrator off, he left it unmoving but pinned between her body and the chair.

"Fuck yeah." Her lips spread into a wide grin, and she gave a soft laugh. She really thought she'd won. Oh, it was going to be a hard reality for her. No need to drag out the wait; better to just rip off the bandage.

"Last chance. What made you change districts?" He shifted to his knees, The squat burned his thighs, and this wasn't supposed to be giving him any discomfort.

She dragged in a long breath, pressing her head back against the leather cushion, and peered down her nose at him, a sneer on her lips. "I thought you were better at this. I've already gotten what I want. Why would I—" Her snide commentary cut off when the vibrator erupted into high speed. "Oh!"

Even with the binds on her legs and arms, her ass could wiggle just enough she could possibly get away from the vibrations. If she were playing with another dominant, maybe she would succeed. But lucky for her, she had Scott. And he didn't miss things like this.

He held her hips steady, pressing her ass into the seat and putting more pressure of the vibrator into her.

Her wide eyes sought him out. If she was searching for pity, she wouldn't find it from him. There were two ways out: safeword or confess. Anything else was bullshit.

"Scott!" She shook her head. Strands of hair stuck to her face, enlaced with a layer of shimmering sweat.

"Either tell me or come." He grinned up at her, twisting the head of the vibrator and sliding it even farther down her slit, closer to her entrance.

"Fuck you!" she screamed, threw hear head back, and wiggled her hips. The protest didn't fool him. Another twist, a little more lift to the back of the vibe to put extra pressure on her clit, and she unraveled before him.

Another cry and more huffing as she came down from her orgasm. Steady eyes landed on him when he flicked the vibrator off. Her chest heaved with each ragged breath. What had been neatly brushed hair when they started now hung around her face in loose strands. The rugged beauty of a submissive in the twilight of a scene was never lost on him, but it went deeper with Sophie. He didn't just want to plow his cock into her, he wanted this connection—he wanted her trust. Not just to tie her up and spank her, or flog her tits, but enough trust to give him this piece of information she kept stored away from the rest of the world.

He brushed away her hair again, tucking it behind her ears and wiping the strands from her cheeks. As she regained her breath, he ran the back of his fingers over her jaw, down her chest, and petted her, stroking her softly and continuously until she raised her chin to meet his gaze.

The fire hadn't died.

Perfect.

"We won't stop until you tell me," he assured, waving the vibrator in front of her. "That was only two. I've gone up to seven."

Her eyes narrowed at his confession. Maybe during a scene wasn't the time to mention past lovers.

Noted.

"I've never had more than one." Her confession surprised him. He expected a smart-ass remark, a jab at him for his blunder.

He laughed. "Well then, I'll give you a moment to think about it. Give me the reason, or you'll give me another orgasm." Standing, he pressed a kiss to the top of her head and walked over to his bag of tricks. He could try more impact play, maybe use a small crop on her tits, but she loved pain. He had seen it when he'd flogged her earlier. Getting her lost in subspace wouldn't get the answer he wanted.

No, he had the right course. He just needed a new tool.

A smile crept across his lips when he found it. The perfect little bullet to help. Some pain mixed with the pleasure would drive her wild, and the little purple toy was just the vibe for the job.

Palming it, he walked back over to Sophie. She still breathed heavy, but she'd relaxed during the time he gave her. The muscles in her arms were less strained. Still, he worried.

"How are your arms?" he asked, grazing his fingers over her shoulders. He hadn't raised them over her head, but being trussed for any length of time could fatigue the body.

"My arms are fine, but my shoulders are starting to burn a little, sir."

His breath caught at her easy use of the title. They hadn't talked about it, and he hadn't demanded it, so to hear it so naturally fall from her lips made him take a moment to sink into her submissiveness.

Tucking the bullet vibe in his back pocket, he released her arms from the restraints. "Fold your hands in your lap," he directed. She nodded, shook her arms a bit then steepled her hands between her thighs.

He went back to his bag and grabbed the black leather cuffs. Squatting behind her, he reached around to pull her arm back. "If you wiggle too much, your shoulders will hurt more, so I suggest you don't." He smiled widely since she couldn't see him.

"How's that?" he asked once he'd linked the D-rings of the cuffs behind her.

"Better, thanks." She glanced up at him as he rounded the chair, once more palming the vibe.

"Not sure you want to thank me just yet, sweetheart." He winked at her and grabbed the larger toy. Settling back in place between her thighs, he observed her body, her breathing. As each softened, he brushed her hair from her face. "Ready to start again?" He reached up and pressed a kiss to her warm cheek. A tint of rose covered her face, hopefully from exhilaration.

"Why is this so important to you?" she questioned. Her expression softened as she brought her gaze to his.

"For one, you don't want to tell me, which means it's something important to you. And if it's important to you, then it is to me, too. And two I have my own suspicions about you, but I need to find out if they're true."

"I can safeword out of telling you, can't I?" She posed the question void of hope weighing down her words.

"Of course, you can. Call your safeword, and we stop. I'll unbind you, and we can go get a drink in the lounge." He sat back on his heels. Making the decision to cry off or stay in the scene wouldn't be determined by him; he'd keep his touches to himself until she gave the blaring green light.

She took in a slow breath and pushed on a smile. "Then let's go."

Oh, how silly this girl could be.

Flicking on the large vibrator, he once again maneuvered between her pussy and the chair. She squirmed but couldn't get away.

"Wait. Oh fuck, wait," she huffed. She had to be sensitive by now. The lightest touch probably shoved her right to the edge of an orgasm.

Time to crank it up.

"Tell me," he ordered, his fingers hovering over the speed switch.

She clamped her mouth shut and shook her head.

A spin of the dial and the vibrations intensified, the chair made more noise from the shaking, and she squealed as another orgasm ripped through her.

"Ow. Oh god! No! Fuck!" Jerking her hips did nothing since he was completely focused on her, he followed her and twisted the toy along with her body, not giving her a moment of peace as her orgasm waned into something more intense.

"Scott!" she screamed and jumped in the chair as best she could manage.

"Whoa," he chuckled. "Just tell me and you can stop." He pulled the small bullet from his back pocket and twisted the bottom with this thumb, springing the miniature toy to life.

Her eyes were squeezed shut, her body writhing within the restraints, and her mouth hung open taking in breaths and whimpering at the same time. Almost there. He knew the signs, could see the fatigue. She'd cave. And he would catch her when she did.

Leaning forward he swiped his tongue over her large nipple, bringing it to a hard peak.

She groaned, but he wouldn't stop, not until he had what he wanted.

"Why'd you leave?" he asked, the little bullet positioned.

She half sobbed but shook her head. At least one part of her was beginning to understand how this worked. He asked, and she answered. If only she would stop overruling her mind and let herself fall into the moment.

"Okay, then." He moved the bullet closer to her nipple, his attention refocused on her face. Her eyes flew open just as the tip touched the little bead.

Another moan. A moment of pleasure that wouldn't last, but she didn't know. How could she?

He licked his lips, watching her expression. The parting of her pouty lips, the crease in her forehead as the vibrations worked their way through her breast. He scooted the vibe at her pussy higher, putting more pressure on her already overworked and over sensitized clit.

"Oh." She rolled her head to the side.

One more click of the dial and the bullet sped up. Her pouty lips pressed together firmly. The soft crease between her brows deepened, and her eyes flew open as the vibrations started to take effect. A little sensation could be great; too much would make her feel like her nipple would ignite.

He didn't bother suppressing his laugh when her eyes filled with betrayal and she glared at him.

"Why?" he asked, softening his tone.

"Oh fuck." She inched her hips closer to the edge of the chair, seeking or avoiding, he doubted she could tell the difference at the moment.

"Scott, too much." Her head bowed making her hair fly back in front of her face. "Okay. Okay!"

He removed the bullet from her breast and turned the speed down on the vibrator at her pussy.

"Tell me."

"Give me a second to breathe." She shook her hair away and took several gulping breaths. Stalling.

"Nope." He brought all the toys to full speed and went back to work.

"Travis Dixon!" she screamed just before she groaned and her body jerked. Another orgasm had taken hold of her. The chair shook along with her movements, her mouth open in a silent scream.

He dropped the bullet to the floor and eased the vibrator away from her, replacing it with his hand and rubbing her gently until she relaxed into his touch and she leaned her head back to catch her breath.

Travis Dixon.

Just hearing the name sent his blood to a simmer, but he had more pressing business at the moment than thinking about that prick.

"Good girl," he whispered, pressing kisses to her shoulders and chin while he worked the restraints. "Such a good girl." He unclasped her ankle restraints and brought the legs of the chair back together, reattaching bolts before setting his attention to freeing her hands.

"I'm never going to orgasm again," she whispered.

He chuckled.

"You will. I promise." Once her arms were free, he scooped her up and walked with her to a set of chairs in the corner.

He kept her in his lap, lifted her legs onto the chair beside them, and finagled a blanket around her body to keep her warm. Even with the thin layer of sweat on her forehead, she smelled fresh from a shower. He snuggled her closer to him.

They sat quietly. He wouldn't disturb her too soon.

"You played dirty with that vibrator on my nipple," she accused in a light tone. "It felt really good until it felt really bad."

He grinned and rested his chin on her head. "I know."

"Of course, you did.

"So. Travis Dixon," He clamped down on the blunt wording he wanted to use to express his feelings about the man. "What did he do?"

She sighed and pushed away from him enough to meet his eyes. "We dated. It ended badly."

"How badly?" If that asshole put one fucking hand on her, he'd wreck him.

"Badly enough." She whirled her legs off the chair and pushed away from him, wrapping the blanket around her.

"Were you partnered with him?" Travis didn't work well with others, and if he hadn't changed much in the five years since he'd worked with him, he really didn't work well with women.

"No. He worked the gang unit, and I was homicide."

He didn't stop her from pacing around the room. As long as she kept talking, she could keep walking.

"So, what happened?" He remained in his seat, unwilling to interrupt her by moving toward her.

"I took a trip home to see my mother in Chicago and made the mistake of asking him to stop in and feed my cat. He took it upon himself to have a look around and found my toy box. When I got home, he teased me about it and said I was into some sick shit." She wandered over to her pile of clothes and scooped them up.

"Asshole," Scott muttered.

"Yeah. Well, it got worse. I broke it off. Aside from the sheer disrespect of that comment, it was obvious he'd never step up into the dom role."

The idea of any woman submitting to a prick like Travis made his fists clench.

"When I got back to work, people would snicker when I walked past them, stare at me."

She didn't seem like the type to give in to pressure, but he didn't comment.

"It wasn't their childish shit that got me. Travis made every day harder than it needed to be. I think he was pissed that the chubby girl in homicide blew him off. He thought I should have been on my knees begging him to be with me instead of breaking up with him."

"You didn't report him? Go to HR?"

She dropped the blanket and worked her way back into her clothes.

"For what? So an investigation could be opened and we'd all be questioned? The last thing I needed was to talk to my union rep about my kinks. So, I took leave and got myself a transfer." She shrugged and slid her shirt over her head.

He'd heard of people being outed at work or in their personal lives and how hard it could be for them, but knowing Sophie had to change districts because of that son of a bitch made it more real. But that was the exact reason Black Light existed. To keep those situations to a minimum. A safe place for them to play.

"You think I'm some weak little woman, now, don't you?" She folded her arms over her chest and leaned against the table where he'd laid out his toys for the night.

Just minutes ago, she'd been in the throes of an orgasm. His cock had been steel hard. But here she was, dressed, the evening winding down. His cock had been completely ignored, yet he didn't have regrets. Satisfaction came in many forms, and hearing her open up to him meant just as much as any orgasm he might have.

"No." He shook his head and stood. "I'm still trying to wrap my brain around you being a cat lady."

CHAPTER 12

*S*usan James was a first-class bitch.

Sophie opened the digital files Craig had sent over. So far, she'd only uncovered emails throwing co-workers under the bus and blatant attempts to steal clients.

No wonder there hadn't been any memorial services planned at McAnistor. Not a soul mourned her.

Between the stealing and the conniving, the suspect list grew each time she opened an email. Rubbing her eyes, she sat back in her chair.

"Hey," Scott touched her shoulder as he rounded her desk to his own. A light brush of his fingers, nothing more. Yet her body reacted as though he'd just stripped her naked. "Find anything useful?"

She waved at the computer. "Nope. Not at all. Forensics got back to us, though. There are exactly three sets of fingerprints in the apartment. Susan's, the maids, and the super's—which can be easily explained with the leaky faucet he fixed the day before." She pointed to her computer screen. "Which is also backed up by the nasty email she sent him requesting the service."

"Not a gracious woman, huh?" He sat in his chair. Having their desks facing each other made conversations easier, but it also eliminated any privacy.

"Not someone I'd like to deal with on a daily basis." Sophie grabbed her coffee and took a sip, keeping her eyes on the computer.

The weekend had been spent mostly with Scott. Saturday they'd had lunch together, then seen a movie that turned into dinner. Sunday breakfast at his place had been followed by another session of panty melting make-outs and a solid spanking before he fucked her against the kitchen island. But she'd passed on spending the evening with him at his friend's house.

Friend dinner bordered on meeting the parents, and they weren't there yet. Hell, maybe they would never be there, but for right now, she just wanted to embrace the fun they were having. And get to work on the case.

Telling him about Travis had been easy once the flood gates had opened. The judgment she feared had never come.

"Have the IT guys been able to find any leads on the email?" he asked.

"They promised to have it this afternoon. But in the meantime, I've been combing through her crap. Hoping to find someone who stood up to her, because fuck, she was a bitch." She put her coffee cup back on the desk.

"Nothing?" Scott leaned back in his chair. So many parts of working a case involved waiting for analysis and test results; without a witness or suspects to grill, they were left staring at each other.

"Nelson! Russo! Got another one for you!" The captain jerked a thumb toward the interrogation rooms.

Scott arched both eyebrows. "He can't be serious. Another one?"

"This is just stupid." Sophie grabbed a pen.

"Well, the last one did give us some information. Maybe this one will have more insight." Scott stood and stretched his arms over his head, his shirt hem lifting enough for her to get a glimpse of his abs. Not too hard bodied, but enough fitness to dry her mouth by watching him move. She blinked, reminding herself they were at work. They had a case to solve. No matter how much of a bitch the victim was, she didn't deserve to be murdered.

Scott cupped her elbow as they walked toward the interrogation room. Her first instinct was pull away; the little touch could be misread by other officers. The mind reader he was turning out to be must have understood her too well; he closed his fingers around her arm and held her close to him.

"Just being a gentleman," he whispered while he pulled open the first set of glass doors. His hand released her but found a new position on the small of her back. Even when he wasn't in the lead, he led her.

Scott stopped just outside the interrogation room. "Have we heard back yet from the vic's family?"

"No, which is a little weird. She has a sister who lives in New York. You'd think she'd be interested in finding out what happened. We'll need to talk to her."

Scott nodded. "You wanna get some dinner tonight?" He posed the question with his hand on the door handle.

"We're at work," she said.

"Partners have dinner all the time," he pointed out.

And that's what they were, partners. But she didn't see a friendly smile beaming down at her. She saw possession.

With too much to think about, to process, she turned back to the closed door. "Fine. Dinner. Now, open the door." She hadn't meant to sound so pissy. A girl being taken to dinner by Scott should be thrilled to her toes, yet for Sophie, it stirred up unease. She'd agreed to see how things progressed with them, but she hadn't expected so much normalcy to invade their relationship.

Nights at the club, learning tricks of the trade, that sort of thing, sure. But he wanted dinners and movies and hanging with friends.

And when it all failed, where would that leave her? Them? Would she have to transfer districts again? She'd let herself get taken in with the promise of Scott's dominance, and now she worried it would all crumble again anyway. Hadn't she learned her lesson already?

Too much uncertainty for a Monday.

"Let's get in there."

Scott hesitated a moment, wrinkled his brow, and she thought he was going to drag her into a long conversation. Thankfully, he let the matter drop and opened the door.

A man, mid-thirties, sat facing the door, his hands folded on the table. Wide dark eyes, clenched jaw, his mouth downturned. For someone ready to confess to a murder he probably hadn't committed, he gave more of an impression of terrorized animal than martyr.

"You're—" He paused to clear his throat, and hopefully straighten out his nerves. "You're the detectives working on Susan's murder?" A little wobbly at the end, but he made it through the sentence without wavering too much.

"Yes," Scott answered pulling back the chair opposite the man and sat down. "I'm Detective Russo, and this is my partner, Detective Nelson."

"And you are?" Sophie asked. They should have stopped to get the preliminary information before jumping into the room.

"Clark Simmons," he answered but kept his eyes glued to Scott.

"Well, Clark. I understand you have some information for us about Susan." Sophie perched on the table beside Clark, letting her leg brush his elbow.

Still he didn't face her.

"I think she was murdered by her ex-boyfriend. I saw them a

few days ago, arguing in front of our office building. It looked…
heated." He interlaced his fingers, whitening his knuckles.

"And you worked with her?" Sophie asked tapping her pen
against his shoulder to draw his attention to her.

"I did." He nodded. "Well, in the same building."

"So, you aren't here to confess?" Scott sat back, folding his
arms over his chest. She knew him well enough to hear the relief
in his voice, but suspected their new friend, Clark, would take it
as disinterest.

"Confess? Why would I do that?" Clark's back straightened,
and he dared for the first time to look up at Sophie.

"Tell us more about Susan. Were you two close?" Sophie
skipped his question.

"No. She worked on the floor above mine. We only knew each
other casually. Lunchroom, elevator, that sort of thing." Clark
went back to staring at Scott. Did he think Scott had more clout
because he was the man in the room? Could he really mistake her
for a sidekick of sorts?

Scott didn't make a sound. He kept his arms folded over his
chest, giving off the formidable presence he was while Sophie slid
from the table and walked behind Clark.

"I'm confused. You knew her or you saw her, which was it?"
Sophie questioned from behind him.

His back tensed, and he shift in his seat.

"We spoke casually," he explained.

"And what was your impression of her?" Sophie asked next.

"Impression?" he parroted.

"What did you think of her? Generous, adventurous, warm
hearted, business shark? Like, how was she?" Sophie tossed the
pad of paper she'd brought with her on the table and took the seat
beside Scott. The bastard could keep ignoring her, but she'd be the
one asking questions.

"I don't know. She seemed decent enough. I heard her talking about trying to make partner where she worked, but there was a lot of competition. She worried she wouldn't get it."

Scott unfolded his arms and leaned forward. "You heard her?"

Clark blinked several times and swallowed hard. "Yes. On her phone, talking to her boyfriend."

"How did you know it was her boyfriend?" Sophie asked.

"She used his name, I'd heard it before when she was making dinner plans with him." Clark fidgeted in his seat.

"So, you never had any real conversations with her? You sort of stalked her?" Sophie leaned closer to him. From what she had learned about Susan, this guy seemed more likely to be devoured by her than befriended.

"What? No! We rode the same elevator many times, took lunch at the same time. But I didn't stalk her." His jaw clenched, and Sophie watched him for a long, silent moment. This was definitely an admirer from afar. He wasn't looking up at her because he thought her a mere woman. He couldn't make eye contact because girls scared him.

"What about this ex-boyfriend. What about him?" Scott pressed on, probably having come to the same conclusion.

"She was mad because he didn't make time for her. So, she broke it off." He squinted at Sophie, not quite meeting her eyes. "I heard her telling him on the phone to stop calling her. She told him she didn't want to see him anymore, and she'd call him if she needed him."

"You ever meet him?" Sophie asked.

"No." He unlaced his fingers and spread them flat on the table. "That afternoon I saw them arguing was the first time I'd seen him in person."

"How'd you know it was him?" Scott asked.

A blush grew over Clark's cheeks. "His picture was on her contacts. I saw the screen when he called once…or twice."

"You ever ask her out?" Scott asked. "I mean after she broke up with her boyfriend," he added.

Clark's eyes widened briefly. "No. Of course not." He swallowed hard, his Adam's apple bobbed. Never ask, never get rejected.

Sophie exchanged a glance with Scott. Once she was confident they were on the same page, she continued. "So, you saw them arguing. Did it get physical?" Sophie asked. "Did he push her maybe, slap her?"

"No, he just, well, he pinned her against the building. And he… well, he kissed her. But it wasn't a nice kiss, and she pushed him off." His jaw tensed again.

"And you charged in to save her?" Her attempt to keep the sarcasm from her voice failed on an epic level. Clark turned his gaze to her; a flash of disgust was quickly disguised once more behind his eyes. Was he disgusted by his own cowardice?

"She didn't need me to. I only came down here because I heard about what happened to her, and I know he had something to do with it."

"Because he kissed her a little rough a few weeks ago?" Scott asked. "You sure you weren't just a little bit jealous? I mean, she was really good looking. Successful. Maybe you didn't like being ignored? Rejected?"

"She never rejected me," Clark said firmly.

"Right. Because you never asked her out. You just sort of followed her around like a lost puppy? Hoping for some scraps from the table?" Sophie pushed.

Clark shook his head and slammed his hand down on the table. "I knew you'd make something out of nothing. It's why I didn't come down right away." The fear from earlier crept back into his expression.

"You thought because you had a crush on her, we'd pin this on you?"

"I figured you'd turn this into some sort of jealousy plot, and it's not. I'm not. I wasn't interested in her, not like that. She was a good lady and didn't deserve what happened to her." He ran his fingers over his eyes, pinching his nose.

Sophie raised her eyebrows in confusion. "A good lady?"

"You didn't even know her, Clark." Scott pointed out.

Clark's blush deepened, and he took a deep breath through his nose.

"Do you know the boyfriend's name?" Scott kept his tone even. No one they'd talked to so far had mentioned a boyfriend. From what they knew of her, she didn't have anyone in her corner.

"That's the other thing." His hands clenched together again, and the vein on the side of his neck throbbed with his pulse. "He's a cop." The sentence came out like a moan. Like he didn't want to say it. Understandable, walking into a precinct uninvited to accuse an officer of murder. Now his fear really became palpable.

"What's his name?" Scott asked again. His tone didn't change, but she'd seen the tension build in his muscles.

"Look, Clark, you came in to see us. We didn't come find you. And I know it's hard coming into a police station pointing the finger at a cop. It takes a lot of strength to do that." She reached across the table and placed a gentle hand on top of his hand.

At first, she'd thought he only wanted to deal with Scott because he had a strong sexist gene flowing through his dick, but Clark was just a guy who didn't have the balls to talk to women, no matter how attractive he found them. It was probably worse with the attractive ones. He found Scott less scary because he was a guy. She couldn't completely blame him. It wasn't like Clark had seen Scott carrying a flogger with that intense glare of his. And she did tend to give off a bitch vibe when in the interrogation room.

Clark dragged his gaze up Sophie's arm to meet her eyes. The fear eased away a fraction, but she could still see the hesitation.

"You've come this far, not telling us now would be such a waste, wouldn't it? And if he's really the guy who did it, who hurt her, we might not get him without your help. None of our current leads are getting us very far."

He took in a shaky breath and nodded. "His name is Steve Renner."

Scott tensed beside her, but she didn't let on she noticed. She kept her eyes steady on Clark, he visibly relaxed.

"I'm not sure which station he works out of." He added, his tone softening. He'd just tossed a boulder off his shoulders.

Unfortunately, he'd tossed it onto theirs.

CHAPTER 13

"*I*'m telling you it's weird. He had such a rose-colored view of Susan. Nothing like we'd heard yet. How could he get such a nice piece of her when everyone else got megabitch?" Sophie said as they walked down the street toward the first precinct. Scott had parked the car a block down, wanting a few more minutes with her before they headed inside. And the slight winter chill turned her nose a sweet pink.

"Well, it's not like he actually knew her. He just let himself get caught up in his attraction to her. Probably fantasized about her more than he even actually spoke to her," Scott offered. His hand brushed hers as they walked. Taking her hand would be the natural thing for him to do, but she wouldn't let him, he was sure. Not so close to the precinct. The exact house she transferred out of because of Travis Dixon.

As though he needed another reason to hate that prick of a man. Getting through the academy hadn't been hard for Scott, not after all his military training. Making it through graduation without ruining everything by turning his weapon on the creep had been challenging. Whatever made Sophie consider dating the asshole in the first place?

He hadn't brought it up after their scene on Friday night. She'd given him the answer he required, and digging into her past relationships hadn't been part of the deal. If she had said any other name, he wouldn't pry, so he let go for the time being.

"I doubt a woman like her would ever go for a man like him. He was nearly pissing himself to see me walk into the room with you. He is not confident enough to take on a woman like Susan James. Besides, we've interviewed co-workers and neighbors, and not a single one had a nice thing to say about her. Hell, her own sister hasn't shown up to claim her body or get the memorial ready."

Sophie stopped in front of the precinct doors and took a deep breath.

"It's going to be okay," he assured her, rubbing her back.

"It's going to be awkward as hell. I know the captain said he called and got the okay to come over to question Steve, but my history here makes this even more awkward." She unzipped her coat— one of those long down coats that made it feel like it was springtime but looked like you rolled yourself in a sleeping bag. She could have wrapped herself in potato sacks, though, and he'd be able to see the beauty beneath.

"Well then, let's get it over with. I'm getting hungry."

She shot him a snarky grin over her shoulder. "For food?"

"Not if you're with me." He winked, reached around her to pull the door open, and gave her a gentle shove to get her going. "Now stop trying to eye fuck me. We're on the job."

Her snort made him smile.

They had just stepped into the back offices of the building when Steve Renner greeted them.

"Hey, Sophie." He flashed a smile at her first before turning to Scott. "Russo." He gave him a brief nod.

"Thanks for talking with us." Scott offered his hand. Steven responded in kind with a sympathetic nod.

"No problem. It probably looks bad. Happy to help any way I

can." He hooked his fingers in his duty belt, obviously ready start his shift on the street in his full uniform.

"Want to use a room, or is here okay?" He signaled to where they stood.

"Up to you." Sophie's smile was forced. The little crevice in her right cheek when she gave a genuine smile wasn't there.

"Here's fine," he said and leaned against the desk.

"Okay, then. We're investigating the murder of Susan James, and we were told you and she dated a little while back?"

"Susan. Yeah, we did. I was sorry to hear what happened." Other than a grimace when Scott said her name, he didn't give the appearance of being overly sorry. Much like everyone else they'd talked with regarding her death.

"A witness reported he saw you and her having an argument outside her office building about two weeks before the murder," Sophie stated. "Any truth to that?" She used her professional voice, but Scott detected the little waver in her tone. She knew this guy. They'd been in the same stationhouse. It couldn't be easy to question him like any other creep on the street.

"Yeah, we did. She was a hothead, that one. Nothing made her happy. Everything I did was barely acceptable to her. I mean, she was hot but, I'm not chasing after any woman the way she wanted to be chased."

"How do you mean?" Scott asked.

"She wanted to be completely adored. Like there was no one else in the damn world. Which works fine, if, you know, there's no one else in the damn world. She'd get pissed if my shift ran long, or if I had to work a crime scene. Everything was about her. Too much. And we'd only been dating maybe a month. Neither of us were having fun, so I broke it off."

"That was a few weeks ago?" Scott clarified.

"No, that was two months ago. But I ran into her a few weeks ago. She acted like she didn't even know me. I admit I got a little pissed off. When we broke it off, to be honest, I don't think she cared."

"So why argue?" Sophie questioned.

"Not really a plus for the male ego to be forgotten so easily." He smirked. "I thought she was playing with me, acting like she didn't know who I was. I thought it was a game. She liked those." He shrugged. "So, I kissed her, you know, to jog her memory." The smile faded slightly. "But either she really didn't remember me or she had upped her role-playing talent. After I pulled away, she smacked me one. I took the hint and left it. I hadn't talked to her since."

Scott scratched his jaw. "Her sister hasn't gotten back to us. Do you happen to know anything about her?"

"Her sister? She had an adoptive sister, but they didn't talk." Steve nodded at a group of men walking past them.

"Anything else you can think of that might help us? She have any friends at work, someone close we should talk to?" Scott pressed.

"Work?" Steve laughed. "She was a workhorse, really went after accounts hard. I doubt anyone in that office would be considered a friend. No, as far as I know, she didn't have time for friends. She really only put up with me because I wasn't battery operated." He glanced at Sophie and cleared his throat. "Sorry."

"I understand what you mean." She smiled, probably to assure him she hadn't been offended.

"Where'd you two meet?" Scott asked. Susan James didn't seem the sort to give a great first impression.

Steve quickly glanced around them; a soft blush crept onto his neck. "Online. Just the usual dating site. You know, long-walks-on-the-beach sort of stuff."

"Think she might have gone back on the site after you two split?" Sophie asked, stuffing her hands in her pockets.

"I don't think she ever left." He made a face, clearly explaining that Susan wasn't a one-man woman. "She was out for whatever suited her at that moment. We weren't a good fit, I saw that right away, but the sex was good." He grimaced again. "Sorry."

"If you think of anything that might help, make sure you give us a call." Scott handed him a business card.

"I will." Steve pocketed the card. The walkie-talkie strapped to his chest sprang to life. "That's me. We good here?" he asked with hand hovering over the button.

"Yeah. We'll be in touch if we have any other questions," Sophie said.

Steve nodded and walked away, already answering the call from dispatch and hurrying to the motor pool.

"You believe him?" Sophie asked him starting to work up the zipper of her jacket.

"Yeah. But that doesn't mean he doesn't know more than he's told us." He brushed her hand away when the material of the jacket got stuck in the zipper and she struggled with it. A quick yank, and zip and she was bundled back up. He couldn't help but grin down at her. "Warm enough?"

"Shut up, it's freezing outside." Her smile countered the stinging words, and a soft blush blossomed to her ears. Damn she was edible.

"Sophie!" a dark voice boomed from across the room. The smile dropped from her full lips, and Scott's hands fisted at his sides.

"Travis." Sophie pulled her hair out from where it had been tucked into her coat and turned to face the asshole.

"Good to see you." His smile bordered on a sneer. "I didn't think I would after you ran away." He ended his sentence just as he stepped up to them but held enough volume a few officers walking by turned to stare. Bastard.

"I transferred, not ran," she said in a tight tone.

"Ah, so you're working over in the seventh district now? This your partner?" He jerked his chin toward Scott. "Scott, right?

Yeah. I remember you." He waggled a finger in the air. "I understand the two of you make quite the pair."

"What the fuck does that mean?" Scott stepped toward him.

"It means it looks like my girl couldn't get what she wanted here, so she ran off to find it on the other side of town." Travis flashed Sophie a knowing grin.

"She's not your girl," Scott said with clenched teeth. Just being near him was enough to get worked up, but for him even to pretend to have a claim on his Sophie was too much.

"Scott." Sophie's expression morphed into shock, her nostrils flared, and her lips pressed together. Letting out a huff, she turned to Travis. "Scott and I are working a case, but we're done here. It was nice seeing you." She'd started to turn when Travis put his hand on her shoulder.

Scott clenched his hands, reminding himself where they were and who they were. Taking his fist to the asshole's face would feel good, for a moment, but ultimately it would end badly.

"Sophie, don't run off. Look, I know things were a little embarrassing for you, but you didn't have to change districts."

Sophie shoved his hand from her shoulder and squared off with him. Travis had two inches on her, but she didn't cower.

"I had nothing to be embarrassed about. You should have been embarrassed. Going through my apartment like some creep, digging around in my underwear drawer? Seriously, Travis. It was weird. I'm good where I am now, and it's only a bonus that I don't have to see your stalker face every day."

Travis ran his tongue along his bottom teeth while regarding her. His upper lip curled under, and his nostrils flared. Tension built in Scott's chest, but he couldn't stop it from happening.

"Yeah, well, I don't mind not having the reminder of my chubby-chaser phase. Thankfully, it was a short phase."

"Are you fucking kidding me?" Scott stepped forward, despite Sophie's hand on his arm tugging him back. "Can you really be that big a prick, still? Did you forget the part where you're supposed to grow up and be a fucking man?" He wedged himself between Sophie and Travis.

Travis's eyes widened, and he licked his lips like he was getting ready. Maybe the little bitch thought if Scott threw the first punch, someone would save him. Travis's head reached Scott's eyebrows, and his build hadn't grown over the years like Scott's had. Apparently, there wasn't as much tail to chase at the gym, these days.

"Scott. Scott!" Sophie tugged on his arm. "Stop it."

Travis huffed a laugh. "What, you taking a turn now?"

Heat burst through Scott's body, and an explosion built beneath his skin. Getting his hands around this asshole's neck would be just the soothing medicine he needed. How could Sophie ever have dated this guy? Could she not see what a buffoon he was?

"No. He's not." Sophie yanked on Scott again. He bit into the side of his cheek and took a step back. They were in the damn precinct. Getting into a barroom brawl wouldn't do anything other than cause a few appointments with internal affairs.

"We have to get back to work." Sophie turned away from Travis, but her eyes blazed with fury. She could be angry at Travis for his shitty comment or pissed at Scott for getting involved. He would sort it out when they got to the car.

"Yeah," Travis said, giving Scott another sneer. "Need to get back to work."

Scott took half a step toward him, making him retreat a full step before turning around. Sophie couldn't just brush off a comment like that; it had to sting her. Meanwhile, Travis just walked away looking completely unphased. He should be feeling the pain of a broken fucking nose after talking to her that way.

Fuck.

When he was in the military, he wouldn't have thought twice. Back then, he would have swung first and thought about consequences later. But after bunking down with Grayson and

Sammy for over a year in a war-torn country, he'd learned to use his head before his fists.

Sophie was already on the sidewalk before Scott caught up with her. She had her cell to her ear, and when she noticed him she turned her back to him.

Great.

She walked down the street, and he fell in step beside her.

"Yeah, no, I get it. Think you'll have something by tomorrow?" she asked into her phone.

Scott stuffed his hands into the pockets of his leather jacket.

"Good. Let me know as soon as you have it, thanks." She clicked off the phone and slid it into her pocket.

"Anything I should know about?" he asked after several long moments went by in silence.

"Craig can't find the original email. He's gone through the vic's computer from home and work."

"Well, why would she send the email out? It has to be from somewhere else."

"That's what I said. He checked the server at her firm and found nothing. He's going to see about getting access to Mrs. Singleton's computer and server at her new job. If she got the email, he should be able to track it down that way. He should have something tomorrow." Her clipped tone, along with her speed walking didn't give him the opening he hoped for.

"And Steve was pretty much a dead end, although I'm going have IT check into her dating profiles. Maybe there's something else there that can be helpful. Her parents—I guess adoptive parents—passed a while back, so, other than her sister, there isn't any other family. We'll have to send a uniform out to the sister's house and try to contact her that way." Sticking to the case until they were in private would work in his favor. Professionalism was on the forefront of her mind, and having seen Travis, he could understand her hesitation to let anyone inside their precinct know they were anything more than partners.

"Yeah. We'll start with the dating profiles up tomorrow." She let out a long puff of air. "I'm really beat. I think I'll just get an Uber and head home."

And get out of having to talk about what bothered her? Uh, no.

"I don't think so." He shook his head and grabbed hold of her elbow before she got the idea of walking away from him. Looking over his shoulder, he gauged the precinct far enough way they wouldn't be spotted, or at least not overheard.

"Scott." She sighed, like she was annoyed at his attention.

"No. You're obviously upset, and we should talk about it. You know, like adults. No running off to pout in separate corners."

Heat blazed in her eyes. If only it were arousal instead of anger.

"Talk about what, Scott? How you just bulldozed your way into a conversation? How you got all Neanderthal back there?" She yanked her elbow free and jerked a thumb toward the station. "I don't need you to fucking protect me against verbal assaults. I'm not a little girl. I can take the insults just fine. And I sure as fuck can stand up for myself."

Of course, she could. He'd never doubted for a moment she could hand Travis his ass if the situation called for it.

"I want you to lower your voice," he commented.

She laughed. "What?"

"I get that you're mad, and I understand the point you're trying to make, but you don't get to yell at me."

She jabbed a finger into his chest. "It's your behavior that's being discussed right now, not mine."

"That is the case, yes, but if you don't stop pointing that finger at me and raising your voice to me, the tables are going to turn— and not for the better." He could admit when he'd stepped over the line, and he would apologize immediately once his mind wrapped around his error. But he would not allow his girl to act like some screaming banshee when she was angry.

"You can't be fucking serious."

"We'll talk about this when you're calm." He laced his arm through hers and took a step forward. When she gave slight resistance, he leaned down. "I'm happy to throw your ass over my shoulder and really show you what a Neanderthal I can be. Or maybe you'd like me to bare your ass right here in this alleyway"— he nodded toward the entrance—"and give you a spanking before we get in the car."

Anger flashed in her eyes, but she started moving. "You were the one who acted like an ass."

"Not a word until you're ready to talk about this calmly and without cursing," he said.

"But—"

"Two minutes with a gag when we get back to my place. Keep talking if you want to make it five." He stared at her, watching her lips twitch, the need to defend herself simmering in her expression until she regained control of herself and pinched her lips closed. He nodded and started for the car.

She had valid points. Jumping into that conversation hadn't been needed, and definitely could have drawn more attention than she was comfortable with at the moment. The idea was to ease her into a grander picture of them, and there he had been shoving her right into the fire.

But he could not tolerate her being disrespectful. And she didn't want him to tolerate it either. She may not see it at the moment, or even during her ass whipping, but once it was settled, once the heat of her ass worked its way into her core, and her heart stopped hardening against the injustice and allowed softness to take over, she would see he was only putting them back into place. He was giving her what she wanted. What they both needed.

But he doubted she would go quietly over his knee.

And a part of him really hoped she wouldn't.

116

CHAPTER 14

*W*hen Sophie was a child, her mother constantly warned her about pushing limits. If she was told to sit quietly in the corner, she just had to whistle or do something equally obnoxious until her mother gave up and let her out. Unfortunately, the same need to needle thrived inside the adult version of Sophie, and she managed to earn herself ten minutes with a gag.

It would give her time to calm down, she figured. At least then she could come up with an idea of how to derail his thought of any sort of punishment. He'd been the one misbehaving, not her, and once she could rationally discuss it with him, surely he would see it.

Scott rode beside her in the elevator to his condo in silence. The little tick in his cheek had stopped. That had to be a good sign.

Once inside, he helped her out of her coat and hung it in the closet, along with her purse. He made sure her phone was tucked away in a pocket of her bag and left it in the closet as well, shaking his head when she protested.

He crooked a finger, which she assumed meant she should

follow him, and follow the leader she did, right to his bedroom. No, she didn't want to be in there yet. Bedrooms were for couples, and they weren't a couple. They were, well, partners both on the job and sort of the same off the job. Friends who were having some fun.

"Can I wait in the living room, please?" she asked, holding her hands behind her back and digging her nails into her wrists.

He glanced over at her where she hung out in the doorway, his brow furrowed slightly, but he didn't deny her. "There's a guest bedroom if you'd rather we took care of this in there."

She released her hands. "Yeah, that's fine." At least he wasn't pushing her. It had to seem weird, her unease at being his bedroom. But since he was focused on the current issue, it seemed she'd be able to skirt having to talk about that as well.

"To the right." He jerked a thumb. "Might as well disrobe while you're waiting," he said and opened his closet. Whatever he was looking for, she could contain her anticipation to find out. A moment to breathe openly had been granted, and she hightailed it to the next room.

A simple room furnished with a double bed, dresser, TV. More like a hotel room than a guest room, but she supposed it got the job done. Shaking her head, she reminded herself she needed to get her game in order. She needed him to understand she could stand on her own two feet. That just because she was interested in exploring her submissive side, and she agreed she enjoyed the idea of discipline being part of a relationship, she did not need him to be her body guard, especially against stupid apes she could easily take care of on her own.

"I guess you aren't in the mood to follow directions tonight." Scott walked into the room, straight to the dresser, and plunked down several items.

"I wanted to talk to you. This isn't all my fault." She pointed out. Not really the way she had thought to go, but it was at least a start.

"Never said it was. Now. You have ten minutes with the gag, so strip down and kneel at the foot of the bed." He picked up the black ball gag from the dresser and unbuckled it.

She swallowed back the refusal burning on her tongue. Ten minutes—not so bad. Sophie pulled off her clothes and neatly piled them on the dresser beside his arsenal. She could have done without seeing the hairbrush paddle. Her mother also always told her she was her own worst enemy.

"I just—"

He clamped a hand over her mouth. "You just nothing. You will just kneel in position and open your mouth wide for me. That's what you'll just do." Had he ever used that deep tone with her before? She would have realized it if he had. Because it sent a chill down her spine but warmed her insides at the same time. Who knew a tone of voice could turn a human body into a weather report.

Deciding compliance would serve her better, she nodded. Once he released her, she stepped over to the bed and sank to her knees. Thankfully, the room was covered in plush carpeting, so her knees weren't on bare wood. Though she had a feeling the worst of the pain she would feel by the time he finished with her would be spread throughout her ass.

He shoved the ball between her teeth and strapped it around her head, buckling it behind her. She winced at the few hairs he pulled, but overall, she let him get the job done. Compliance.

Another chill went through her when he stood, towering over her kneeling form. Not so much because of the force he represented, but from the lack of his presence. The soft touches he'd given her that morning, the minor brush of his hand across her back as they walked down a hall seemed to have happened so long ago. Replaced now by a separation between them. Though he stood only a few steps away, he might as well have been in the next apartment.

Could it all be because he was displeased?

After the silence made her skin itch, she looked up at him. His arms were crossed, his eyes set firmly on her.

He glanced at his watch. "Ten minutes."

The ball already stretched her jaw, but she'd bear it. She could handle it.

Scott sat on the edge of the bed, hooked his finger into the leather strap running from her mouth to buckle, and pulled on it until she moved to face him. He removed his finger, and she moaned internally for the loss.

"You aren't a woman to be fucked with." He caught her off-guard with his statement. His eyes still screamed displeasure, but there he was complimenting her.

He leaned forward enough she could smell his aftershave, but not close enough for her to truly feel him.

"It's one of the things I'm attracted to about you. So, yeah, you could have handled Travis on your own, and you did. You didn't let him get under your skin and make you react out of anger. You did better than me in that department." His tongue wet his lips. "I'm proud of you for that."

He was proud? Then why the fuck was there a ball gag in her mouth and a string of drool getting ready to jump ship down her damn chin?

"I'm also sorry I didn't let you take care of him in your way. I got protective, not just as your partner, but as your dominant. I let that seep into the situation, because I'm not just the guy who spanks you for fun, or decides where we're having dinner. I see myself as your protector. I won't let anything bad happen to you, not while in a scene, and not while we're in our daily lives. So yeah, I jumped the gun. I'm a big enough guy to say I'm sorry for that."

He took a slow drag of breath.

Her chest tightened while he talked. She'd expected some male chauvinistic bullshit to fly from his mouth. A long lecture on her being a sub and to just follow the dom's orders would have made some sense to her. But apologizing and explaining it so clearly?

He was her protector.

Had she ever had one of those before?

More importantly, did she need one?

She'd agreed to this arrangement because she thought she knew him. She had him pegged for a casual guy with no real depth she would have to concern herself with.

Fuck had she been wrong. And now he was dragging her right to the bottom of the sea with him. Why wouldn't he just fucking touch her already? Just a hand to her hair, or her shoulders. Something.

The puddle of drool she'd worried about finally broke the damn and spilled from the corner of her mouth, landing on her breast.

He leaned farther still, no touching.

"But."

Of course, there was a but.

"When you have a problem with something I've done or said, you bring it to me in a respectful and submissive manner. You don't ever yell at me on the street, and you sure as fuck don't jab your finger into my chest."

His breath hit her face, and she inhaled it. Finally, something from him touched her.

"Do I raise my voice to you? Or poke at you to get a reaction?"

She ran her tongue over the ball, hoping to block more spit from falling and making a fucking mess of her chest. But she failed.

"Answer me." His voice went stone hard; his eyes darkened.

She forgot about the spit and shook her head. He hadn't. Ever. He treated her with respect at all turns. Even if he didn't agree with her on a case, he'd never mocked or raised his voice.

"You don't like the drool, do you?" he asked, his tone serious and still no smile in sight. Couldn't she have just waited until they got back to his apartment to talk to him about what she was upset about? Why did she have to push him, to sour the evening with discipline instead of sweeten it with play.

Again, she shook her head. Lifting her hand from her thigh, she tried to wipe the string now freely falling from her chin, but he wouldn't allow it. Swatting her hand away, he shook his finger at her.

"Keep your hands down. Let it leak down onto your tits, making you all messy. Look at all the spit collecting on you." He moved his gaze lower, but she didn't follow it. How could she? To see the mess would make it too real, and the burn of her cheeks at his chastisement was all the reality she needed for the moment.

Moments ticked by with him staring at her, and all she could do was stare back. She'd move her gaze to his chin, or his shoulders, but always find his eyes again. She didn't like the stern expression, the disciplinarian side of him. She wanted his playfulness back.

She wanted a fucking bib.

"When you're disrespectful to me, it's not just me you're doing it to. It's us as a unit. The only way this works is if we are in this together. Every time one of us derails, we both go off course. And in this relationship, I'm the one who puts us back to on track. I decide how and when we do that, but you will always have a voice. Do you get that?"

Tears built in her eyes. He might as well have smacked her; pain blossomed inside of her. She'd hurt him. Simple words, a harsh tone, and she'd hurt him—and her.

She'd hurt them.

"I think you do." He ran the fat of his thumb over her cheek, catching a tear. Bringing it to his mouth, he sucked the moisture away.

She nodded. What else was there to do?

He checked his watch, a slim Fitbit on his left wrist, then back at her. The hard edges of his jaw softened. He ran the back of his fingers down her cheek, and she leaned into the touch. The warmth of it, the gentleness of it, the expanding power of such a simple act overwhelmed her senses. More tears fell until she found herself cradled in his arms.

The buckles of the straps were undone, and he gently pulled the ball from between her teeth, whispering soothing words and placing soft kisses on her forehead. She sniffled, fighting the urge to wipe her chin, which was now covered in her spit.

"When you're being naughty I'll always take control of the situation. Always. Even if it means ruining our night out with having to come back here and teach you a lesson." He continued to speak while tossing the gag toward the dresser. "Stand," he ordered and leaned back on the bed. She pressed her hands on his knees to give herself leverage and moved to her feet. Her knees expressed their displeasure at being held hostage for so long, and she shook out each leg until the pain subsided.

He didn't let on if he minded the extra moment she took to get into position.

"Your knees okay?" he asked, leaning over to take a look at them.

"Fine. They're fine," she whispered, not wanting to break the moment of peace growing between them.

He touched her right knee then moved upward until he found them. She squeezed her eyes closed. Embarrassment flooded her where tranquility had formed.

"You were digging your nails into your thighs," he stated and ran his finger over each half-moon shaped indention.

"It's just a coping thing. I'm fine." She waved her hand over the marks, hoping to distract him.

"You almost broke the skin, Sophie." He stood to his full height and pulled her to his chest. "If you feel like you need that in the future, you need to tell me, okay? I don't want to cause you distress to the point you need to do that."

"It's just normal for me, I was—well, I am sorry. I fucked up our evening." It was partially true. She'd begun burying her nails into her flesh with each passing moment he denied her his touch.

"Do you think you'll be yelling at me on the street again?" he asked, cupping her chin and pulling it upward, wiping her chin with his fingers. She'd forgotten all about the mess on herself when he began to soother her and touch her again.

"No. I was mad, but I should have waited to talk to you until I wasn't so pissed and could handle it better."

He pressed his lips against hers in a warm kiss that ended entirely too soon. But she wasn't going to rock the boat just yet.

"Instead of going out, how about I make us some sandwiches and we watch a movie?" he suggested.

She peered over at the wooden paddle sitting so lonely on the dresser beside the used gag. Not that she really wanted further punishment, but, well, maybe she did.

"Not all punishments have to involve a spanking," he said releasing her and walking over to the dresser to pick up the paddle. "The point is to teach you a lesson, and this time, we managed it well enough without the aid of my little friend." He twirled the paddle and spoke in the worst Pacino impersonation she'd ever heard.

"But what if I want you to use your, uh, little friend." She made the attempt and failed worse than him at the accent.

He laughed and slid the paddle into the back pocket of his jeans, so the handle was tucked away but the rest could be seen.

"Well, then, I suppose you'd better be a really good girl the rest of the night so I can blister that sweet ass of yours after the movie." He picked up her shirt from the pile of clothes and tossed it to her. "Just that, for now."

She snagged it midair and watched him walk out of the room, whistling, the paddle swaying n his back pocket as he left her behind.

He hadn't spanked her, but he'd managed to put her right where he wanted her, where she wanted to be. She snaked the shirt over her head and pulled her hair free. What little of her saliva that hadn't already dried on her breasts stuck to the shirt, but she left it. A small reminder of what bad actions would cause.

"Hope you like salami," he called from the kitchen.

She stopped in the hallway and grinned. "For the sandwich, or you talking in code?" She stepped into the living room and headed toward the kitchen.

"A little of column A and a whole lot of column B," he said with a smile when she entered the kitchen.

CHAPTER 15

*I*f she could look less fuckable while they ate their sandwiches, his cock might be able to take a rest. She'd messed her hair all up while having the gag in, and her makeup—what little she did wear—had smeared on her cheeks from the delectable tears she'd shed during her punishment. While she nibbled on the bread and licked the crumbs from her lips, he tried to convince himself it would not be gentlemanly to throw her to her knees, fist her hair, and plunge his cock into her mouth. Protest or not—better if she did.

Fuck. He adjusted his dick in his pants. Pressing too hard against the zipper was making sitting still impossible. He needed to do something to take the edge off.

"So, you and Travis have history?" she asked, popping the last bite of sandwich into her mouth.

That worked well enough.

He took a swig of beer and nodded. "We were at the academy together."

"And?" she pressed when he didn't offer any other information.

"And he's a prick," he offered with a wide grin.

"Oh. So, I'm supposed to be open and honest with you, but you don't have to answer my questions?" She raised an eyebrow at him. "Just like today, you're allowed to be rude, and I'm not."

He pulled the small paddle from his back pocket and slid it onto the table, resting his hand on it. "Just a reminder of what a bad tone will get you." He drummed his fingers. "I apologized for this afternoon. Yes, I let him get under my skin. But it's not your job to discipline me, is it?" He quirked his own eyebrow. They'd covered this in the guest bedroom, but maybe she didn't fully get it.

"That doesn't sound fair." Her lower lip protruded in a sweet pout.

"It shouldn't. It's not. It's the balance of power we play with. Fair doesn't play into it," he said.

"Kind of like when we were at the club, and I had all those orgasms, and you didn't even get one?" She tilted her head and grinned playfully at him.

He laughed. "Sort of. I got what I wanted out of that scene just as much as you. Coming would have been the icing on the cake, but I survived."

"Well, can I strike a deal with you? Obviously, I don't get to punish you, and I wouldn't want to, either, but I can barter, right? Like, you give me the story about Travis, and I give you a nice long blow job before we watch the movie."

Silly girl. She was going to do that anyway.

"I think what you're suggesting is called topping from the bottom. Not really my kink." He picked up his plate and took it to the sink.

"Okay, fine. Don't get a blow job out of the deal." She pushed her chair back and crossed her legs. "But I'm still interested in knowing what your problem is with Travis. Other than the obvious assholeness of his personality."

Scott leaned against the sink, crossing his ankles. Talking about her ex didn't score high on his list of arousal topics, but he'd seen how persistent she could be.

"He's just an ass, Sophie. Doesn't take shit seriously. He nearly got a cadet killed during firearm training. And considering the number of safety protocols they have in place so that sort of shit doesn't happen, I'd say he's really good at being an idiot."

"Yeah, I think he told me that story." She frowned. "We got into an argument about it. I didn't find his lack of safety funny."

He clenched his fingers around the countertop. Even after all the years on the force and all the training, the jerk still didn't get that almost fatally wounding a fellow officer because you forgot to put the safety on while swinging your loaded weapon around in some stupid attempt at *Top Gun* humor wasn't a laughing matter.

"Aside from that, he's not really the type I'd see you with."

She scrunched her lips and let out a sigh. "I admit it. I was swayed by the muscles and the tight abs."

Her hands flew up in the air as though she were surrendering to an arrest, and he laughed.

"Is that why you said yes to dating me?" he laughed.

"Dating you?" Her smile dropped a fraction.

"Isn't that what we're doing here?" Oh, hell. Excellent way to make her bolt for the door, to bring up the *what are we* conversation. He couldn't even get her into his bedroom. How could he think she'd be ready for this talk?

"We're having fun." She stood from the table and pressed against him. Fuck she smelled good. She'd spent all day at work with him and then been put through a discipline session. She shouldn't smell so damn fuckable.

"I bet we'd have more fun if that shirt wasn't on." He pressed a kiss to her lips and pulled at the fabric covering her breasts. "I believe there's a pretty submissive's mouth that needs filling." He traced her lower lip with his thumb.

"Do you have ice-cream?" she asked with a coy smile.

"Get down on your knees," He fisted his hand in her hair, finally rewarding himself for the tortuous evening of waiting to get her soft curls in his hand and shoved her to her knees. She gave him a disgruntled look, but he chalked it up as showmanship. The strong woman inside her needed to at least pretend to protest, but when he maneuvered her body until he had her pinned against the cabinets, her pupils told him the truth. Arousal had taken her over.

"My shirt," she said and pulled the hem toward her head. He released her, letting her draw it free of her body then took it from her. He rolled the shirt lengthwise and wrapped it around her head, covering her eyes and tying it in the back.

"Much better," he mused out loud. He worked the buckle of his belt, while watching her pink tongue dart out and wet her lips. Her full, pouty lips that could only make him hotter wrapped around his cock.

"Open," he ordered once he had his hand wrapped around his shaft. He needed to get inside her. Her mouth, pussy, wherever as long it was her.

Her lips opened wide, and she stuck out her tongue.

Sliding the round head of his cock over her tongue, he bit down on his own. Why did he torture himself? She knelt right there. He could plunge into her and take her mouth as his own. He could pump his cock down her throat and come all over her round, full breasts.

"Second thought." He reached down and hauled her up by her armpits, not just bringing her to her feet but clearing her off the floor and plopping her on the cabinet. "I'm still a little hungry myself." He covered her mouth with his hand when she started to speak and used his free hand to drag her leg to the side, uncovering the sweet beauty of her sex.

Still holding his hand firmly over her mouth, he dipped low and pushed his lips into her pussy. He could get high just from smelling her arousal. His nose pressed against her clit while he maneuvered his tongue lower until he found her entrance.

"Scott," she muttered beneath his hand.

"You taste too good to be real," he said into her flesh as he swiped his tongue from bottom to clit, taking the bundle of nerves between his teeth and applying pressure.

Her legs kicked out, and her ass bounced on the counter, but he didn't let up. Releasing her mouth, he used both hands to keep her legs spread wide. Little whimpers escaped while he suckled and nipped, but she didn't try to push him away. Not that she could anyway.

"Oh fuck." Her chest heaved.

"Not yet." He smiled and stood, taking her face between his hands and kissing her deeply. His tongue lashed against hers. And she met him full force, the sort of kiss that had their teeth clashing and their tongues dancing and left them both breathless when he pulled back. "I want to fuck you."

"Yes. Do that. A lot of that." She nodded with vigor.

He couldn't help but laugh. "Sometime soon, we should go over protocol and proper responses."

Her brows furrowed.

"But right now, I just need to be in you." He scooped her off the counter and hoisted her over his shoulder. On the way past the table, he snagged the wooden paddle, just in case his girl got mouthy again.

Bypassing the damn living room, he went back to the guest bedroom. She had less of a terror-filled gaze in there than when he'd brought her into his own room earlier.

She made a humph sound when she bounced on the bed, and quickly scrambled up, until she rested against the headboard.

"Flat on your back, legs wide," he ordered, reaching out and grabbing her ankles. He dragged her down until she was in the position he wanted before he went about shedding all his clothes.

Kneeling between her legs, he skimmed his gaze down her body. Beautiful. Curvy and imperfect.

She couldn't see him, not with the shirt still tied around her eyes, and he left it that way. She didn't get to see him fawn all over her. Staring at her and taking her all in couldn't be ruined by her noticing. No, this moment was for him. Private.

"Scott." She lifted her arm, searching him out. "You're still here, right?"

"I wouldn't leave you, baby," he said, grabbing her outstretched hand and lacing his fingers with hers. Moving closer to her, he ran the head of his cock through her heated folds. So fucking wet. And hot.

"You're wet as hell for me," he said, pushing into her sweet softness. Her mouth parted into a perfect ring when he thrust himself to the hilt. "And so fucking tight," he ground out, pressing her hand to the mattress. "Don't. Oh fuck, Sophie."

She lifted her legs, bending her knees, her sweet pussy gripping tighter around his cock.

"Don't slow down," she begged, wrapping her arms around his neck. "Please. Not slow. Not gentle."

He kissed her, withdrawing until only the tip of his cock nestled inside her warmth.

"Beg," he uttered against her lips.

She huffed.

He didn't move. Pushing himself up on his elbows, he remained in position, not inside her enough for either of them to be satisfied.

"Please," she whispered.

He turned his head, leaning down until her lips were a breath away from his ear. "Say again?"

"Please."

"Please what?" He pushed his dick farther in but stopped again.

"Please fuck me," she whimpered, moving her hips trying to

get him to give her what she wanted. But she didn't want him to just play a role for her. She needed to let him have the control, and she wasn't going to come until she realized it.

"Please fuck me, what?" he asked, pressing her hips into the mattress. "The more you try to control this, the more disappointed you're going to be," he warned. He'd have to jerk himself off in the shower as soon as she left, but he would follow through.

"Please fuck me hard, sir?" She sucked in her lower lip and dropped her hands to her sides. "Please, sir." There it was. The soft plea coming from her submissive side. Not a huff, or a sigh, but a genuine quiet plea.

"That wasn't so hard, was it?"

"No, sir. But please, don't make me wait anymore." She wiggled her hips from side to side..

He pulled the shirt from her eyes. She blinked a few times but once focused, she stared up at him.

One quick thrust, and he was inside her again, fully imbedded. He kept his hands on her hips and drove into her over and over again.

"Clit. Rub your clit for me, Sophie," he urged.

She did him one better. She licked the tip of her fingers and ran them down her body until she was between their bodies. He could feel the slickness of her fingers as he thrust into her.

A shiver ran through her body. The little tremor started and blossomed into pulsating waves that he could feel along his cock. She called out, screaming his name over and over again.

"Fuck!" He dug his fingers into her hips and plowed into her a few more times before his orgasm tore through him, and he froze above her. His vision faded in and out while powerful burst of energy slowly ebbed to a soft throb until it completely calmed, leaving him sucking in air, and pressing fast kisses to her face.

"You make me lose my train of thought," he accused, slipping from her body and reaching for his T-shirt on the floor to wipe her down. It seemed every time he had a plan of what to do with her for the evening nothing went according to plan.

"Yeah, you have that effect on me, too," she whispered, though it sounded a bit more forlorn coming from her than him.

CHAPTER 16

"*E*xcuse me, are you Detective Nelson?" a hard voice interjected into Sophie's thoughts. A new report had been sent over from the M.E.'s office, and she was trying to read through it. Not exactly light material.

"Yes, that's me." She swiveled in her chair and stood to greet the woman attached to the voice. An inch or two taller than herself, and at least fifteen pounds less around the middle. Colorful tats across her chest revealed by the loose-fitting tee she wore only increased her attractiveness. She had bad girl written all over her. In fact, she might actually have it written on her body somewhere with the amount of ink she showcased.

"Hi. I'm Dani. Scott said you'd be here. I'm supposed to be meeting him for lunch, but he's running late. Said to hang with you until he gets here?" She tucked her chestnut hair behind her ear, displaying a silver earing that crawled up her ear.

"Uh, sure. I guess. I thought he'd be back by now." Sophie looked at the time on her phone. He'd gone to check on the IT information they were still waiting on, trying to get them to hurry with the server searches.

"Last text said ten minutes, tops." Dani smiled and dug out her phone from the bag she had strapped across her chest. Definitely an artsy type, one who probably was up for anything at any time and never had to plan out her day or clench her teeth while meeting someone new. No. Dani probably didn't feel the uncomfortable heat rising while they stared at each other.

Damn, she hated this. Small talk might as well be Chinese, as fluent as she was either language.

"I've seen you somewhere before," Sophie said, tapping her fingers against her chin. She'd heard about her, of course. Scott had filled her in his friendship with both Dani and Grayson, even before they'd agreed to put the benefits in their friendship. He'd been in the military with Grayson and Dani's older brother, Sammy. Unfortunately, Sammy had been killed on the battlefield and didn't return home from deployment.

"Yeah, Black Light." Dani nodded with a sweet smile. "I was there on Valentine's Day."

Sophie cringed. Of course, she had been.

"Ah, you were there for the spectacle that was my first night out in the world?" Sophie pinched the bridge of her nose, wishing she wore a rubber band to snap against her wrist.

Dani laughed softly and leaned forward to touch Sophie's arm. "It wasn't that bad. You're not the first person to pass out in a crowd like that. I'm just glad Scott was there. Probably made it a little easier when you came to, having someone you knew in the room."

"Or insanely awkward," Sophie couldn't help but laugh.

"Yeah, or that," Dani agreed with a grin. "So, was that your first time at Black Light or in a club like that, period?"

Sophie turned her head to see who could overhear them, heat spreading through her neck.

"Shit. Sorry, forgot for a minute where we were."

"Forgot what?" Scott walked up to them, place a hand on Dani's back and pressed a kiss to her cheek. "Sorry that took so long."

"No problem. Just chatting with Sophie here." Dani readjusted the strap of her bag.

"Anything new?" Scott asked Sophie.

"Still nothing, but I'm going back down there this afternoon and sit on him until he gets what I need." His eyes found Sophie's. Did he even know when he turned on the Dom stare?

"I'm sure that will help," Sophie said, rolling her eyes. "While you're at lunch, I think I'll go visit the M.E. I don't understand something I'm reading here. It looks like he found bruises on the vic's forearms." She picked up on Dani's stare and shook her head. "Sorry."

"No, I'm fine. Scott's talked work before with me. Kinda used to it by now." Dani glanced up at Scott then back at Sophie. "Why don't you come with us for lunch. I don't want to steal your guy from you."

"No, no, that's okay." Sophie shook her head. Friend lunch ranked right next to friend dinner—which was only one tip toe away from meeting family. "He's not my guy. It's fine," she added hastily once Dani's words registered.

Dani's eyebrows furrowed, and she looked up at Scott.

"Yeah, Sophie, you should eat something. Just come with." Scott shifted his stance until he towered over her.

"No, really. I'm just gonna grab something after I talk with the M.E. I don't want to eat before that conversation." She forced a laugh, which no one joined.

"It's just lunch with a friend, Sophie," Scott said, mostly under his breath. Dani must have heard, though, because she became interested in the adjustment buckle of her messenger bag.

"I really need to get down there before Dr. Greene decides to dig into another body. I hate walking in on that shit." She scooped up the file on her desk and held it to her chest. "Go have lunch, I'll meet up with you later, after you've bullied IT into finding that email." She plastered on a smile that ached all through her face into her chest.

Dani's eyes softened like she'd just been wounded, but she nodded and gave a polite smile. "Maybe next time, if you aren't busy."

"Of course," Sophie said. Having lunch with them wouldn't be the end of the world. She'd survive. But it wasn't just lunch. Not with Scott. Nothing was just as simple as a meal when it came to him.

"I need to give Gray a quick call." Dani pulled out a cell phone and waved it in the air. "I'll meet you out front. It was nice meeting you." She gave Sophie's arm a squeeze and stalked off through the desks toward the front office.

Scott watched Dani leave before turning to Sophie. His irritation heated the space between them.

"You can't even do lunch with a friend?" he asked, annoyance clear in his voice.

"I'm not hungry. Besides, you said yourself, you haven't really had time to talk with her since the Valentine's party. It's fine. Go catch up, and we'll meet up later." She shifted from one foot to the other.

Friends with benefits. That's where they were, but the sense of rejection she saw in his expression tore at her. No matter how much she wanted to toss the manila folder on the desk, link hands with him, and walk off to lunch, she couldn't. She wouldn't. One of them needed to keep their head on straight.

"Dinner, then? Just us?" He positioned himself in front of her, blocking her view of the rest of officers in the room.

"Something more substantial than salami sandwiches?" she asked, hoping she'd managed to get her tone right. Lightened the mood.

He huffed a laugh. "If the princess would prefer a full meal, then we'll have all four food groups present."

She screwed up her face. "Not all four. Don't get crazy on me. We can skip the veggies."

He leaned closer to her, making like he was reaching for

something on her desk, but stopped when his mouth came close to her ear. "Eat lunch, a real lunch, and I'll let you get away without veggies at dinner. Be a naughty girl and order a sandwich, and you'll have a paddling as your appetizer and orgasm denial for dessert."

She took a deep breath. One. Two, and let it out slow.

He snagged a pen from her desk and waggled it near her nose.

"Salad for lunch. Got it." She managed to at least hold back the smile.

He took a step back and pocketed the pen. "Sounds like a good idea, Sophie."

She watched him walk out of the area. His jeans hugged his ass especially tenderly today. His black leather jacket cut just right, giving her a first-person view of his physique. Fuck he was delicious.

How had she been his partner for two months before opening her eyes to the beauty that was Detective Russo?

"Sophie!"

She jumped.

"Where'd you run off to?" Camille, a detective at the next desk over, laughed.

"Just tired," Sophie lied.

"Well, sleeping beauty, I just got a call about your case. Dispatch patched it to the wrong desk. A Ms. Elizabeth James called about your vic. Said she received the messages. Said she's not the next of kin and gave me this name and number." Camille handed over a piece of paper.

"Did she say who it is?" Sophie looked at the scribbled name.

"Just said she's the next of kin and to please stop contacting her, then disconnected." Camille shrugged. "Sounded more afraid than angry, like she just wanted this off her plate."

"Huh." Sophie bit down on her lip. "Thanks."

Tossing the manila folder on the desk, she grabbed the phone and dialed the number on the piece of scratch paper.

No answer.

She hung up, tapped her fingers on the receiver then tried once more.

No answer.

And no answering machine or voice mail, either.

She handed off the bit of information on her way down to meet with the medical examiner.

"Hey, David, can you do a reverse phone number look up for me? I have a first name and a number, but I need who the number belongs to, and anything else you can find on them. Previous arrests, divorces, birth certificates, whatever. I just need to know who it is and how they connect to my vic."

David shoved the last bite of an Italian sub into his mouth and nodded.

"Sure thing," he said out of the side of his mouth while chewing. "Give me a few hours."

"Thanks." She patted his shoulder and headed down to the medical examiner's office to discover more about bruising on a corpse.

Who wouldn't love this job?

At least it would distract her from thinking of Scott. Doing that was dangerous. Too dangerous. She'd rather spend the afternoon dodging bullets in the literal sense than navigating the mine field that was her mind. Any thought about how she really felt about Scott threatened to blow her whole afternoon. Better to avoid the entire topic.

CHAPTER 17

"Leave it be, Scott," Dani said for the third time during their walk back to the station house.

"Easier said than done," Scott replied.

"She'll come around. You said she got burned dating someone she worked with, right? She's just being cautious. If you push, she'll bolt."

He'd told himself the same thing, knew she was right. Pushing Sophie into a relationship talk would make her freeze up. Offering to keep things casual had been a fucking bonehead thing to do, though.

"I guess if you could wait on Gray like you did, then I can give her a little more time," Scott conceded."

"I didn't wait. I was too scared to act; there's a difference. You are with her, just not as intense as you want. So, take it slow. Burrow under her skin, like I know you can. Hell, you did just fine with me. And it couldn't have been easy dealing with someone as angry as I was when you guys got back from Afghanistan." She linked her arm through his.

"You were a kid who'd just lost your brother. It was easier with you."

"That's because there wasn't much pressure. I was like a sister to you. So, take some of the pressure off with Sophie and just let things happen." Dani had good advice—for other people.

"For a kid, you're pretty smart." He ruffled her hair until she smacked him away, laughing.

"Uh, huh. You don't think I'm so young when you sit in my chair. By the way, you still haven't come by the shop to work on the design for your new tat." She poked his forearm. Dani had done all the tattoos on his body, and he was itching to add another.

"Yeah, things have been a bit crazy with this case and Sophie." He scratched the back of his neck. The sun beat down on them, warming the winter air enough to an almost tolerable temperature.

"Well, when you're done solving your case and you've gotten the girl firmly attached to your hip, come by, and we'll get the design down." She flashed him a smile. It was a wonder Gray had managed to wait years to put his mark on this beautiful girl.

"I will." He stopped outside the station. "How about we have Sunday dinner near my place this week."

Dani's smile dropped a fraction. "Why?"

"'Cause I'm tired of hauling my ass across town to your apartment then having to listen to Gray bitch about that damn window you haven't gotten fixed yet," he grumbled.

"The window is getting fixed." She sighed with her response. "He's even more overprotective now than before."

"Well, that's what we do. We take care of our girls, and you're a hell of a lot more to him than just his buddy's little sister, now. You're his."

A blush crossed her cheeks, and she gave him a shove.

"Yeah. I get enough of that talk from him. You don't have to explain it to me, too. Now, get back to work. I have an appointment coming in soon." She gave him a hug and headed toward the bus stop. Any offer of a ride would be rejected, so he didn't bother. But he would ask Gray about letting her take the fucking bus around everywhere. She had the means for a damn car and shouldn't be hoofing it so much.

He shook his head at himself and headed back into the station. If only taking care of Sophie could be so easy. Not that she needed taking care of. She didn't need any help in the adulting department. But he'd noticed the way she dug her nails into her palms when she was flustered. An easily missed tell if he hadn't seen her do the same with her thighs during her discipline the other night. But now he noticed she did it often. If she'd just let him in, he could help her. He could give her the stress relief she was looking for, show her she didn't have to rely only on herself.

"Hey, Scott, I have what you wanted, but you aren't going to like it." Craig signaled from his office.

Unless it was a signed confession by someone who'd actually committed the damn crime, of course he wasn't going to like it.

Scott followed him into his office, maneuvering around the tech equipment. "So what'd you find?"

"Nothing." Craig plopped down in his chair. "I have searched through her personal emails, her work servers, the emails of Singleton who said she got the email. Nothing. If that email did exist, whoever put it out there has more knowledge than me about this stuff."

"You don't think there was an email?"

"Nope. I don't. You've had two people come in about it, right? Two people confessing to her murder? Any chance they were part of all this? Trying to throw us off?"

Scott sighed. "It's possible. It'd be risky. I mean, we could have just taken their confession and run with it."

"Yeah. Well, I'd say they probably had a good reason to go along with it, then. Maybe whoever had them do it was holding something over their heads? And you did say you saw through them pretty easily. Right?" Craig swiveled back and forth in his chair.

Scott groaned. "This case is really starting to piss me off. So, no email. Anything of worth at all?"

"Not from my end. Sorry." Craig held up his hands.

"Thanks anyway." Scott unzipped his jacket, taking it off as he made his way to his desk. False confessions, phantom emails, what next? The wrong victim?

CHAPTER 18

$\mathcal{S}$ophie stood at the doors of Black Light, willing herself to go inside. She'd made the trek through the tunnel from the psychic shop easily enough. Aside from the twisting in her stomach.

Usually when she worked a case and it started to stall, she'd bury herself in it, combing through the files, the evidence, looking for something she'd missed. But she couldn't focus. Her mind kept wandering over to the man sitting across the desk from her.

She'd known getting involved with her partner would be bad. She'd warned him they couldn't keep it just outside the station. Going along with him had been stupid. He invaded her thoughts, her fucking dreams, and every fantasy she conjured ended up with him in it.

When she'd found out about demonstration night at the club, she had decided to get there and get her mind straight. Maybe focusing on something completely non-Scott and non-murder case would get her thoughts back in order.

Her stomach hurt; she should have skipped lunch. But doing that would have tipped Scott off something wasn't right. She hated lying. It made her want to punish herself. She weighed herself down with the guilt of it, but if she'd been honest and told him what she was up to for the evening, he'd have insisted on taking her, and she really needed the night to focus on herself.

Then again, maybe if she had told him the truth about why she wanted to go alone, he'd have backed off. Too late, now. He thought she was at home watching chick flicks.

Groaning at herself, she stomped her foot.

"Dammit, you're here. Just go," she chided herself then looked behind her to be sure she was still alone. If someone heard her, they'd probably alert security a crazy person was trying to get into their high-end establishment.

Scott was making her lose her damn mind.

With another grunt at herself for the lying coward she'd turned out to be, she flung the door open and rushed inside. Better to get it all over with. The sooner she could sink into the atmosphere, the sooner she could stop thinking about the weak lie she'd given Scott to keep him off her trail.

Danny checked her in at the security podium. He tried to make small talk, but her stomach was too twisted for her to do much else other than smile and give one-word answers. If she acted so damn timid at work, she'd find herself in a hell of a lot more dangerous situations.

"Don't forget to lock up your phone," Danny flashed a smile when he handed her back her membership card.

"Right. Almost forgot," she secured her phone and purse in a locker and headed in for the demonstration.

Folding chairs faced the platform where she assumed the demonstration would take place. Most seats were taken by couples, which only worked to remind her Scott would have absolutely wanted to come with her. Sophie sat down in the back, at the end of the row in case she wanted a hasty escape, and settled in.

She'd expected one of the suspension rigs to be on stage since the demonstration was supposed to be about suspension. Instead, she saw a straight-back chair, illuminated by a spotlight. Off to the right stood a man with his arms crossed and his jaw set. A shudder went through her at the utter fierceness in which he stared at the chair.

"Hi, everyone." Chase, one of the owners took center stage with mic in hand. She recognized him from his modelling career, but holy fuck did he look even hotter in person. If she hadn't been trying to keep on her feet at the roulette game, she probably would have noticed him more then, too.

"I know we advertised a suspension class tonight, but Owen, who was giving the demonstration had a fender bender on the way in." Small gasps came from the crowd. "He and his sub are fine," he assured. "But it was enough to keep them away. Instead of cancelling, we have a demonstration that hopefully will be of interest to you all. I know not everyone who comes to the club practices their kink full-time. Some of you may want to keep it to the bedroom, but a lot of us, like Jaxson, Emma and I take the dom/sub relationship with us everywhere we go. And in doing so, there will be more times when the sub may need redirection or punishment for misdeeds. Stephanos"—he gestured to the fierce man still standing in the corner of the stage—"and his submissive, who is also his wife, Anna, are going to demonstrate what a punishment can look like between a dom and sub."

Sophie sank into her chair. How fucking fitting.

"Just like everything that happens in this club, this scene is completely consensual. Anna has agreed to accept her punishment publicly. She has safewords to use if she needs them." Chase glanced off stage. "For now, I'll turn it all over to Stephanos who'll start the demonstration."

The large man stepped forward to a round of applause. The spotlight amplified his stern, set features and seemed to make him a few inches taller at the same time. Who in their right mind would agree to be disciplined by this mammoth of a man?

"So, like Chase said, I'm Stephanos." He moved the mic from

his right hand to his left. "Every relationship is different, so don't think what you see here is how you have to do things in yours. That said, there are few components I believe are extremely important when administering a punishment." He pressed his hand to his chest.

He walked across the stage, continuing to talk about trust and commitment, while she tried to tune out the guilt building in her chest.

"And there's mindset. Now, your sub, slave, wife, whatever you label her—or him—most likely already feels guilty for what they did. They knew they were breaking a rule, or acting badly. They aren't kids. They know these things. But accepting the consequences can sometimes be harder to get their minds around. Especially when they've been at work all day, had to deal with the kids when they got home, and cook dinner, pay bills, etcetera. Real life can hamper their willingness or their ability to enter into the discipline session with an open heart and mind. So, it's up to the dominant." He pointed at himself again. "To help the sub get there, because if you take a sub over your knee who really has their mind firmly planted outside the session, thinking about work, or what they have to do with the kids the next day, you can spank them for the rest of the night, and all you'll get is a physical reaction. They may not break through the barrier to get to the submissive state you both benefit from."

Sophie squirmed in her seat. He was talking about real life. A real relationship. Not a fantasy. Her chest tightened, and she had to clear her throat to keep it from closing.

"Because that's one of the reasons we enter into a discipline relationship, right? It's not just so I get to have my way all the time. Because hell, I'd rather be having a beer and watching the game when the kids are asleep than having to punish my wife. But it's what we do to keep our relationship on the right track. Real life happens to Doms, too. So, what do you do about your own mindset? Well, there are a few things you can do."

As he went on to explain how the Dom might prepare himself for punishing his or her sub, Sophie took several calming breaths. This was supposed to get her mind off Scott, not draw her attention to all the elements she wished she could pursue in their relationship.

"When we're at home and it's time for Anna to face the consequences for whatever she's done wrong, I like to put her in the corner. I strip her down myself. I don't let her do it at all because this isn't about her pleasing me, this is about her accepting what's about to happen to her, and I'm completely in control during this time." He took a few steps toward the back right of the stage and pointed at what could be considered the corner of the room.

"Once I have her nude, I walk her to the corner, explain again why she's being punished, and make her face the wall with her hands on her head. I give her time to contemplate what's going to happen, and why. While she's doing this, I take the time to get whatever I need for the session and to get my head on straight. Clear it of anything other than her and why we're doing what we're doing. Because mindset, right? We both have to be there with the right intentions and the openness to get through it. As much of a sadistic bastard as I am, I hate to see her cry from pain, like real pain. And when I punish her, it's not pain-slut sort of pain. So, I have to prepare myself to put her in a place neither of us really enjoys."

Sophie swallowed hard. He probably wasn't intending to get the audience aroused just by his description, but damn if she couldn't already feel her pussy dampening at the image of Scott performing those actions with her.

"But like I said, this might not work for you. You have to find the right actions, the right words that work for both you and your partner."

As he finished his statement, a woman who could easily fit into the back pocket of his jeans walked on stage.

Stephanos turned his head toward her then put the microphone down and went to her. As he approached, Chase set a microphone on a stand near the couple, but not close enough to interfere with their conversation.

Stephanos picked up the woman's hand and walked her to behind the chair. He turned her to face him, her back to the audience. While he untied the robe, he talked to her. The mic didn't pick up every word, but Sophie got the gist.

Anna had lied.

Anna had gotten caught.

Sophie's heart sank even deeper.

Once he had her naked and her hands on her head, he walked back around the chair and picked up the microphone. "Before we get started, are there any questions I can answer?"

Two men asked questions about setting the right mindset, and a woman questioned how he decided what sort of punishment to give out. Had Scott sat through these sorts of demonstrations before? He'd gotten the job done well enough with the ball gag, but he hadn't spanked her.

She started to raise her hand, to ask about alternative punishments, but Stephanos had put the mic on the stand and walked over to his wife.

He brought Anna's hands down from her head and kissed her forehead. How hard a punishment could he be giving her if he was being so loving?

As though Stephanos heard her thoughts, he dug his hand into his wife's hair and pulled her to the chair. Without releasing her, he sat down and dragged her over his lap.

"Hope you're taking notes, Sophie. So, you can compare during the spanking you're going to get after this is done," a deep, authoritative voice vibrated in her ear.

She sucked in her breath, not daring to turn around. She didn't need to. She could feel him.

Scott.

149

Fuck.

"No, don't you dare take your eyes off this. You watch her as she gets her ass spanked, and every time his hand lands, you think about it being mine. Because you're in for one hell of a spanking when it's over." His voice shook.

He probably wasn't dragging her out of the class to deliver the punishment because he was too angry.

She'd lied.

She'd gotten caught.

Double fuck.

She tried to focus on the scene in front of her. Anna cried out when the spanks landed, and Stephanos didn't give her any time to recover from them. A full arsenal was being deployed on the little woman's upturned ass.

Sophie didn't think Stephanos would go easy, he seemed downright terrifying, but holy shit did that woman take a walloping. From where she sat, she could see the vibrations of her ass with each stroke. Her white flesh blushed then quickly turned a deep crimson.

No amount of wiggling helped her, as her massive husband just wrapped his arm around her waist and continued to punish her.

"Lying is unacceptable, and it breaks down what we have," he said, taking a momentary break from swatting her to speak.

It would be completely okay with Sophie if a sinkhole opened up right beneath her and took her away. Scott didn't say another word throughout the punishment, but he didn't need to. The tension rolled off him, enveloping her—trapping her.

Anna's cries for mercy went unheeded, her pleas for him to stop ignored. She finally broke down into a sobbing, contrite mess, lying over his lap, completely accepting each spank to her ass. The fight left her, but she turned into something else. Something stronger.

When Stephanos stopped spanking and starting rubbing her ass, she sniffled but didn't try to escape him.

The distance from the mic made hearing his words hard, but Sophie could make out his tone. Loving. He loved this woman he'd just spanked to tears. Although he kept a stern demeanor while had administered the spanking, Sophie could almost feel his own pain at having to dish it out. But they were reconnecting now.

Several couples rose and quietly left the area, seeming to know Stephanos and Anna needed private moments now.

"Let's go," Scott whispered in her ear and gripped her upper arm.

Sophie didn't fight back, didn't pull away. She continued to watch Anna as her husband helped her from his lap and brought her into his chest for a cuddle. Stephanos kissed her forehead, her cheeks before kissing her lips and wiping away all of her tears.

Envy seeped into Sophie.

"I know the club's closed, but if it's okay, I'd like to use one of the semi-privates. Need to take care of something." Scott's voice pulled her attention away from the aftercare taking place on stage to the immediate danger of her ass.

Chase, who had looked so damn hot only minutes before, suddenly appeared more like a prison warden. He swept his gaze over her with a frown.

"You good with this?" he asked her.

She could say no. She could get loose and just go home.

Lowering her head, she nodded. "Yeah. I'm good with it," she muttered.

"We need to clean up still, and everyone's milling around for a bit in the lounge, anyway," Chase said, not an ounce of pity in his voice. "Not sure what she did, but I've seen that same look of guilt written all over my Emma's face."

Sophie shot her head up to look at him. Still no empathy for her, but at least she found encouragement in his tone.

"Thanks." Scott gave a curt nod then pulled her along with him to the same semi-private room he'd used the last time they were at the club.

"What are you doing here?" she asked once they were inside and the curtain had been closed.

He laughed. "What am I doing here?"

Okay, she probably shouldn't have led with that particular question. But she was still curious.

"I didn't think you'd be here." She changed tactics, though it seemed to get the same result.

He grinned, but not the sexy, come-fuck-me grin she usually got from him. No, this one made her spine tingle. Danger danced in the room with them.

"Obviously, since you were supposed to be home watching chick flicks and chilling out." He let her arm go and strode to the chair in the corner. Lifting it with one hand he carried it to the middle of the room and put it down. She swallowed back a defense because she had none, and watched him jerk the zipper of his coat down and pull his arms free.

She'd left her jacket in the demonstration room, but it didn't seem like the right time to mention it.

"You lied," he stated with his hands on his hips. The dark T-shirt he wore stretched across his chest. His tense muscles didn't do much to ease her panic. She'd thought he was mad with the ball-gag punishment, but this was different. This made her chest twist and her stomach flop. He wasn't just a little irritated because she didn't stop talking when he told her to. No. This went deeper.

"I did." She nodded. What else was there to say?

"Why?"

Easy answer, I'm a coward. But he'd want more. "I wanted to get my mind off things for a night." Mostly true.

"I get that. I'm not mad because you needed a night to yourself. That's understandable; we've been spending a lot of time together." If his voice hadn't softened at just that moment, like the time meant something more to him than just casual play, she could harden herself.

"But I told you I was staying home and then came here." She finished his thought for him. No point in arguing once you've had your hand in the cookie jar for a full hour.

"Yeah. That's what I want to know. Why not just tell me you were coming here?"

"Because you would have wanted to come with. You would have said it wasn't safe for me alone." She rushed out her answer, although every word now seemed fabricated.

"So, you lied because you thought you knew how I'd react?" He quirked an eyebrow.

"Would you have let me?" she asked, meeting his gaze. Maybe if she could win that point, he'd take it easier on her.

"I'm not your owner, Sophie. If you wanted to come here alone, I wouldn't stop you. Yeah, I probably would have suggested I tag along, mostly because I like the demonstration nights. That's why I'm here, because of the demonstration. But fuck me. When I walk in, I see you, my fucking submissive, sitting in the crowd when you're supposed to be home tucked under your blankets, binging on chick flicks and popcorn." His lips thinned more with each sentence.

Okay, she was not going to win the point.

"But…" His voice deepened. "If you'd been honest with me, that you wanted to go it alone, I wouldn't have stopped you. I would have just stayed home or gone out to dinner with Gray and Dani."

She flattened her hand over her stomach. Lunch had been a horrible idea.

His gaze flickered to her belly then back up to her face. His sigh filled the space between them.

"I'm sorry I assumed your reaction," she murmured, folding her hands in front of her.

"Lying breaks down communication and trust," he said.

"I know," she agreed. She knew this but had done it anyway.

"I'm going to punish you, now, Sophie. Not a little spanking, either. It's going to hurt, and it's going to last a while, and you'll remember it tomorrow morning when you sit at your desk."

She swallowed and took a shaky breath. Watching it on stage had been like watching a dirty film, made her hot and wanting. Having the words aimed at her, the disappointment in his eyes focused on her, made the experience humbling. Painful.

"I kinda figured." She tried to smile, to bring some lightness to the dark tension surrounding them, but he didn't return it.

His hands went to his belt and unbuckled the leather strap. Her ass clenched in reaction, and she bit down on her tongue to keep from begging him to forgive and forget. He might be able to, but in the end they would both walk away resentful. Because once again she wouldn't have taken what she needed, and she'd have that craving digging at her.

He ripped the belt from the loops in one quick pull, the sound making her jolt. It wasn't like she read in books. It didn't sound sexy. It was like a dark beacon, calling her to her punishment. No, she didn't like that sound. The books got it all wrong.

"Step over to the chair," he ordered.

Her feet must have heard the same deep dominant voice she did because before she even thought to move, she obeyed.

"Take down your pants and your underwear to your knees, lift your shirt, and place your hands on the seat of the chair. I want your ass high in the air for me, presented for my belt. You'll take fifteen lashes, not one less. If you get up, you get an extra. If you try to block with your hands, you get an extra. If I have to stop to put you back into position, you'll get a second spanking when I take you home."

Take her home? Three words. Simple and probably meant nothing to anyone else who might have heard them. But it meant he wasn't just going to punish her and leave. He wasn't going to let this ruin them. Stephanos had been right. This was going to put them back on the track her lie had derailed them from.

"Okay," she whispered.

"I want to hear, yes, sir." His voice hardened.

"Yes, sir." Tension eased in her chest with the phrase. Shouldn't it be difficult, saying it to him? They were casual—this was all just part of their roles. Not real. Nothing substantial.

"Now, Sophie," he urged when she remained motionless.

She reached under her blouse and yanked on her leggings, pulling her cotton briefs with them until they bunched at her knees. She pushed harder on the back side to be sure they were even. Such a silly thing to be concerned about with him standing there gripping a belt in his hand.

Lifting her shirt up her back until her full ass was exposed, she bent and pressed her palms into the wood seat of the chair. Even with the heat on in the club, she felt a chill on her exposed skin, sending a light tremble through her. It wouldn't be chilly for long, she knew.

She kept her eyes down as he stepped around her, his booted steps echoing. Didn't matter the walls were basically hanging fabric. Everything amplified in that moment.

His fingertips rested on her right cheek, and she whimpered.

"I'm not going to warm you up for this. I'm just going to use the belt," he warned, and she nodded. What else was there to do? Have a discussion about it? He wouldn't go harder or longer than she could tolerate or harm her. Trust. One of the single most important elements of the relationship she claimed she wanted. And she'd broken it with a dumbass lie.

Tears burned her eyes before he lifted the belt. But they spilled upon first contact.

"Ow!" she grunted with the first fiery stripe. He pulled back and unleashed the second and the third.

Just like Stephanos, he didn't give her a moment to recover

from the first before going to the next. Tears dropped onto the seat below her.

She wiggled a little at first, but on the fifth stroke, she moved her ass to the right, making him miss his mark. The tip of the folded belt lashed at her hip, and she squeaked.

"Get back in position," he ordered.

She nodded and moved back to where she'd been.

Had he stopped? Did she just earn an entirely new spanking?

"That's an extra one," he declared and brought the belt down again, this time lower, right on the crease where her thighs and ass met. Oh fuck, it burned like hell.

She bit down on her tongue, her lips, everywhere trying to persuade her mind to dwell on the pain somewhere besides her ass. This wasn't like when she dug her nails into her palms, or when he smacked her while buried deep in her pussy. This was raw, urgent pain.

The strikes kept coming, and her mind continue to focus on him.

Her fault. This was all her fault. She'd done this. She'd made this happen.

By the twelfth lash, her elbows buckled, and she had to push herself back up. He paused, giving her a moment to reposition and suck in much-needed air.

"Almost done," he said, his fingertips once again touching her ass. The lightness of it a promise, a possibility of reconnecting. Throughout the spanking, it had been his belt touching her, not him. She'd been disconnected.

He flattened his hand on the small of her back. Not to keep her in place, he was bringing them back together.

She sniffled and blinked a few times, shedding more tears.

Each time the belt landed, she moaned. Light sobs tore through until she finally gave in and let her chest explode from the guilt, letting it all fly out in tears and shaking limbs.

He gave her the last lick of the belt, reminding her she was getting it for moving, then stood back from her.

She pressed her face into her arm and continued to cry. She expected him to put his belt back on and get her a tissue, but she didn't know him as well as she thought.

He carefully pulled her panties over her ass, letting the elastic snap in place at her hips. Hanes again. Dragging her leggings up, he didn't protect her burning cheeks from the material as he put them in place as well.

"Come here," he said, urging her to stand.

She faced him, quickly wiping the tears and what little snot had snuck out from her crying. He shooed her hands away and pulled her into his chest, smoothing her hair from her face and planting soft kisses on the top of her head.

"That was hard," he said as though confessing. "You okay?"

"Yes, sir." She nodded and clutched at his shirt, not wanting to let go. Just needing him to keep holding her in place, because if she looked up at him, if she saw the care and adoration matching the tone in his voice, she would fall apart.

And she worked so hard to keep herself together.

"The next time I rip off my belt like that, I want it to be right before I sink my cock into you and make us both fucking explode. Understand?" He kept running his fingers over her hair, soothing her.

"Yes, sir." She took a trembling breath. "I'm sorry. I shouldn't have lied, and I shouldn't have assumed."

"Thank you," he whispered and kissed the top of her head again. "I didn't see your car in the lot. You cabbed it?" he asked, not letting her go yet.

"Yeah. I wasn't sure if I'd be drinking or not, so I played it safe."

"Good girl." He kissed her again then patted her back. "I'll get you home and put you to bed. Straight to bed. No touching your pussy, either. You'll have to wait until I give you your next orgasm." Pulling away from her, he raised her chin with his fingers until she met his gaze.

She had to look like such a fucking mess, but he still appeared to be something from a Greek mythology book. "Yes, sir. I understand." But she didn't like it.

He dragged his fingers through her hair and tilted her head back farther, bringing his lips down on hers. The warmth of his lips spread through her body, momentarily making her forget the pain in her bottom, and the weariness in her body. With such an easy touch, two lips touching hers, he wiped away the residual fears, the lingering doubt, and left a calm, confident heat.

When he broke the kiss, he pressed his forehead against hers, breathing heavily. "I'm trying to go slow, Sophie. I'm trying to keep this casual for you, but nothing about you is casual."

The heated words simmered through her. He didn't tell her anything she didn't already know.

She didn't know what to say, how to respond. Her heart ached to scream back that she agreed, she knew what he meant and wanted to dive in all the way with him.

She opened her mouth, ready, willing, but clamped her lips closed. There were too many what-ifs. Still things that weren't decided. It wouldn't be fair—to either of them.

"They probably want to finish closing up," she whispered after a long moment passed in silence.

He kissed her forehead. "Yeah. We should get going."

He grabbed his jacket, buckled his belt, and slid his hand into hers.

For the moment, she'd find comfort in his touch.

But only for a moment.

CHAPTER 19

"How is that even possible?" Scott glared at the medical examiner in the M.E. office.

Dr. Greene slid his hands into his the pockets of his lab coat and shrugged. "It happens. There wasn't a question of the identity, as far as we knew, so there wasn't a rush on the testing."

"But now there's a question of identity?" Sophie asked, coffee in hand.

"It's complicated. You see, we ran the results of your victim through the data base. We do that to see if it triggers anything in cold cases or missing persons. And we found a match, but it's not an exact match."

Scott pinched the bridge of his nose. Obviously, he should have spent more time studying biology in high school instead of practicing his chemistry with the homecoming queen.

"Can you explain that in English?" Sophie asked, her tone tight. At least Scott wasn't the only one confused.

"Yes, there's a small mutation in the sample we sent off. So, the sample from your victim matches another profile almost identically, except for a tiny mutation that wouldn't have been caught except for some really stellar work on the part of one my technicians. He's got a knack for finding the little details. It's actually quite—"

"Yeah, I'm sure it is, but I still don't get it. The match was a match, but not really?" Scott pressed on, running low on patience.

Dr. Greene cleared his throat and rolled his shoulders back. "Yes."

"Okay, so how does that change things here?" Scott tried to focus all his attention on the doctor. He shifted his body to the right, bringing himself a little closer to Sophie. She didn't move away. He took it as a good sign.

"Well, the profile we found is for Susan James. A rape case that went unsolved about ten years ago," Dr. Greene said.

"Wait. But you just said the DNA you sent from our victim doesn't exactly match that profile," Sophie pointed out.

Dr. Greene huffed. "Yes. Your victim doesn't match the profile. But the profile has your victim's name on it. Same age, appearance is identical. You're dealing with twins, detective. And you have the wrong one in my lab."

Scott closed his eyes. They had the wrong victim. He could laugh. It would feel good to relieve some of the tension, but he held back.

"So, who the hell is the victim if it's not Susan James?"

"The unfortunate woman in my lab's name is Sabrina Charleston. I took the liberty to send a request out for all of her records and get you more information on the real victim."

"So, where the hell is Susan James if it's her sister who's dead?" Sophie asked, irritation seeping into her tone.

"That's why you're the detectives, and I'm just the lab rat." Dr. Greene smiled.

"Right," Scott said. "Thanks."

"Thank you, Dr. Greene. Did you have any more information about the bruising on the report?" Sophie asked.

"Oh yes, I'm sorry I missed you yesterday. It was such a slight discoloration, I nearly overlooked it. That's why it wasn't on the preliminary report. The bruising is around both forearms, but just over the tops, as though she'd been tied down to a chair. There was also some fingerprint bruising under her arms, like she'd been dragged."

"Okay, thanks. That actually makes sense now." Sophie nodded.

"If you need anything else, just let me know." The doctor gave them each a dismissive smile and went back into his lab.

"That makes sense?" Scott asked with raised brows.

"Yeah. She was tied down to the chair so she couldn't get up and leave, but when she was shot and fell over, she would still be too close to the chair, right? The force of the bullet would have thrown her further away, but the binds kept her secured. So, the murderer had to reposition her body at least a few inches to make it look like she fell from the chair. We should get forensics to examine the blood splatter again and see if it matches my theory."

"If the shooter manipulated the body afterward, there should be more evidence," Scott added as they climbed the stairs toward their department.

"I think everyone jumped on the suicide bandwagon too quick and overlooked things. We'll have it all combed through again. But in the meantime, what I don't get is where the hell is Susan James. I mean, her twin sister is killed in her own apartment, but she's nowhere around? And what about that email?"

"The email doesn't exist. I have the two confessors coming in this afternoon for more questioning. Obviously, they were put up to confessing, especially since the person they were claiming to have killed isn't even fucking dead." Scott stopped at the top of the stairs. "This is one of the most fucked up cases I've had."

"Yeah, me, too." Sophie laughed. A light sound, easing the tension between them.

After his slip in letting her know he was having trouble keeping things casual between them, he worried she'd run for the hills. But he couldn't help saying it.

Sure, he was pissed she'd lied to him. When he arrived for the rope demonstration, he was disappointed it had been changed, but once he saw her sitting in the audience, he chalked it up to fate.

He had expected her to take her punishment; she had too much pride to walk away from it. She knew she'd lied, and Chase had been right. The guilt had been written all over her. To not punish her and relieve her of the heavy burden would have been cruel. But he hadn't expected her reaction. He hadn't spanked her as hard as he would have a more experienced submissive. She'd never had a belt spanking before as far as he knew, so he went lighter. Still marked her ass pretty good, and holy fuck did those marks play through his mind all fucking night, no matter how many times he jerked off.

Seeing her cry, feeling her chest heave against his own with her sobs had taken the little seed of hope she could be something more and fertilized it until he lay awake most of the night trying to figure out how to make her his. Really his. Like, forever his.

That she wasn't hiding from him this morning gave him more hope. That she actually texted him with a good morning and offered to pick up coffee for him on her way to work nearly sent him through the roof of his Mazda.

But it was small steps. Like Dani said, let it simmer, until it all comes to a boil. Until then, he needed to keep things as casual and as aloof as possible with her. He didn't need her running scared now.

"So, where do you want to start?" she asked.

"Let's watch the security footage from the apartment again. I know they said they only saw her going into the apartment, but since we know she isn't really her, we might be able to see something else," Scott offered.

"Good idea. I can handle the witnesses, unless you want to join in?"

"If you need me, call me. I'll be watching hours of footage." He smiled then gestured for her to move to the side of the hall with him. "How are you feeling today?" he asked in a soft voice so not to be overheard.

She glanced around, a light pink taking over her cheeks before she answered. "I'm fine, thanks."

"And your—" She pressed her fingertips to his mouth to stop him. He smiled, savoring the scent of coffee lingering on her, and pulled her hand away.

"Naughty, naughty," he teased in a low whisper.

"I'm fine there, too." She looked away but smiled. "Sir."

Did heartbeats actually skip? Maybe he was coming down with a heart murmur, brought on by the sweetest tone speaking such a heavy word.

"Good. Let's not repeat that lesson anytime soon." He wanted to brush the errant strand of hair from her face, cradle her cheek, and kiss the breath from her. But they were at work. So he straightened to full height instead. "It will be worse if we have to."

Her eyes widened, and she jerked her head up to look at him. Her hair fell over her shoulders in thick waves. Running his fingers through the curls became a priority, and he mentally counted down the hours until they could get the hell out of the station.

"Got it." She blew out a burst of air, making her lips vibrate in a less than ladylike fashion. "I need to get to work, or we may have to take a really long smoke break to your car. And neither of us smokes."

He laughed, and how fucking good it felt to laugh with her.

"Okay. I'll get to my stuff, you get to yours, and we'll meet with Captain Peterson at four thirty. He wants an update, and then we can wrap for the day. Sound good?"

"Absolutely."

"Think you need alone time tonight? You didn't really get it last night," Scott remarked.

"I dunno. I feel like there's a few things on my list you haven't gotten to yet." She winked. Was she trying to make him walk through the damn precinct with a fucking hard on? Not that she needed to try. Her formfitting black slacks achieved the goal easily enough. Even if they were offset by the sneakers she wore.

"Ah, teasing. Well, you'll have to see where that gets you. Now get back to work," He spun her around and sent her off with a resounding smack to her ass.

She gasped and set a hard glare on him while stomping away.

Shit. They were still in the hallway. She made it so easy for him to forget everything other than her. A quick glance around assured him no one had seen. Thankfully.

Giving her a smack when they were alone was one thing, jeopardizing reputation at work was completely different. And he wouldn't do that to her.

Keep your fucking head on straight! Work then play.

And play he would.

.

CHAPTER 20

"Okay, we'll go over this one more time and then no work talk. Got it?" Scott pointed a finger at her while he maneuvered his car through the evening D.C. traffic.

They'd worked later than either of them wanted, and she was tired. Feet-aching, mind-burnt tired.

"Deal."

"Good. So, neither witness showed for their interview."

"Right. They took a flight to Mexico early this morning. I spent most of the day checking into them. Michael Carmichael's wife did have a baby several weeks ago, but healthy as can be. No heart defects. Mrs. Singleton's husband, although is sickly, was more than happy to explain his wife had left him for another man."

"Michael Carmichael?" Scott guessed.

"Yep. Apparently, he has a thing for older women. Susan James found out about the affair and was blackmailing them both. Mostly to get accounts, it seemed, but I have a feeling they came in with their stupid confession because she had them do it. Once they did their part, they weren't needed. But to keep them from fucking her over and giving us real information, she made sure they hightailed it out of the country."

"No longer caring their spouses would find out?"

"Mr. Singleton didn't seem to mind. I think he had his own thing going, if you know what I mean." Sophie waggled her eyebrows. "Mrs. Carmichael had less-than-kind things to say about her husband, but I think she'll land on her feet."

"The next case we get better be a straightforward robbery gone bad," Scott mused.

"What did you find on the video?" Sophie changed the topic.

"I saw her go into her apartment then, two hours later, I saw her go into her apartment again."

"Twins." Sophie nodded. "That makes sense, if they were sisters."

"Yeah, but the records that I pulled showed they grew up in separate states. They were both adopted out to separate families." Scott glanced over his shoulder and merged into the left lane.

"Yeah, I was researching what Dr. Greene was telling us about the DNA sample. Sometimes an identical twin can have a mutation in one of the strands due to environmental influences. So, growing up apart would account for the variation he found." She leaned back against the headrest. Science had been a big enough pain in school; she found no joy in relearning it.

"Okay, so they weren't reared together. Maybe they just recently met, and that's why she's around. No one knows about the twin because Susan James wasn't exactly friendly. But what about Sabrina? Have we gotten hold of any of her relatives? Adoptive parents, siblings, friends?"

"No. But Susan's adopted sister did know about the twin. She's the one who gave me her phone number and said she was the next of kin to contact. I finally got her on the phone today, and she told me she hadn't seen or heard from Susan in two years. I guess when their parents died, Susan, tried to take the full inheritance from Elizabeth. It ended up in court, a real mess. No love lost there. But Susan told her about Sabrina, so she at least knew of her twin sister two years ago."

"Such a tangled fucking mess." Scott sighed.

Sophie sat straighter in her seat. "And remember what Steve told us? He said he ran into her a few weeks before the murder, but she acted like she never knew him. Put up a real fight when he tried to kiss her."

"He probably ran into Sabrina, not Susan."

Scott turned onto his street. "Okay, so the twins have met, and both were in her apartment that day. The security footage didn't show anyone leaving the apartment once she entered until the next morning when the maid showed up. So, what happened?"

"No one left? The patio doors were locked from the inside, so they couldn't have left that way."

"Maybe we should check out the apartment again tomorrow," Scott said, parking the car.

"I guess it wouldn't hurt at this point," Sophie agreed. The overhead lighting of the garage filtered through the windshield and cast a light shadow over Scott's features, still wearing the tension from the day. "If you'd rather just chill out tonight, I can grab a cab home. I don't mind. It's been a hard day."

His eyes snapped to hers, and he reached across the car, wrapped his hand around her neck, and pulled her to meet him. "All I need right now is you." He pressed his lips against hers hard, like he'd been waiting all day to get his lips on her.

She had been.

"Upstairs, then?" she muttered against his lips when he eased up.

Not moving from her, he smiled. "Fuck yeah."

The elevator worked against them. Three other people crammed in on the way to his condo, and, of course, each lived on a separate floor. If the damn thing stopped once more, she was going to throw an all-out tantrum.

Scott took it all in stride, holding her hand and running his thumb up and down her palm. The action was probably meant to soothe her, but the only thing that would accomplish that feat was him naked in bed.

"Dinner?" Scott teased once he had the door opened and they were inside.

"I had a really big lunch," she said. "Do you still have my list?" She dropped her purse and coat on the living-room couch.

"Your list is somewhere in my room, and I'm not getting it. I have it memorized and categorized, and I don't want to hear another word about that fucking thing. Got it?" He picked up her coat and purse and moved them to the loveseat.

"Okay. Got it." She leaned against the couch and stared at him. "If you really want to eat, we can."

"I think you're turning into a bit of a brat. Maybe you should have taken a nap today?" He moved closer to her, taking away the space that usually comforted her. Except him being near her was better.

"I don't believe I've ever played a brat before," she mocked with a tapping finger to her chin.

"You've never played anything before." He captured her hips in his hands and pulled her against his body. She leaned into him, inhaling him, wanting to devour him.

"True enough."

"But, if you want to be a brat, I'm happy to play along. In my experience, a nice long spanking usually quells the urge to mouth off, especially when coupled with some ball-gag and corner time."

He wouldn't.

"That sounds horrible…well, unless there's a happy ending?" She looked up at him with some hope.

He screwed up his face and shook his head. "Unless you consider being used like a fuck toy and put to bed hornier than hell, no."

"You did that last night. You didn't let me touch myself." She pushed against his chest. Playing. She was flirting and playing with this massive man who could tan her ass with three swats of his hands. And enjoying it.

"That's right because you'd been a very naughty girl, and naughty girls don't get to have their pussies played with, and they sure as fuck don't get to have orgasms." He tapped her nose. "I think some corner time would do you good, actually."

She pulled back.

"Not as a punishment. Just a little way to get your head in your submissive space. We've had a really fucked-up day, and we're both run down mentally. I think this will help. Both of us." He laced his fingers through hers and started to bring her toward the bedrooms.

At the familiar cramp in her chest, she pulled back on his hand. But he didn't give in, didn't take her down to the next room.

The fight in her softened. It was just a room, right? It didn't necessarily mean anything. Just a room.

With his bed and his clothes, and his intimate desires housed in it.

Just a fucking room.

He brought her to a corner of the room next to the nightstand. Turning her to face him, he began to unbutton her blouse. The style she wore to work every day, making her fashion choices easy and predictable. Comforting, even. And now, his big fingers slid the small pearl-colored buttons through the holes.

She watched him finish the row, enjoying the feel of his hands as he ran them under the shirt, over her shoulders, and pushed the fabric away from her body. He discarded the blouse onto the bed and reached behind her, pulling her into his chest to unhook her bra. She inhaled hard, taking in his scent, memorizing it, bathing in it.

Her bra slid down her arms, the cups freed from her breasts, making them jiggle a little.

"Fuck these are so beautiful." He cupped her breasts and lifted them to his mouth, taking one between his teeth while he rolled the nipple of the free one between his fingers.

She inhaled a sharp breath and whimpered when he released them.

His eyes moved from her chest to meet her gaze, and he kept her locked, almost entranced while he worked the button and zipper of her slacks and pushed them down until they pooled at her ankles.

"No panties?" He tsked, releasing her from his tractor-beam stare, and ran his hand over her bare hips.

"My ass was a little tender this morning, I thought it would be better without them," she answered. It hadn't been bad, not like she couldn't sit, but one of the marks from his belt lay along her panty line. Having the extra pressure on it all day would have left her more uncomfortable.

"Ahh, well, maybe a spanking tonight isn't a good idea, then. Let me see." He grabbed her upper arm and turned her around. His fingers found the mark and ran along it. "Just this one?" he asked sounding disappointed in his handiwork.

"It's just in a bad spot." She looked over her shoulder down at him while he continued his inspection.

"We need to get you in the corner before I forget my plans again. You have a way of derailing me." He gave a soft smack to her ass and moved out of her way. "Just face the corner and fold your arms behind your back. If your shoulders start to ache, you can drop your arms to your sides."

She moved nose to corner. A shudder ran through her. She felt him watching from behind. Folding her arms behind her like he commanded, she widened her stance to get comfortable.

"Just let your mind sort of empty. Think about what you get out of your submissive side. How peaceful do you feel? That sort of thing." He spoke softly, as though he didn't want to interrupt her thinking.

"And what do you do while I'm going on this mental voyage?" she asked.

He delivered a sharp smack to her bare ass, completely avoiding the bad spot. "Remember what brats get and what they don't get, Sophie." Warning delivered loud and clear.

"Yes, sir." Going to bed without an orgasm for a second night was not on her agenda.

"Good girl." He kissed the middle of her back. No one had ever kissed her there before.

A little peck, nothing really, but it reached into her. Intimate. He'd brought her into his room, undressed her, placed her in his corner, and now he gave her tender kisses.

Her stomach twisted, and her throat constricted.

"Relax, Sophie. I'm here, and it's fine." He ran his fingers down her spine. "Don't dwell. Just let the thoughts go."

Curling her fingers, she dug her nails into her forearm. The little bite was enough to center her. Intimate, he was being intimate, and she would have to cope with it. She would have to handle it. Because for the first time in, well, ever, the idea sent warmth rippling through her instead of dark terror.

His touch left her, and she heard the bedsprings creak. If she dared to check, she was sure he'd be watching her.

As the moments ticked by, she let her mind wander into what she wanted. How she imagined serving him meals, or fetching him coffee, how she would sit at his feet while they watched a movie. She let the images fly by, settling her nerves, soothing her to the core, until all she had left was warm haze.

"Come here, Sophie and kneel." His silken voice broke through the internal noise.

With a revived calm, she obeyed, finding the act simple. She moved to her knees before him, placed her hands on her thighs, and looked up at him.

"Give me your arm." He pointed to her left arm. The one she'd been pinching.

Reluctant to make him angry, she hesitated, but he snapped his fingers, and she quickly obeyed. He touched the marks her nails had left, lifted her arm and kissed each one of them. "I told you to tell me if you felt like you needed to do this while you were with me. Did the corner set you off so much, then?" he asked, still holding her arm.

"No, I just… Well, at first, but after a few minutes, I think it was just habit. I didn't want to disappoint you," she confessed and lowered her gaze. In not telling him, she had done the same thing.

"You don't disappointment me. You have coping mechanisms for stressful situations. This isn't a terrible one, and not even one I would refuse you, but I would like the opportunity to help." He dropped her arm. "How do you feel now?"

"Relaxed." She chanced a look through her lashes. His jaw wasn't set. Maybe she'd managed to avoid ruining the evening.

"Good." He leaned over to kiss her. "I want to fuck you, Sophie. And I don't want to be gentle. Are you good with that?" A kiss on her cheek.

"Yes, sir," she whispered, turning her face to capture his lips when he tried to kiss the side of her neck.

He laughed. "You don't control this, remember?" He tapped her nose. "Do that again, and I'll have to find a way to make you sorry."

"I won't," she promised herself and him.

He placed a softer kiss on her chin. Something clicked, and his hand fisted in her hair.

"Up on the bed," he ordered in a hard tone. Not waiting for her to move, he dragged her from her knees and shoved her onto the bed. "Open your legs, Sophie. I want to see that pussy." He unbuckled his belt and tore off his shirt, like he was a starved man being served an entire feast who didn't know where to begin.

Unsure of where to put her arms, she slid them under her ass. Better to rid herself of the temptation to grab for him. And with the way his muscles were flexing and moving while he disrobed, plucking him up and tossing him down to have her wicked way with him seemed like a really good idea.

Except she didn't want the control. He was right. She just needed to give over and let him have it. Ease into his dominance. He'd already shown her he wouldn't let her get by without being satisfied and would give her exactly what she needed. It was knowing the difference between what she needed and what she wanted she had to focus on.

Right now, she needed his cock. And if she made the wrong move, he'd deny her.

He climbed onto the bed, his hand wrapped around his shaft.

"Keep your hands where they are," he growled and pushed her left leg farther out, exposing her pussy to his stare. His touch.

Two fingers traced the outside of her sex, light touches. She mewled when he continued to explore her without sating her need for the rough touch.

"You sound like you're in heat. Are you, Sophie? Does my little sub want my cock?"

"Yes!" She bit down on her lip to keep the demand buried inside. Let him control the moment.

He chuckled and plunged two fingers into her pussy. She sucked in hot air and arched her back. After pulling his fingers out, he thrust them forward again. Not enough! She spread her legs wider and pushed her ass up at him.

"More? Does my little slut want more?" He leaned over, swiping her clit with his tongue while his fingers fucked her harder. The zap of electricity running from her cunt to her core burst through her. "Like this?" He bit down on her clit.

She moaned. Fisting the blanket beneath her couldn't anchor her well enough, not while he sucked and bit and thrust. Her hips gyrated with his movements. She was fucking his damn face.

And loving it.

"That's my girl." He smiled up at her between nips. He kissed her thigh then bit down hard, making her scream. "One more time." He turned to her other thigh and did the same, this time sucking while he bit.

"Scott!" It wasn't a plea for him to stop. He couldn't stop. She would kill him if he stopped.

His fingers moved faster his tongue dancing over her clit.

"I'm going—fuck I—" Where the hell had the words gone?

"No, no, not yet." He withdrew his fingers and the pressure in her belly building, ready to explode, slowly rolled back.

She whimpered. How could he?

Pulling her hand out from beneath her, she found her clit and gently rolled her fingers over the sensitive bud. It lasted a moment, a breath before he swatted her hand away.

"No touching, remember? You don't get to come until I give it to you, until I say you can come." He held her hand and brought her fingers to his mouth. Taking two of them inside his mouth, licking at the tips before biting down hard. "Do you understand?"

"Yes!" She tried to yank her fingers out, but he held her firm.

"Now, put your hands over your head and grip the headboard." He released her.

"This is where you tie me down?" she asked, unable to keep the grin from her lips.

He gave her a serious look. "No. This is where you obey. Hold the bars of the headboard, and if you let go, you'll be punished. Maybe you won't get to come. Maybe I'll spank this pussy until you're begging me to stop." He slapped her sex to make his point, and she jumped.

Point taken.

"Then, please hurry." She reached over her head, gripping the wooden posts.

"Since you said please." His grin tilted. She couldn't read it, though. Did that mean he was pleased with her using her manners, or was he taunting and torturing her by going even slower because she'd shown him her cards.

"Scott," she whispered as he moved his body between her open thighs. His gaze traveled from her face to her breasts, farther still until he stared at her sex. She closed her eyes and turned her face.

She didn't get obsessed with her body image. She knew what she was, how she looked, and she wouldn't apologize for it. Except when lying completely nude beneath a man who had all the power in the world to crush her with a simple look. Her breasts weren't perky when she lay on her back, and with her hips flattened out, she resembled more of an overstuffed pancake than anything he might think of as sexy.

"Sophie, open your eyes and look at me." The order came softly but held the authority of an emperor.

Opening her eyes, she breathed through her nose, afraid to say something stupid. She never worried about that. Why now, with him so close to her, did she get so tongue twisted and nervous.

"You are fucking gorgeous," he said with a straight face.

She had no response.

"I can't go slowly, not now, so you have to tell me if you need me to stop." He ran the head of his cock through her slick folds. Just the brief touch of him against her clit spiraled her back toward the edge. "Keep your eyes on me, do you understand? Don't close them again."

She nodded.

"No, say it." His voice tensed, like he stood at the brink with her.

"I understand, sir."

He captured her mouth beneath his, sweeping his tongue inside hers and taking her. Completely conquering her thoughts and any breath she'd been holding.

In one swift thrust, he was inside her, and she cried out against his mouth. Perfect. He fit perfectly inside her.

He growled. "Holy fuck, Sophie." Nipping at her lip, he pulled back, nearly retreating all the way before plowing forward again. "Spread your legs more," he ordered, and she pulled them toward her chest, spreading them wide.

Another grunt.

His hands moved to her hips, pinning her to the bed, and pulled halfway out again then thrust back into her. She couldn't move. His body and his command immobilized her beneath him. She reeled from the knowledge, the feelings, his power, being at his mercy while he continued to withdraw and plunge.

The bed creaked beneath them. She didn't care, and he didn't stop.

He fucked her like she'd been made for the act. Like he couldn't get enough of her body, and she accepted every grunt, every bite, every thrust of his cock as though it brought her next breath.

"Fuck your pussy is so hot, so tight," he groaned and kissed her again, drawing her lip between his teeth before releasing hit.

She hooked her feet behind his back, and he dug his nails into her flesh. All she could do was grip the posts harder. She'd break them if she had to, but she would not let go. Not until he gave the okay, not until then.

His loud grunts and murmured words of how sexy she was, how fucking tight and hot she was, spurred her on.

"I can't, Scott. I can't." She wiggled her ass, gaining the friction she needed. "Too much…oh fuck too…good." She moaned.

"Not good enough, Sophie." He let go of her hip and plucked her nipple.

"Oh fuck. I can't!" she yelled, tears forming

"You can. Wait. Obey me, Sophie. Trust me." He thrust again, grinding into her clit. The added pressure made it worse. Hot pain shot through her. She had to come. If she didn't release soon, she'd lose her mind.

"I do!"

Scott plucked her nipple again.

"Oh fuck." He looked up at the ceiling. "Fuck. Come, Sophie. Now!" He fucked her harder. Like he was going to fuck her through the bed and through the floor.

Any resolve to hold back vaporized with his command. Arching her back, she felt him fully imbedded, felt him crush her clit with his body. Violent tremors shook her. She screamed with each pulsating wave, pushing herself toward him, trying to drag out the utopian sensations for as long as her body would allow.

"Fuck. Fuck," he chanted over her. He pumped hard then stilled, his words freezing on his lips while his release took him away.

His forehead pressed against hers. She loved the little ways he connected with her.

"Spend the night," he whispered. "I'll drive you to your place in the morning to change before work." He gently brought her hands down from the headboard.

Her spine stiffened.

"Do you feed your overnight guests?" she asked softly, trying to filter the fear from her tone.

He laughed. "If you give me five minutes, I can definitely feed you." He shifted his body, slipping his cock out from her, but she could feel it pressing against her.

"How can I say no to that?" She pulled him toward her and kissed him.

CHAPTER 21

"No luck on tracking down Carmichael and Singleton?" Sophie plunked a cup of coffee on Scott's desk.

"No. No credit card usage, no phone calls on their cell phones. Nothing. They got to Mexico and disappeared."

Sophie leaned against his desk and sipped her coffee. "Nothing on Susan, either, but she went to a lot of trouble to make it look like it was her death."

"So, you really like her for this?" Scott asked, tilting back in his chair and avoiding staring at her breasts. She'd worn another button-down blouse, lavender, and had left the top two buttons undone. If he peeked, he'd get a glimpse at her cleavage, and all blood would redirect to his pants.

"On the security tape, we only see the two of them going into the apartment. No one leaves. It has to be her, right? But why?"

"I think this might help." A file folder dropped on the desk. Detective Cartwright stood over them. "I took the names you asked me to run for background and financials and came up with some interesting information. Probably would have come across this sooner if the false vic's sister had come to claim the body, or maybe not at all. But…" He flipped open the folder and stabbed a finger at the top page.

Sophie turned around, slanting over Scott to see better. Damn, she smelled like his soap. His scent on her body smelled right.

"Life insurance?"

"Yeah, on Susan James. Look at the beneficiary."

Scott picked up the paper. "Shit. Sabrina gets the money."

"So, Susan James kills her identical twin, takes her identity, and collects on her own insurance policy?" Sophie asked. "But I checked with the hospital this morning. No one has requested a death certificate. And you can't claim on a policy without it."

"Maybe she's waiting this out. Once the case goes cold, she'll request and collect. The policy is for a million. She's got to be worth more than that, right?" Scott dug through the file. "This her financials?"

Detective Cartwright nodded. "Yeah. She's been putting out money left and right but not bringing much in. Apparently, she likes the high life. That apartment she lived in? She can't afford that. The rent is 75 percent of her salary. After she pays utilities and association dues, she's got next to nothing to live on. Stealing those accounts was her way of beefing up her commissions, but it wasn't enough. And if you checkout her credit history, she's drowning in debt."

Scott leaned back. "So, all this for money." He shook his head.

"Okay, so now we have motive. We still don't have her. I have a car stationed outside Sabrina's house to see if she'll go there. So far nobody has stopped by except for the mailman."

"Look who underwrote the policy." Sophie pointed at Clark Simmons' name. "He said he didn't speak to her, just sort of knew her from the building." She turned to Cartwright. "Can you look further into this policy. See if there's a clause allowing the policy to pay out without a certificate or something like that."

"Sure thing. I'll drive over there now and corner the guy." Cartwright nodded. He'd been on family leave from the precinct while his wife fought an unwinnable battle with breast cancer. After she passed, he'd taken time away to grieve, get their affairs in order, sort out things.

It was good to see him back. Hopefully, he'd be ready to take the lead on his own cases again soon. But for right now, Scott appreciated the help. It gave him an excuse to keep Sophie with him and not split the tasks up between them.

"Let's stop at Steven Renner's place, see if he knows anything about the policy or the sister. Maybe he can help steer us in the direction of where she might be hiding." Scott grabbed his coat off the chair and stood to slip it on.

Sophie downed the rest of her coffee. "Sure." She grabbed her purse from the drawer of her desk and met Scott near the doors.

"I didn't realize the captain had put Cartwright on the case with us," Sophie said as they made their way to Scott's car.

"Yeah, he told me about it yesterday. I forgot to mention it last night. Someone distracted me with her sexy body." He laughed and opened the car door for her.

"I'm pretty sure you were the distracting one, but I won't argue the point." Sophie stuffed her purse on the floorboard by her feet and buckled herself in.

Scott pulled out of the parking space and into traffic.

"Seeing as you benefited as much as I did, I don't see why you'd argue at all," Scott said with a grin.

The easy banter between them relaxed him. Every baby step they took together made him tense, waiting to see her reaction to it. She'd spent the night. In his bed. He'd woken up half afraid to feel the pillow beside him, fearing she'd run off in the middle of the night.

But she'd been there. Smiling at him when he opened his eyes. He expected her to be cute in the morning, but she blew him away. Adorable with her messy hair and smeared eye makeup, yes, but sexy as all fuck when she slipped from the bed and made her way toward the bathroom completely naked.

Her hips swayed so gently, so sweetly, he didn't see anything else while she made the trek across the room. He'd noticed her reluctance the night before while she was splayed out nude before him in bed, and he'd wiped it away for her. She wasn't the self-conscious type, but anyone would be a little hesitant when being examined the way he had been doing to her.

He hadn't been judging her; he'd been devouring the sight of her. He'd been enjoying every imperfection, every curve, every little mark on her body. Because he was making it all his. Every little step, every time she gave him an inch, he was making her belong to him.

It had been euphoric.

Sophie checked her phone. "So, he's off today. Swing by his apartment." She rattled off the address and gave him the directions before stashing her phone back in her coat.

"You know him pretty well?"

"Who? Steve? Not really. He never worked with me directly. He's a beat cop," she answered and leaned back against the seat. "When this case is over, I'm taking the hottest, longest, most bubbly bubble bath known to man, and while my skin is getting all wrinkly and nasty, I'll be downing a bottle of wine."

"I kept you up too late last night," he said, pulling the car into a parking garage.

"No, you woke me too early." She laughed. She'd been awake when he opened his eyes, but the sun hadn't even risen yet. He could have told her to go back to sleep. They could have easily gotten another hour or two of sleep.

Instead, he'd rolled her onto her belly, raised her ass in the air, and taken what was his.

"I don't recall hearing a complaint. I do remember there being a lot of begging, though." He glanced sideways to catch the blush creeping up her cheeks. She begged so fucking prettily, he couldn't help but delay her orgasm until she was nearly clawing his eyes out to have it. Playing her was so much fun, he didn't think he'd ever tire of it.

"Yeah, well…" She seemed to lose her retort when her gaze met his.

He shook his head with a laugh and found a spot to park the car. "Maybe tonight I'll put you to bed early."

She didn't respond.

"Apartment five C," she said and stepped out of the car.

Diving into the case. Her way of avoiding the topic of having another sleepover, but that was fine. Get the work done, then he'd have his play time.

Steve opened the door to his apartment wearing only a pair of jeans.

"Oh. Hi." He stood straighter, closing the door to press it against his body. No visual of the apartment.

"Hi, Steve. We just had a few more questions about Susan, and we're really hoping you can help us," Sophie said, keeping her hands tucked into her overstuffed coat. She really hated the chill of winter.

"I already told you, we broke up a while back." He plastered on a civil smile.

"Yeah, but we have a few questions about her maybe a boyfriend might know. Family, friends, that sort of thing," Sophie pushed gently.

"We're having a hard time finding her next of kin," Scott added, taking Sophie's lead and not telling him is ex-girlfriend wasn't really dead.

"She never talked about her family," Steve said quickly. He hugged the door tightly to his body.

"I'm getting hot in the hallway." Sophie unzipped her coat. "Mind if we step inside?"

"I-uh." He glanced over his shoulder. Sophie and Scott exchanged a glance. "Sure. Come in." He opened the door and shoved his hand through his bed-head hair.

"Thanks so much," Sophie said with a smile and a pat his bare chest.

"So, how can I help?" Steve clapped his hands together loudly and placed himself between them and the living room. The apartment was pretty open space, but he clearly didn't want them walking any farther inside than they already had.

"Well, for starters, she had a twin. Did you know that?" Sophie asked, removing her coat and draping it over her arm.

"I, uh, yeah, I think she mentioned it once. They didn't really talk, though." He folded his arms over his chest.

"Oh, cause you didn't mention that before. When we asked about her sister, you only mentioned the adopted sister, nothing about a twin. That might have been helpful." Sophie pointed out.

"Hmm, any idea where her sister might live? We're having trouble tracking her down. I was hoping you might be able to help," Scott said, stepping closer to him.

"Uh, no, like I said, they never really talked."

"Shame, really. So far, her adopted sister has refused to come down and claim her body, give her a proper burial, and now we can't locate her biological sister," Sophie said. She went on asking him about his thoughts on a memorial service, other family while Scott maneuvered away from them to get a better look at the apartment.

Relatively clean. The couch was a bit messed up. Cushions shifted, crunched like they'd just been rolled around on. TV wasn't on. No drinks or food on the coffee table.

Scott narrowed his eyes, just to be sure he saw what he thought he saw.

"No. Like I said, we weren't that into each other. She was kinda private," Steven answered. He untangled his arms to scratch his elbow, and his gaze flew to Scott between questions.

"I was really hoping you'd have something for us. Oh." Sophie pulled her phone out of her pocket. "I'm sorry, it's the lab." She took the call and walked off into his kitchen with the phone. Steve went to stop her, but Scott stepped in front of him.

"Hey, man. Did we catch you at a bad time?" he asked in a low voice, putting on his man-to-man tone.

"What? No, why?"

"Uh," Scott jerked his head toward the living room and pointed to the used condom on the floor beneath the coffee table.

Color seeped from Steve's face, and his throat constricted with his sudden hard swallows.

"We can come back later if you're in the middle of something," Scott suggested. "Sophie and I'll go to lunch and let you finish up here..."

"No, it's fine. I'm not—" Steve turned to the doorway of the kitchen where Sophie stood on her phone.

She finished the call and stared at them silently. What had she just found out?

"I have a quick question for you." She aimed her phone at Steve and closed the gap between them while dropping her coat onto a chair.

Scott moved closer to the couch, blocking Steve from retreating. The tip of Sophie's tongue touched her upper lip, and her eyes narrowed a fraction. He knew that expression; she'd learned something important.

"So, Susan's apartment was dusted for fingerprints. Makes sense that yours weren't among those we found that day since you'd been broken up for a while. But..." She finished closing the gap. "Your prints were found on the exterior of the front door. And a few other places, and at first it wasn't looked into, because we already knew you had been dating her. But..."

She waggled her phone in the air between them.

"I had forensics go through the evidence again, make sure your prints weren't on anything they were holding. Just to be sure. Routine." She nodded.

Steve's nostrils flared. The muscles in his neck tensed, but he remained silent.

"They didn't find your prints, but they did find an evidence bag with your name on it." She spoke to Scott. "It was a crazy day. Crime scenes can be a little chaotic, witnesses to question, taking in the whole scene, right? But I don't remember seeing him, do you, Scott?"

"Naw, I don't recall. But her apartment is outside his district. He wouldn't be there." Scott stared down Steve. "Would you?"

"I—"

"See, another thing that's been tripping me up is we didn't see anyone leave the apartment after the murder. We saw her enter the apartment. We saw her sister enter the apartment. But we never saw anyone else leave that day." Sophie backed up a step. "Here's what I think. And it's a bit farfetched, so stop me if I'm way off. I think you came home with Susan the night before. You were already in the apartment when Sabrina showed up. Then, after Susan kills her twin sister, making it seem like a suicide with some help from a police officer who's worked a few crime scenes, she gets out using the patio door. You stay behind, lock the door so it looks like no one left that way and hide in the apartment."

"Huh. I'm with you so far," Scott said. "That would explain him not showing up on the video feed, leaving."

"You guys are really crazy. Why would she kill her sister? She didn't even talk to her sister," Steve rambled.

Scott nodded to Sophie, let her finish what she started. Go in for the kill.

"No, I think it works. You stayed behind, hid, waited for the crime scene to start being worked, and blended in with the crew. You had your uniform on, you knew procedure, and you bagged and tagged evidence!" She laughed. "That probably wasn't so smart. But I'm guessing someone noticed you, told you to do it, and you couldn't not do it. That would raise suspicion. And then you just walked out while the scene was being worked."

"Why would I help her kill her sister?" he asked with a weak undertone.

"Shouldn't you be asking why we would think you killed your girlfriend?" Sophie asked with a triumphant grin.

Steve shoulders sank; his mouth dropped open. "Fuck."

A loud thump came from the bedrooms. "Stay here with him," Scott ordered, pulling out his weapon, and headed to the bedroom.

He flipped the bedroom door open. Empty bed, closet door wide open, wind billowing through the open curtains. A lamp lay on the floor beside the windows.

"Get back in here!" he commanded. A tall barefoot blond stood outside the window on the narrow fire escape. In pair of sweatpants that hung off her thin frame and an oversized shirt, she clung to the railing. The ladder of the fire escape was on the opposite side. She'd stepped to the right of the window when she should have stepped to the left.

He could grab her easily if she moved for it.

"Get inside, Susan!" He holstered his weapon and reached for her.

"That fucking asshole! Such a stupid prick!" She stamped her bare foot on the metal flooring.

"Inside. Now." He grabbed hold of her hand.

She didn't fight him, though he chalked it up to her having to hold the elastic of the sweatpants to keep them from falling off her hips.

The lovers obviously thought they were completely safe from being caught.

Susan jerked her arm out of his grip once she was inside the bedroom. Her hair was a tangled mess from the wind, her nose red from the chill.

"It wasn't me, you know," she spat at him, charging into the living room. "It was him. He fucking killed my sister." She brushed her hair away from her face. "He made me go along with it, but it was him!"

"You fucking bitch!" Steve turned on her, his face red, the vein in his neck throbbing. "This…woman, is a conniving, manipulative crazy person. She swore to me, if I didn't help her, she'd end my career. She'd claim I raped her."

Sophie put her hand on her weapon. Scott didn't worry she'd act rash. She'd assess before reacting, but with the way the two of them were standing off with each other, precautions were smart.

"He pulled the trigger. He put the gun to my sister's head and shot her," Susan yelled. "I was so scared. So, terrified he'd do the same to me."

"Liar."

Scott waved Susan away, knowing Sophie had her in her sights, and focused on Steve. "She pulled the trigger, then?"

"Yes." He nodded so hard his neck cracked.

"And where were you?" Sophie asked.

"I was in the dining room. I told her to stop, to just scare her sister. Get her to help out with some money. I never told her to kill her." He pointed a finger at Susan.

"Bullshit," Susan spat.

"Who untied her?" Sophie asked.

Steve blinked, like he just woke up. He shook his head. "No. I'm not saying another word until I have an attorney."

"You're going to need one," Sophie agreed. "But you know as well as I do you have a better chance with a deal from the DA if you come out with the whole truth now." Sophie pulled out handcuffs and recited the Miranda rights to both of them.

Scott pulled out his own cuffs and worked Steve's wrists into them.

Steve huffed. "I know how this works. I want to see a real deal in front of me, on paper."

"Of course. I'm sure we'll get the D.A. to put you top priority.

You'll only have to sit in the holding cell a few hours before we get it squared away." Sophie said with a non-caring shrug.

"Or we can put him in an interrogation room, you know, if he's going to be talking." Scott pushed.

Steve pressed his lips together, screwing them up tight and let loose a string of curses.

"I pulled the trigger," Steve said once his arms were bound. "I don't know what about her makes me so fucking crazy. She needed the money. Her sister had this huge inheritance from her adoptive parents but wouldn't give half over to Susan. She needed the money. I couldn't afford to pay her bills anymore. I just needed her sister to help. But I'm not signing anything other than a deal from the D.A. I have more information on Susan they'll want."

"I'd save the rest for the district attorney." Scott grabbed his phone to call in the collar.

CHAPTER 22

"Well, we did it." Sophie lifted her beer in Scott's direction before taking a hard swallow.

"Yeah. What a fucked-up case." Scott dipped a tortilla chip in the salsa and chomped down on it.

A celebratory dinner after pulling a double shift getting all the details from two twisted fucks. Neither took full responsibility, and both blamed the other.

"The D.A. is going to have a hell of a time with them. At least the district attorney will have the evidence backing them up, and since Steve admitted to doing the actual killing, that might help sort it all out," Sophie said.

"I don't know how it's going to play out, but they are both behind bars. And since we have the right ID on the vic, family of hers is going to come out and take care of the burial."

"Good. At least she can rest, now." Sophie took a chip.

"So, what are we doing for our day off tomorrow?" Scott asked, sounding excited to have a full day with her.

She'd be excited, too, but reality was setting in. The case was finished. They worked it together because they were great partners. They'd been lucky so far that their personal fooling around hadn't got in the way. But that didn't mean it wouldn't eventually.

"I was sort of thinking of taking a day to hit the salon. I could use a pedicure and a haircut."

Scott's smile dropped, but he recovered. "Sounds like a good plan. Maybe dinner?"

"I think I'll just make something small, binge-watch old *Friends* episodes. I've gotten behind on my binge-watching since you and I started goofing around."

His eyebrows furrowed. "Yeah, okay. Well, then we'll just play it by ear."

"Right. Casual," she said and sipped at her beer.

"Yeah." He nodded again. "Casual." Except when he said the word, it twisted her stomach into a knot she wasn't sure she'd be able untie.

The main courses arrived, and Sophie choked down half her order of enchiladas. Scott ate in silence, sipping his beer in between bites and glancing at her from time to time.

The mood, apparently, had been killed.

Her phone buzzed on the table. After glancing at the caller, she swiped to ignore.

"My mom. I'll call her tomorrow," Sophie said when Scott looked up at her with concern.

"You haven't mentioned your mom before," he said around a bite of his burrito.

"She never came up." Sophie shrugged, knowing full well there was a hell of a lot more to it than that. If he'd asked her about her family a few days ago, she would have avoided the conversation altogether.

"She live in the area?" he asked.

"No, back home in Chicago. I came out here a few years ago." Taking the plunge, she continued. "Chicago apparently wasn't corrupt enough for me, so I got in my car and drove east."

He chuckled. "Our station is pretty clean, though I've heard of some really shady houses."

"You're right. The captain does run a pretty clean operation here."

More silence stretched between them. Was he afraid she'd run if he continued to probe into her personal side?

Well, who's fault is that?

"How about you? Parents in the area?" She swigged the last of her beer and pushed her plate away. Her stomach couldn't handle food.

"No." he shook his head. "My folks passed a while back. Mom then Dad."

"I'm so sorry." How could she have missed him never mentioning family. Aside from Grayson and Dani, he'd never mentioned anyone else in his life. She'd been so caught up in putting distance between them, she'd completely not seen him.

"Oh, no, it's been a while. Thanks though. I was a bit of a surprise for them. Mom was nearly retired when she had me. I was grateful I had them both for as long as I did."

"Retirement?" Sophie mulled over the concept. If she waited much longer to figure out what she really wanted and who she wanted it with, she may find herself in the same situation.

Although, him smiling at her from across the table didn't put too much of a question mark on the who question.

"Yeah, she was really surprised." He laughed. "Or so the story went."

They fell into an easy conversation. One she would have blocked the moment it started only a week ago. This was her partner, after all. They'd be going into dangerous situations together; they needed each other at all times while working a case.

The fact that if they didn't work out as a couple it would impact their jobs still remained blaringly true. She needed to find a way around that.

"So, I'm having Gray and Dani over for dinner on Sunday."

Scott eased into the topic while he drove her home. She'd eaten too much, drunk too much, and worked too much.

"Oh, will they be dining on your famous salami sandwiches?" she joked.

"No, babe, you're the only one who gets to have my salami," he said while driving and managing to keep a straight face.

She laughed. "Oh my god. No. You can never say that again. That was horrible."

He cracked a smile. "Yeah, it was."

Pulling up outside her apartment building, he shifted into park. "It's true, though. I haven't thought about being with anyone since we started seeing each other."

Neither had she, but her mind already whirled from the day. Between questioning a couple of dirtbags for hours and then dipping her toe into the pool of personal data with him at dinner, she couldn't think clearly.

"Me either," she whispered with her hand already on the door handle. "I'd better get inside before the drinks really kick in."

"Sophie—" He put a hand on her arm. "I didn't mean to spook you, I was just being open about it."

A guy who could express his feelings without having to be cattle prodded, and her chest clamped up.

She'd wanted casual. He'd promised it. Said he wouldn't push, but he was pushing.

"I know. I'm good. Thanks for dinner." She leaned over the console and kissed him. A soft, sweet kiss to his warm lips. Lips she could lean into and kiss until the sun rose.

She needed space.

She needed to think.

She needed him.

Fuck.

He started to say something, maybe to ask her what was going through her mind, but she'd hopped out of the car, shutting the door on his words. Without looking back at him, she jogged up the steps to her building and the stairs to her apartment.

He wanted more.

He deserved more.

It was time to make a decision.

CHAPTER 23

"Okay, explain this again." Gray leaned against Scott's kitchen counter with a beer in his hand. "You're seeing her, she's your submissive, but you're not really seeing her?"

"They're playing it by ear, Gray." Dani breezed through the kitchen, working her magic with the meal. Scott had bought everything needed for the chicken alfredo, but he couldn't put it together like Dani. "Keeping it casual."

"Casual?" Gray asked, cynicism dripping from the word.

"Yeah," Scott answered. "She wanted to keep it light."

"So, what, you're like a tour guide for her? This is what a spanking is, this what a limit means?"

Gray's tendency to put things in blunt terms grated on Scott at the moment. And after not hearing back from Sophie for two days, it didn't take much. They'd agreed to meet for dinner, but after that she'd taken an extra day off and hadn't returned his phone calls.

Obviously, he scared her with his proclamation in the car.

"No, asshole. She just didn't want a firm commitment, you know, like we are able to see other people if we want."

"So, you've gone poly?"

"No." Scott grabbed a beer from the fridge and twisted off the cap.

"You gotta help me out here, man. You don't do casual. I mean, you've gone through women like some women go through shoes, but you've always been a one-sub, one-woman guy."

"She's not seeing anyone else. I'm not seeing anyone else. I'm just giving her the space she needs."

"So, no commitment whatsoever. You're in a dominant submissive relationship that's not just bedroom kink, but she won't come over for dinner if your friends are here, because that would be too intimate?"

"It's not that simple," Scott muttered into his beer bottle.

"Leave it be, Gray. He's working on it. It's obvious he really likes her. Just let him do this his way." Dani poured the alfredo sauce over the noodles.

"This is the dumbest thing I've heard you do. And you've done some stupid shit with women. You've basically let her run wild. If she wants to be your sub, she should be your fucking sub. If she wants to see other people, then you two work out an open relationship, but this back-and-forth crap, and you can't even be honest with her about how you really feel because she might run and hide? No, this is dumb."

Dani put her hands on her hips and glared at him. "Oh, and you and I played it so smart? Exactly how many years did you fist your cock thinking about me before you finally did something about it?"

"We're not talking about us right now," Gray responded, holding a firm tone for his girl, but she'd obviously won the point.

The doorbell rang.

"She's here."

"Sophie?" Dani asked with confusion. "You said she wouldn't come if we were here."

"Well."

"Scott." Dani turned her glare on him. "I told you not to push her."

Scott was already in the living room. "I'm not pushing. I'm nudging." And he yanked the door open.

"Hi." Sophie's smile crept upward. Her body went from tense to soft all with a quick word of greeting.

"Hey." He took her coat and purse, waiting for her to dig her phone out first, then tucked them away in the closet. "Uh, so Dani and Gray are here." Better to give her a heads up than to have her walk in on them and be shocked.

"Oh." Her brows knitted together. "I thought you said your dinner with them was tomorrow."

"It was, but plans changed."

"Oh." She looked toward the kitchen where Dani could be overheard laughing at whatever ridiculous thing Gray said to her.

"It's just friends, Sophie. They won't bite, but I will—if you're good, anyway." He patted her cheek. A little more nudging.

Her eyes focused on the kitchen. Tension built back up in her shoulders.

"No," He grabbed her hand when she fisted it. "You don't need to do that." He pried her fingers open.

"I-uh-need to talk to you. Maybe I should—"

"Sophie! Good. You're here. Now I can open the wine!" Dani hustled from the kitchen over to Sophie and hugged her.

Sophie shot Scott a hard glance as Dani pulled her toward the kitchen. "I hope you like pasta. I made too much."

"I thought Scott was cooking," Sophie commented, sarcasm clinging to her words.

He'd accept the thinly veiled poke at his cooking skills, but only because she hadn't tucked tail and run at the first sight of his friends. Maybe things were warming up. Maybe she just needed that little nudge.

Dani laughed. "Scott cooking means he shopped and picked

out the meal. I do the cooking for this group. Well, unless, you cook?" Dani paused mid pour of the white wine she'd opened.

"Yeah, but only when I have to." Sophie accepted the glass of wine and turned to Gray who watched the interaction with smug appreciation from the corner.

"I'm Gray," he introduced himself with an outreached hand and a warmer smile.

"I figured. You've got that brooding thing showing that Scott told me about. I'm Sophie." She smiled back at him, then sipped her wine. "I wasn't expecting anyone but Scott," she said, running her hand down the long sweater she wore over a pair of brown leggings.

"It's just us," Dani said. "Oh. I forgot the salad."

"I'll help," Sophie offered and put her wine and her phone down on the counter.

"I don't brood," Gray stated once the girls were working on the prep for the salad.

She didn't take off, and now she was helping? Yes, definitely signs his little nudge had been the right thing to do.

"Stop looking so confident over there," Gray said, pulling Scott from his mental high fiving. "This is going to backfire."

"I'm not actually supposed to be taking romantic advice from you, am I?" Scott laughed.

"You can't have a relationship based on such a flimsy foundation, Scott." Gray's toe-the-line tone cut to the heart of it, all right.

"There's no flimsy foundation here."

"Yeah? So that woman was thrilled when she saw us here? She didn't have a moment of pure panic at meeting the family?" Scott understood him just fine. The air quotes he used when referring to family really weren't needed.

"The point is, she stayed," Scott said. "And look, she's helping with the salad." Scott waved his beer at his girl. She stood over the salad bowl, tearing lettuce and chatting with Dani.

"Yeah, way over there. She's been here ten minutes, and has she even spoken to you? Or looked at you?" Gray sipped his beer.

"You're real supportive tonight," Scott shot at him. "She might be a little nervous."

I need to talk to you. There weren't many reasons women used that phrase. Scott swallowed more beer and watched her movements. Stiff, but if she was anxious about the dinner, especially since it was sprung on her, that would be normal.

Gray studied him for a long moment, his forehead wrinkling. "Hey. I don't know her like you do. She's probably just nervous. You're right. It'll be fine. She'll have some of Dani's pasta, we'll share a great dinner, and by the end it'll be like we've known her forever."

The words were right. Given in a more positive spirit, and said in the right order, so why did the weight in Scott's stomach get heavier.

I have to talk to you.

"Right. Yeah." Scott finished off his beer. "Dani, I'm taking the pasta to the table." He grabbed the large bowl overflowing with creamy goodness.

Once all the food was settled, Scott poured the last of the wine into Sophie's glass. She thanked him but still didn't look up at him. His eyes hadn't met hers since she arrived. Maybe she was just upset with him for springing the friend dinner on her. It had been risky, but he'd figured the reward would be worth it.

"I'll get the other bottle," he said and went into the kitchen while Dani told a story about one of her customers' strange tattoo requests.

Scott pulled down the bottle of red from the rack and grabbed the opener from next to the sink. Sophie's phone vibrated beside the bottle while he screwed into the cork. He glanced down at it briefly then worked the cork out of the bottle with a pop.

Again, her phone danced, and the screen lit up. She didn't have a passcode on her phone? He should remind her to put one on. Anyone could get into her personal information without it.

Another message game through, and the bubbles all popped up on the screen.

Mom: Hey, hon. Sorry I missed your call.

Mom: Congrats on the transfer! So happy! Can't wait to see you!

Scott dropped the corkscrew onto the counter and stared down at the phone, rereading the bubbles, sure he'd missed something. Transfer? The screen faded back to black, but he kept staring at it, willing the words to change. Willing the message to mean something other than her leaving.

She was transferring to Chicago?

I need to talk to you.

She hadn't gotten mad about his friends being there because she had no intentions of keeping their relationship going anyway. She probably had her bags packed and ready to go already, and just stopped by to tell him goodbye.

He should be grateful she gave him at least that pinch of respect. She could have simply left town and let him hear the news from the captain.

Transfers didn't just happen. This wasn't a quick call and decision. She had to have put in for it before they'd started seeing each other. She knew they had a time stamp, knew she'd be leaving, and she didn't think to mention it.

Well, of course not. They were casual. Just fuck buddies. She got a taste of the kink life, and he got a play partner for a little while.

He shoved both hands into his hair and blew out a long breath. His heart needed to stop hammering against his chest cavity so he could fucking think. As much as he wanted to yell, no, not yell, scream like a banshee at her, he couldn't. And he wouldn't. No matter how much what she did hurt him, he wouldn't retaliate.

It wasn't his style.

Pacing the kitchen to get a grip was exactly his style.

"You coming back sometime soon? I'm outnumbered here," Gray called from the dining room.

Scott glared down at the silent cell phone. Stuffing his anger down as far as he could, he snatched the bottle and went back to dinner.

"Scott still needs to come by so we can work on his next tat." Dani said while he poured her a glass of wine. He put the bottle down, probably harder than he should have, earning a quick glance from Dani and Gray. Sophie, he noticed, continued to stare at her plate.

"Another one?" Sophie lifted her chin but didn't quite meet his gaze.

"My forearm needs some ink." He tapped the blank spot on his arm and took his seat.

How could she sit and chat like nothing was happening? Like she wasn't gearing up to rip out his heart and walk away. But she probably didn't see that. He hadn't professed his love for her. Hell he didn't know if that's what was forming in his chest for her, but he'd been damn clear on his feelings. He'd been so fucking transparent with her, probably too fucking much.

"Ah." She grabbed her glass and took a sip. That's it? That was her entire fucking reaction?

"How about you, Sophie? Got any tattoos or piercings?" Dani asked while giving Scott a curious look.

"No, nothing permanent on her," Scott answered for her and took a heaping spoonful of pasta. She probably couldn't handle so much as a wash-off tattoo, much less permanent ink.

"Scott." There was a warning in Gray's voice. But Scott already had been dragged to the edge of his patience. She'd either been hiding the transfer desire from him from the start, or she was running scared and not telling him about it. Either way, she'd completely duped him.

He should have seen it coming.

Nudging. He'd boasted to Dani he was simply nudging Sophie into taking their relationship out of the casual category. When in fact, she'd already hightailed straight into the see-ya-later genre.

"Shit." Dani jumped in her seat and pulled out her phone. "The store."

"What's wrong?" Gray asked, leaning over to see the screen.

"The stupid alarm's going off again. I asked the company to work on that." Her thumbs tapped away on her phone. "I can shut it off from here, but I should go down there real quick to make sure it's just another false alarm."

Gray was already out of his chair before Dani flashed a disappointed smile across the table.

"I'll take you."

"You don't have to. I've dealt with this before. It's just a false alarm." Dani walked behind him toward the front closet. Scott met them at the door. He could feel Sophie behind him. Tension was easy to feel when it was so fucking thick.

"You've gone down there before when the alarm went off? Did the police show?" Gray asked, holding her jacket out for her.

Dani rolled her eyes while she faced Scott. "The police showed up after I got there. It was a false alarm," she reminded him while working the buttons of her jacket.

"We'll talk about that when we get back to your apartment. I told you I don't want you going down to the shop at night without me." Gray pulled his keys from his jacket pocket.

"You realize I had a whole life before you became my dom, right? I can handle—" Gray's deadpan stare seemed to be enough to silence her. "Fine. We'll talk about it later."

"Sorry to cook and run, but—"

"It's fine, go. I hope everything's okay," Sophie said with a genuine smile. At least she made it look realistic. Inside, she probably counted the seconds until they left.

"Yeah, we'll do this some other time." Scott opened the front door. Dani rose on tiptoe to press a kiss to his cheek.

"Whatever your problem is, knock it off. Don't blow this," she whispered in his ear then gave one final wave to Sophie before heading into the hall.

Gray said his goodbyes to Sophie and gave Scott a curt nod before departing after his girlfriend.

"So, seems like it's us and enough pasta to feed the entire department." Sophie smiled at him.

"Guess so," he said and stalked past her.

She followed him to the dining room and started cleaning up the dishes with him. They hadn't even eaten, but he had no appetite.

"So, I'm kinda glad—"

"What happened to your cat?" he asked, dropping a plate into the sink.

Her eyes widened in surprise, and the crease in her brow deepened. "My what?"

"Your cat. You said you had Travis feed your cat when you went to visit your mom. But I didn't see a cat at your apartment, no litterbox or anything. So, what happened?" He leaned his hip against the sink.

"My new apartment didn't allow pets. A woman in dispatch took him." She placed the plates she was holding gently on the counter. Her voice took on calm. "What does that have to do with anything? Why are you acting so mad?"

"Why don't you check your phone," he suggested and walked out of the kitchen to get the rest of dishes off the table.

CHAPTER 24

The evening derailed. Sometime between arrival and sitting down with surprise company, an event occurred to ruin Scott's mood.

When he told her to check her phone, she didn't understand at first. What would her phone tell her?

She realized she'd left it on the counter earlier in the kitchen. Swiping it to life she found several text messages from her mother. Congratulating her on her transfer.

It wasn't a transfer, but her mother never really understood the way government worked.

He must have seen the texts. And jumped right to the wrong conclusion. He had no idea what the text meant. It didn't really matter, though. She'd need to come clean.

"Scott." She followed him in the dining room. He'd grabbed the bowl of pasta— perfectly prepared—and cradled it in his arms.

"Were you going to tell me?" He gripped the bowl harder, like it was the thing keeping him upright.

"You looked at my phone." She couldn't help the accusatory tone. He had looked at her personal phone. She had reason to be annoyed by that. She didn't go digging around his phone, or his drawers, or his stuff. Hell, she'd only been in his bedroom once!

"It went off while I was opening the bottle of wine," he exclaimed. "You're transferring." His face hardened, the usual softness and gentle dominance she loved watching nowhere to be seen. Instead, he blanked on her. His jaw set tight, his eyes almost unreadable. Aside from the white of his fingertips as he held onto the damn bowl of pasta, she might not have known how angry he really was.

"It's not like that." How could she even begin to explain it all? So much time had gone past. She'd almost given up on anything coming of it.

"What's it like then?"

"It's not a transfer. Mom didn't understand." She would have laughed at her mom's mistake. It wasn't like Sophie hadn't explained it to her five times already.

"Then, what is it?"

Her dream, the goal she'd been striving for since she understood right from wrong was there for the taking. How could she think of turning it down, even for someone like Scott? Maybe she didn't need to, but it depended on him. Everything, her next decision, her next thought depended on how he would react to what she said next.

It wasn't fair to put that much pressure on someone's response, but it didn't change anything.

"What, Sophie? What is it? Did things get less casual and too serious? Too much for you, so you put in for a transfer?" The heaviness of his anger smacked at her. She'd rather he yelled. Why wasn't he yelling. The low, controlled voice sent a shiver through her.

"No. If you aren't going to listen to me, then I can't explain it."

"Explain what? What can you possible explain?" He shook his head. "Never mind." He walked around her to the kitchen. She didn't move. She couldn't. This Scott didn't want to hear her, didn't want to listen.

"Scott."

"So, when's this start, this new job? You moving out to Chicago right away?" He popped back up in the doorway.

"Chicago?"

"Yeah."

He really had everything so wrong.

"I'm not moving to Chicago. Mom's coming for a visit; that's why she said she'd see me soon." She took a breath. Everything moved too quickly. His anger over the huge misunderstanding gave her a pretty good estimate on how he'd react when she told him the full truth.

"Just get it over with. Just tell me and then you can go home." He crossed his arms over his chest; the tattoos on his arm peeked out from his shirt. There was a spot that would be perfect for new ink, but from the look he gave her, she wasn't sure she'd get to see it.

Her stomach twisted at the idea. This could be the last time they spoke. She'd spent so much time preparing to be alone, not letting him or anyone get too close, she'd forgotten to prepare for how much it would hurt when it came time.

"I've been accepted into the FBI academy. I've been waiting to hear back about my application. It's taken so long, I thought it wasn't going to happen." A moment that should have been filled with excitement and pride shriveled beneath his open stare. Any reaction would have been better than the nothingness.

"It takes months to get through the application process. Testing and background checks, interviews, you never mentioned it." The calm of his tone unsettled her. He took a soft step toward her, moving sleekly, his eyes narrowing in on her as though she were his prey.

A day ago, she'd have found his predatory movements more than just a little arousing. Her panties would be soaked.

But now. Staring back at his unbridled anger, her insides shook with worry over his next reaction.

"I didn't know if I'd get in. I passed the fitness test, but barely. My run isn't the greatest. There was a good chance I wouldn't make it." She rambled. It's what she did when faced with the hard truth, and the truth of the situation was, she'd hidden it from him.

"And you didn't think to tell me this when we started seeing each other?" With another step, he closed off any space between them.

"I—"

"You know, this sort of makes sense." He straightened his spine. "You had a bad experience with dating a cop at your last precinct, so why try again with me? That's been sort of rolling around the back of my head, but I get it now. You weren't planning to stick around, so no skin off your nose, right? Just so long as no one found out we were together, that way if the Bureau starting really snooping around, they wouldn't find you fucking your partner."

Her breath whooshed from her lungs. "No. That's not it at all, Scott."

"Which is why you made sure no one at the station knew anything was going on between us." He jabbed a finger in her direction.

"No. I was honest about wanting to keep things casual."

"Because you had one foot out the fucking door already," he accused.

She blinked, feeling the droplets of her tears roll down her cheeks.

"No. I mean, yeah, I wasn't looking to get serious because I might be going, but I wasn't trying trick you. I was honest." She took a deep, shaky breath. Her fingers fidgeted at her sides. "I came over tonight to tell you, to talk with you about it, but your friends were here. You were the one doing the scheming. Not me." Her temper overrode the hurt.

"Oh, you're right." He walked to the hall closet and jerked the door open. "I'm a lying scheming bastard because I wanted something more. Because I was trying to build something between us. Because I wanted more than just a fuck buddy." Snatching her coat and purse, he thrust them at her. "You don't have to hide anymore, or run away, or transfer out of the station house."

It couldn't end this way. Not like this. Not with so much anger. Not when he didn't have the whole story. Why couldn't he listen to her?

Because he'd put himself out there. He'd been completely honest about his feelings every step of the way, and she'd just trampled over all of it.

"Scott, listen to me. Please. I didn't—"

"You know, I think I've listened to enough. Congratulations on the new job. You'll kick ass at the academy." Grabbing the handle, he yanked the front door open.

She stared at the exit. Just beyond was an open hallway. And beyond that an elevator. And beyond that, outside.

"I wasn't using you," she said in a soft breath.

"No? Well, it does seem that way, doesn't it? I know I didn't get to everything on your list, but I'm sure the guy you pick up at the club next time you're there can take it from here."

Her chest twisted. No air could get into her lungs. Tears flowed silently.

Gazing up at him would be a mistake, but she'd made so many so far. His eyes remained closed off from her. She couldn't get past the wall he'd put up, to see the real him. Hurt. She could feel that from him, but if he would give her a minute, give her a chance, she could explain.

Words wouldn't come, though. Only the crippling pain shooting through her chest. Maybe hearts really did break. Maybe it wasn't just a saying.

She slid her arms into her coat and slung her purse over her shoulder. The whole while she kept her gaze averted from him.

No point in trying to walk through a wall. She stepped out into the hall. The loud bang of the door as it closed behind her, followed by the metallic click of the lock sliding into place nearly deafened her.

That was it?

Just like that?

She'd lost him?

She'd lost him.

CHAPTER 25

"So, you just left it like that?" Gray narrowed his gaze from across the dinner table. "Really?"

"What was I supposed to do? She was leaving —had been leaving since the moment I met her. I wasn't going to beg." Scott leaned back, pushing the cushions of Dani's couch out of his way. He'd been sleeping like crap for the past week. Since he'd seen her last.

"Nothing at work? Not even hello?" Gray pushed.

"Nope. She took the week off. Guess she's leaving for the academy soon, so the department gave her leave to get her shit in order." Scott crossed his foot over his leg then readjusted the positioning. "This couch is shit," he grumbled, getting up and moving to the armchair.

"We could have had this over at my apartment, but Dani is being a little stubborn about it," Gray said, raising his voice. Dani's head popped into view from the kitchen, and she blew him a kiss.

"Well, having dinner at my place didn't exactly work out, so, better to keep to tradition, I guess." Scott lifted his leg, putting his foot on the secondhand coffee table's edge. "What time does the game start?" he asked, reaching for the remote.

Gray snatched it and plopped back down on the couch, staring at him with a dark expression.

"You really haven't talked to her? Text? Called? Emailed?" Gray asked again.

"I already said no. Stop digging. You know Dani may be right about you being a wee bit on the overprotective side."

"I'm protective of her. Of you, I'm wondering what the fuck got in your head to destroy her like that and just let her leave. You said she was your submissive. You don't just let her go like that. You check in on her. You make sure she's okay."

"You said yourself it was a dumb move, taking on a submissive who needed everything to be hush hush. I mean, she gave me a fucking list of things she wanted me to do, Gray. Does that even remotely sound like a sub?" Scott snagged his beer from the end table and nursed it. Other than diving into work during the week, the liquid Band-Aid was all that kept him in one piece.

Gray blinked. "I can't believe you're this stupid."

"Hey—"

"That sounds like a submissive who's brand new to the lifestyle. Did she know anything about kink before she stepped into Black Light?" Gray demanded, his tone hard. Why did Scott suddenly feel like he was under interrogation?

"Well, no, not exactly."

"So, you took on a newbie, who you worked with but didn't know too much about, and then you're gonna sit here and tell me she's the only one who fucked up? Did she know how serious you wanted things to get?"

"I didn't hide how I felt. I told her."

Gray leaned over and jammed his finger on the coffee table. "Did you tell her you didn't want casual? Were you completely open about that? Or did you go along with her casual condition because you figured you could change her mind?"

Scott lurched forward in his seat, dropping his feet to the

floor, ready to combat his best friend over his accusations. Finger poised and ready, he opened his mouth.

But nothing came.

"Fuck," he burst out, jumping from his seat.

"Did it occur to you that maybe she was hiding the FBI thing because she really thought she might not get in? That maybe she didn't want to face any sort of embarrassment over wanting something she couldn't have. Just like she had to with Travis?"

"Where was this wisdom last week when you were filling my head with all your negative comments about her?" Scott shot at him, throwing his head back and covering his eyes. He'd been wallowing so damn hard all week, he hadn't cleared away his anger long enough to see the full picture.

He'd leapt to conclusions and run with them instead of talking to her about them. Exactly the wrong thing to do.

"I just wanted you to slow down. Not push her if she wasn't ready. You went all melodramatic on your own," Gray pointed out, leaning back in his seat and resting his foot on his knee.

"Okay, well, I was listening to you two prattle on in here and completely burnt the steaks. Like fucking rubber." Dani paraded into the living room, her hair tied up in two large knots on her head, and her stomach tattoo flashing as her crop top shifted as she walked. "I ordered pizza." She shrugged and sat on the arm of the couch.

"Pizza's fine," Scott muttered, still contemplating his own stupidity.

"Scott." Dani's soft voice pulled him from the solitary torment of his mind. "Did she leave yet? Maybe there's still time."

"For what? To tell her I'm an idiot and drive her to the train station?"

"No. To tell her how you really feel and apologize for not listening. To tell her you want to listen now." Dani leaned over and patted his knee. "An apologetic dom is a sexy dom."

Scott opened one eye to peer at her. She smiled softly.

"Although, I'm not sure what Dani said is completely accurate, apologizing when you've been a dick is at the very least the right thing to do," Gray added.

Scott blew out a long, delayed breath and didn't stop until his lungs burned. Grabbing his phone from his pocket, he dialed Sophie's number.

Not needing an audience, he left his friends on the couch and headed into the kitchen, where the burnt steaks sat on the cooling frying pan. Worse than rubber.

A single ring then voice mail. Fuck. Either she'd refused his call or had him blocked.

He tried to remember when Peterson said she was leaving for the academy but nothing came to him. Drowning in your own pity makes it hard to hear things around you.

"I'm going over there," Scott announced, shoving his phone back into his pocket and pulling his jacket from the hook near the door. He didn't wait for their well wishes or suggestions, just took off down the stairs of Dani's apartment building.

Speed limits were pretty much optional for him on the drive across town. Yellow lights encouraged him to hit the gas. He tried three more times to get through to her phone, hoping she was just declining and hadn't really blocked him.

They'd had a fight. Couples fought.

That's what he'd start with.

Then beg.

He'd beg if he needed to.

But he wouldn't spend another night without her.

He found a spot two houses down from her building and threw the car into park before the car had a chance to actually park. Taking the stairs two at a time, he flew up them, ignoring the option of using the elevator because he didn't have time to wait for that rickety thing.

Finally, he stood at her door.

Bracing himself on the doorframe, he took a moment to catch

his breath and listen for signs of life behind the door. The television played. He heard the faint sounds of staged laughter. A comedy. She was home.

He knocked on the door, softly at first, then with a bit more vigor.

The television still played, but the sound of feet shuffling didn't add to it.

He knocked again, harder.

Nothing.

Making a fist, he banged on the door.

The television stopped. Feet shuffled along the carpeting and locks turned on the other side of the door.

Realizing he was still holding himself up by the doorframe, he pushed off and stood fully erect. Smoothing out his jacket and swallowing back the fear of utter rejection, he waited until the door opened.

"Hi, can I help you?" A woman, either in or near her fifties, smiled at him. Wearing a well-worn flannel shirt and jeans, she pushed her glasses up her nose while watching him.

"Uh, hi. I was uh, looking for Sophie," he said, hope quickly draining from his heart.

"Oh. You must be Scott." The sweet brown eyes that greeted him moments before hardened. "She's not here."

"You're her mom," Scott blurted. She had the same facial features. He should have recognized her right away. "Right? She said you were coming to visit. I just need to talk with her. Can you tell her I stopped by? Or could I wait? Will she be gone long?" He sounded like a besotted sick puppy, but he didn't give a flying fuck.

Sophie's mother stared at him for an agonizing moment, studying him. The harshness in her features faded back to the welcoming woman she'd been at the beginning.

"I'll tell her you were here, but she'll be gone for five months. She left this morning for the training academy."

He wanted the support of the door frame again. She'd left.

"Oh." He cleared his throat. "Well, yeah, please let her know when you speak with her that I stopped by. If she has time, maybe she can give me a call." He slid his hands into the pockets of his jacket.

"I will." She nodded. "I promise." She gave him a weak smile then softly shut the door.

It was the loudest sound he'd ever heard.

Had Sophie heard that when he'd shut the door on her?

Blowing out the air from his lungs again, he shuffled to the elevator.

She'd left.

He had been too late.

CHAPTER 26

*D*amn the heat.

Sophie wound her hair into a bun and snaked the ponytail holder around the mess of thick curls. She needed a haircut. And a wax. Definitely needed a wax.

Looking at herself in the mirror in the public restroom of Black Light, she sighed. Twenty weeks of training should have been long enough to forget the impossible.

Yet, as she stared at herself in the mirror, her cheeks tinged pink from the July heat outside and her hair frizzed from the humidity, she couldn't stop her mind from wandering to the past.

But going over the list of could'ves, would'ves, and should'ves didn't take away the simmering pain. Five months had gone by. She wouldn't say they flew, but all the classes and drills kept her going at a pace that let her at least keep him on the outskirts of her thoughts.

But at night? When all was quiet and her mind had nowhere else to hide, it went straight to him.

Scott.

She didn't blame him for his initial reaction. She'd been holding back a secret, and you can't form a foundation of trust like that. Her knee-jerk response made it worse. Blocking him from her phone, getting the captain to let her take leave until she left for training, all had everything to do with avoiding him.

She'd been a coward, and by the time she stepped on campus in Quantico, Virginia, she'd put enough space between them both in geography and spiritual terms, it was too late. Maybe they could have worked things out so she could go home on the weekends to see him. If she hadn't ruined everything so nicely.

She needed to let him go. Let the whole crazy idea of having a relationship with a dominant man free. Because it wouldn't happen for a girl like her. She had too many control issues, too many trust issues. She was a fucking wreck. Who would want her anyway?

So why the hell was she standing in the bathroom at Black Light, tucking the stupid fucking curl back into her messy bun and rechecking her outfit?

Because she hadn't been able to stop thinking about how much calmer she felt after he spanked her. Because every time she dug her nails into her palm, she wished it was his belt across her ass, or his teeth pressing into her neck.

Finally disgusted enough with her self-pity, she flung the door open and went back out to the club. Music played in the background, but the play scenes happening all around her drowned out the melody. The only beats she focused on were those of a flogger striking, a moan floating through the air. A loud grunt and a scream—orgasmic in nature.

Fuck. She'd spent too long using her own damn fingers to get herself off. Her body required more, and hearing all the temptations around her woke the desires she'd been shoving down. Her stomach growled at the smell of food being served at the bar. The sight of a glass of wine being passed to a customer made her mouth water. Wine would be amazing right now. Her nerves were frazzled, and the edge needed to be trimmed off.

But wine on an empty stomach would only make the

problems worse. She'd just wait a little while longer before she indulged in some pretzels then she might be able to handle a glass.

Making that decision, she redirected her feet to bring her the edge of the play area. It had been a stupid move coming to the club. Most people came in pairs or threes, not singles. Even if a guy went stag, there was probably a good reason. Or he just wanted a quick hook-up.

Which might work in her favor. Not to fuck. She didn't think she could handle that yet. Even after months of not feeling a man's touch, she wasn't ready. Not with someone else.

But a spanking. She'd kill for one of those. Something to get the electricity firing in her brain again. Wake her up out of her post almost-had-a-relationship-with-a-fucking-amazing-man haze.

She leaned over the railing of the lounge area, watching a particularly heavy scene. The woman, a thin petite blond, bent over the spanking bench, her ankles and wrists bound to the device. Her ass already bore deep-red marks Sophie could see from where she stood dozens of feet away. Though maybe the lighting made them look more menacing then they were. A man dressed in tight-fitting black leather pants and a matching vest, moved from the woman's right side to her left, admiring his work, holding a thin cane in his hand while he talked to her.

What was he saying to her? Was he comforting her, praising her, lecturing her? If Sophie had more nerve, she'd move closer. Five months of FBI training may have readied her for the field, but it hadn't done much to get her to relax about this club on her own.

Being so engrossed in her voyeuristic activities must have lit a sign over her head signaling her availability, because a man slid up beside her at the railing. He gave her a dark grin.

"What's a beauty doing standing over here just watching the show instead of starring in it?" he drawled. She huffed a laugh before she could stop herself. It was cheesy, but at least he showed interest.

Clearing her throat in a cheesy attempt to hide her own rudeness, she looked up at him through her lashes. Examined his features. Powder-blue eyes, soft and comforting. Trustworthy, at least to the point she was sure he wouldn't gut her right on the dungeon floor. There were enough dungeon monitors walking around to fill in any insecurity she might have. And Black Light wouldn't let anyone past their doors who they had any suspicions was dangerous.

"Just watching the play," she answered coolly. She wouldn't bother trying to flirt. She'd just end up making a fool of herself. It had been so easy with Scott, she didn't need to do any of that crap. He knew her for who she was and liked her for it. Like, really liked her.

And she'd fucking blown it.

So, back to blue eyes.

"Mind if I join you?" he asked. Seeing as he'd already done so, she nodded. "I'm Jason," he said giving her a winning smile and turning his attention back to the play.

"Sophie," she said, following his lead and keeping her eyes focused on the scene wrapping up.

"So," he laughed, dragging his hands through the small curls of his short blond hair. "I'm no good at small talk. I'm looking for a play partner for the night. Just play, no fucking, nothing too heavy. Would you be interested?"

Way to put all the cards out on the table.

She swallowed back the rising fear and nodded.

He laughed again. "Sorry, I'm gonna need a verbal answer."

"So, you're a dom?" she asked.

"No, more of a top. I don't take things outside the bedroom, like I said, just a play partner."

Some of her trepidation slipped away. The pressure eased off. Just play. She could handle that, first time out of the gate on her own. It's what she'd come for on Valentine's Day, and now she could finish what she'd started that night.

A play partner.

"I'm not all that experienced. Would just a spanking be okay?" she asked.

The corner of his mouth quirked up. "Yeah, sounds pretty good to me. The spanking bench over there is open. Why don't we grab it?"

She followed him out of the lounge area toward the open play space. Each step was taken on shaky legs. She hadn't been this nervous when Scott played with her. Not even when he'd disciplined her. She'd been a bit hesitant, but each step hadn't felt like the exact wrong thing to do.

"Do you like pain?" he asked when they reached the station. He'd brought a bag with him, and he put it on the table.

"Uhm, a little?" Her stomach rolled.

"Hmm, well, I can use a paddle if you're okay with a that, unless you want me to use a flogger or my belt?"

He was asking her? She could just direct the whole scene if she wanted. Tell him to use the belt, no, not the belt, not unless it was Scott's belt. Paddle. She could tell him to use the paddle, go slow, not too hard, not too low.

Another sour drop in her stomach.

"Uh, I guess paddle." She said with a forced grin. "Do you want me to take my skirt off?" she asked, toying with the hem. She'd worn the flirty skirt only to avoid having to wear pants in the humid air. Leggings would stick to her, and jeans would just be uncomfortable. And she didn't bring extra clothes this time around. It was just her.

"No, leave it like that, I'll flip it up after I start. Panties under?" he asked with a raised brow.

Were they negotiating a used car sale? God. It had been so much easier with Scott. So much sexier. He'd taken control but never made her feel powerless.

Jason, even though he seemed to be giving her all the power here, wasn't giving her the same comfortable mindset. She was in charge of what he would do to her. She had all the say, and it made her head swim. She'd said paddle, but maybe she should have gone with his hand.

"Yeah, I'm wearing panties." She stepped over to the bench, lifting one knee to the first cushion. People milled around the areas. No one seemed to be watching them, but she could feel eyes on her. Burning her.

She narrowed her gaze and looked again. The lighting over the station made it harder to see the crowd of onlookers. Shaking her head, she lifted her second knee and placed her hands on the thick leather of the bench.

Of course, no one was watching. She was just nervous.

Leaning forward, she pressed her breasts against the cool leather and felt around the sides for the hand grips.

It would be over soon. She'd get her spanking. Her mind would finally settle, and she could get her head on straight.

Jason walked over to her, pressing his hand flat on her back. It felt hot and wet. Were his palms sweating?

Shaking off the thoughts, she closed her eyes to get ready for the first blow. The sooner he started, the sooner he could finish.

His other hand touched her bottom, rubbing her in large circles.

This was wrong.

Her eyes flew open, and she pushed up from the bench, once again kneeling. Jason took a step back with surprise.

"I can't." She shook her head and her hands and stepped off the bench.

He huffed. "What's wrong?"

She smoothed down her skirt that had gotten twisted in her movements. "Nothing. Everything. I don't know. I'm sorry, Jason. It's literally not you." She was babbling again.

Dammit.

220

His shoulders dropped, and his eyes darkened. "Yeah. Fine. Okay." He stalked back to his bag and threw the small leather paddle back inside, jerking the zipper to close it.

"I'm really sorry."

He swung the bag over his shoulder. "It's fine. I don't want to play with anyone who's unsure. It wouldn't be fun for either of us."

She watched him walk away. Although a little put out, he didn't seem mad. Or hurt. She wouldn't want to hurt him.

"You have to clean the bench." a deep voice, a familiar voice said from behind her. "So others can use it."

Her stomach went right back into a square knot. Scott slowly came into view.

Thankfully, he was standing alone. She'd half expected to see some doll hanging off his arm. Her relief quickly changed into panic at seeing his handsome face again. He wore a tight black V-neck T-shirt and jeans. He'd bulked up even more since the last time she'd seen him. Which explained the tight shirt; he probably hadn't bought new clothes to fit better once his muscles started to grow.

Great, now she rambled in her head, too.

"Scott. Hi." She finally remembered to breathe.

His jaw tensed, but his eyes, those warm, revealing eyes softened. "Sophie."

"Did. Did you want the bench? We didn't really use it, but I'll wipe it down," she offered, jerking her thumb at it.

"I know."

"You know what?" she asked. Had she moved? He seemed closer.

"That you didn't really use it. I was waiting to see if you would go through with it." His eyes shifted to the bench then back.

"You were watching me?" She couldn't help the accusation from flying out of her mouth. She hadn't been crazy.

"Not on purpose." He folded his arms over his chest. A new tat covered his forearm, just like he'd talked about. "I mean. I didn't like follow you here."

She laughed. "I didn't think that. It's just… Well, I felt someone watching, but I couldn't see with these lights."

"You graduated?" He pressed ahead with no delay.

She nodded. "Yeah. A few weeks ago. I start at the D.C. office next week." She rolled her shoulders back. She'd busted her ass at the academy. She deserved the pride coursing through her at completing the training.

He stepped closer still. "I'm proud of you, Sophie." He surprised her by saying, "You did good."

"Then why do I feel like such shit right now?" she blurted, her shoulders caving in again.

His fingers ran over her jaw. She could smell the musk of his aftershave, feel the roughness of his skin against hers. To lean into his touch would take away so much of the ache in her heart, her soul. But she remained still.

"Because you've been gone for five months, and we didn't leave things exactly the way we should have." His voice came at her low, controlled.

"I-I overreacted. I shouldn't have blocked you. I should have called you when my mom told me you stopped by."

He moved his hand farther up her jaw, cupping her cheek.

"So, she did tell you. I thought maybe she wouldn't. She looked a little pissed when she realized who I was."

"I may have twisted the story of our fight a little." She turned into his touch, feeling the warmth of his palm against her cheek.

"Fight? Is that all it was? You hid some pretty big things from me, Sophie. And I acted like a complete asshole about it. But I wasn't completely truthful, either. I never wanted casual. Not with you." His thumb rubbed her cheekbone. "I wanted everything, and I figured if I took it slow, you'd come to want the same thing."

"I—"

His hand dropped away from her. "Why did you stop just now? With him? What made you call it off?"

She wrinkled her brow. *Who? Oh! Jason.*

Heat crept up her cheeks.

"I didn't bring my toy bag with me tonight, so I can't get answers out of you the way I did before. So, you'll just have to tell me." He took a small step back, showing her he wouldn't touch her again.

She let out a breath. "In short, he wasn't you."

The corner of his mouth kicked up. "Go on."

"He wanted me to tell him what I wanted. What implement, how hard. You never let me decide those things."

"Sure, I did." He edged closer. "I let you decide to trust me to lead or not. I let you decide to submit or not to. You just always made the right decision." His lips pulled up in a full grin. "Didn't you give him your list?"

"Oh!" She covered her cheeks with her hands. "That fucking list. I made such an ass of myself with that."

He shook his head. "No. You didn't. You just didn't know better. And it's good to have a list of limits for when you meet someone."

When you meet someone.

Her heart sank, and the little embarrassment she felt about her damn list blew up into mortification. She'd thought he'd approached her because he wanted to talk things out.

But, why would he? She'd been crystal clear she didn't want anything serious. And he'd just confessed to not wanting anything casual.

So, she stood there in front of him. Once again with the choice. All in or nothing. But did it have to be all or nothing?

"Scott," she started when he shifted his stance. "I—have you been with anyone else while I was gone?" she blurted.

He shook his head. "No. You?"

She laughed. "Yeah, after a full day of drills and classes, I found time to—" She caught the darkening of his eyes. "No."

"Why do you ask?"

"Because." She closed her eyes. "Because I was an idiot. I should have told you about applying for the FBI academy. I should have told you I was falling for you and casual wasn't on my radar anymore. I should have told you I'm not sure I want any other man touching me." She slowly opened her lids when he said nothing. Maybe he'd walked away to laugh at her without hurting her feelings.

He stared down at her, his lips thin and his eyes focused on her.

"You were falling for me?" he asked softly.

"Why do you think I didn't walk out of your apartment that night when I saw you snuck in a friends dinner? Or why I spent the night with you? I was falling hard and fast, and I couldn't stop myself. And when I got the notice I'd been accepted to the academy I realized how bad it would look. I came over that night to talk to you about it."

He pressed his hand against her mouth.

"Since you were partnered with me, I thought about having you. At first, I figured it wouldn't work, you being vanilla. But then I saw you at the roulette game. After that, it was all I could do not to throw you over my shoulder and claim you as mine. You wanted casual, you wanted slow, and I convinced myself I could do that, but I couldn't. I can't."

She would have melted into her shoes if he hadn't been holding her up.

"We both fucked this up pretty good. You have no idea how much I wanted to charge over here and punch that asshole for even thinking of touching you," he said with heat.

If he didn't kiss her soon, she'd have to kick him.

"Fuck. I missed you." He released her mouth from his hand, only to capture it with his mouth.

It wasn't just a welcome-home kiss. It was a you're-fucking-mine-don't-ever-forget-it kiss. Her toes curled in her shoes. Curled. How could she ever have thought she'd be able to keep anything casual with him?

"I need to clean off the bench," she whispered against his lips when he finally let her loose.

"I'll get someone else to do it. We have to go back to my apartment. The things I want to do to you, shouldn't be done in public." He waved over a DM and asked if he wouldn't mind taking care of the station for them. The young guy looked a little annoyed, but he succumbed to the pout Sophie gave him and relented.

"Do you think you'll give me a spanking?" she asked as they stepped outside into the still-humid night air. It had cooled a degree or so, but still her hair frizzed.

"What do you think?"

"I think we have five months to make up for." She gripped his hand tighter. Needing him, wanting him, and feeling calmer as the seconds ticked by just because he was touching her.

When they got to his car, he spun her around and pressed her against the closed door. Cupping her face with both hands, he kissed her again, leaving her breathless and thoughtless.

"Sophie, this isn't casual anymore. This is full-on relationship stuff. You're mine. My girlfriend, my submissive, my everything. You got it?" His fingers sank into her hair, pulling at the roots.

"Got it." She nodded. "Sir."

His eyes rolled, and he kissed her again. "Enough tempting me, naughty girl." He smacked her hip and opened her door. "Let's get home before I bend you over the bumper of my car."

She laughed, a full bodied, lighthearted sound that spread through her entire body.

Not everything lasted forever. Food spoiled. Flowers died. Relationships wavered.

But for the first time ever, she couldn't see the bad side to this.

Scott didn't fly off to find some new girl to play with. He'd been hurting as much as she had. She'd seen it in his expression when he first walked over to her.

They didn't have to hurt anymore.

They had each other.

And it was more than enough.

It was everything.

THE END

We hope you enjoyed this Black Collar Press Release. You won't have to wait long for our next Black Light installment, *Black Light: Obsession* by new Black Collar Press author, Dani Rene. Look for a release in late August or early September, 2018.

Be one of the first to read this prologue from *Black Light: Obsessed* by Dani Rene:

OBSESSION

əbˈsɛʃ(ə)n/

noun

noun: **obsession**

1. the state of being obsessed with someone or something.

Prologue

Roisin

There's a soft glow from the streetlamp, which bathes the room in silvery light.

The house is silent, filled with heavy breathing and the stale stench of alcohol and sex. Dirty, vile, and putrid. I'm never sure because I stay locked in my bedroom when they have parties.

The two people who are now passed out without a care in the world will soon be left to their own devices. Shoving my clothes into the suitcase, I glance around, taking in the home I've spent the last four years in. But there's nothing more for me here. I waited until I was of legal age before I even thought about running. Any younger and I'd be worse off out there than I ever am in here.

Tomorrow I'll be eighteen and they won't want me here anymore. They'll soon be looking for a younger, more profitable baby.

Nobody wants me.

My parents made it clear when I was born, leaving me on the steps of a church. Talk about a poster child for a cliché'dlife story. Taken in by the pastor and his wife, I grew up Christian, praying and taught to believe in a God that has never been there for me.

Even though they gave me a roof to live under, it was never a home. Each Sunday, I was taken to church, to pray for my sins, and every week, I'd just go out and do them again.

When I turned sixteen, they sent me away. Father Paulson's wife thought I was a devil child, so they put me in the system. No couple wants to adopt a sixteen-year-old, they want a cute baby they can coddle and coo with.

That's when Brady and Dana walked in and saw me. A meal ticket. They weren't parents. Far from it. They didn't give a shit if I was out doing drugs or if I was in my bedroom with one of the boys from school. No, I was only here because the State gave them money to keep me.

All the funds that were meant to go toward my schooling, clothes, and stationery were spent on more alcohol for their friends who visited every weekend. The men who would smirk at me like I was their next meal. I figured I was safe. But that's the first mistake I made.

Sighing, I glance in the mirror as I pull my long red waves into a messy bun. My blue eyes have lost their sparkle. All my life I've spent hiding because of my looks. Floppy jumpers, jeans, and trainers. A tom boy.

Everyone told me I'm pretty. A stunner. I didn't want that. I never did because underneath it all, it's my looks that got me in trouble. It's those big cerulean eyes, the pouty rose-colored lips, and the fair porcelain skin that ensured my life would turn to hell.

Most people would assume it's my adoptive father who did it.

Others would gossip that it was the priest and perhaps that's why I got sent away.

They may have had a part to play in my broken past, but there was so much more to it than that. Until I reached sixteen, I lived in a home that was focused on religion. The man who was a Father to many, took everything from me.

When I went to my second foster home, I knew as soon as I walked into the house, it would not be any better.

School was difficult for me. I didn't have friends. I didn't want any. But it was then when I'd given up hope, that I thought I'd found someone who saw me for who I am. The only boy I had ever trusted. Chad Hollister.

He noticed me. He asked me out.

For a whole year, twelve long, wonderful months, I was happy. He doted on me. Made sure I was smiling from ear to ear every day. I believed he really liked the broken girl he learned I was. I thought that deep down, he wanted to love me.

But life doesn't afford girls like me a chance at love.

I'm broken into so many small pieces of myself that I know I can never be whole again.

When Chad saw me like that, he told me it's okay. He still wanted me. Once again, I trusted someone and got burned in the process. When we walked into prom two nights ago, he had sent photos of me naked on his bed to everyone in our school.

They all saw me for who I really was.

And that's part of the reason I need to leave.

Eighteen and a runaway.

I'm not sure where I'm headed, but it will be better than here. As soon as I step out of my bedroom, the smell hits my nostrils, causing my stomach to roll. Vomit, sweat, and alcohol, mixed with the old cigarette smell that always hangs around the house hit me square in the face.

I pull out my own packet of smokes, tapping a stick out and pressing it between my lips. The silver glint of my adoptivedad's Zippo calls to me. With a smirk, I snatch it up on my way to the exit. To my freedom.

As soon as the front door hits my ass on the way out, I light up my smoke, shoving the expensive item into the back pocket of my jeans, then head toward the bus stop. Since it's after midnight, I'm not expecting any public transport, but I'll wait.

It's not far, and the night is warm, balmy, heavy with the scent of the city. They call it the City of Angels, but it's so far from the truth. Instead, it's filled with devils and broken hearts. Dreams smashed on the sidewalk for all to see.

I won't miss it. My old life will soon be a distant memory.

Upon reaching the road, lights flicker from an oncoming car, the only vehicle out at this time of the night in this part of town. When it nears me, I notice it's a sleek silver Mercedes Benz. One of those fancy ones I know I'll never own.

Perching my ass on the bench, I watch as he slows down, probably thinking I'm some fucking whore. He stops, rolls down his window, and leans over to drag his gaze over me. He looks like he's in his late twenties. Dark hair, big eyes that look blue or silver, I can't tell.

"Where you headed this late, darling?" His mouth tilts into a smirk, ravenous and hungry. That's what they all want when they look at me.

A fuck.

"Anywhere away from here."

He looks me up and down once more, nods, and unlocks his car. "Get in. I'll drive you down to the station where you can get a bus. I'm not leaving LA for a long while, so you'll have to find your own way."

I stare at him for a moment, unsure of trusting a stranger. The last time I did that, it didn't go so well. But, it is the middle of the night and I have no place to go. Dropping my smoke on the concrete below my foot, I stomp it out, twisting my Chucks to kill it, and head toward the car.

"You're no serial killer or anything. Are you?"

He chuckles at my question, shaking his head as he regards me with a small smile. "There's no way I am, darling. Get in, I have to get home to my wife," he tells me, lifting his left hand to show me the thick gold band around his ring finger.

Knowing he's married doesn't change the fact this asshole could do things to me other men have already done. But, somehow, for some inexplicable reason, I get in the car. It's cool inside with the air conditioning blowing wildly from the vents. The leather seat below my ass squeaks as my jeans press against the smooth material.

"What's your name, darling?" he questions, pulling away from the curb.

I don't know why, but I lie. There were many times in my childhood I was whipped for lying, but there's no longer anyone who can hurt me for doing as I please.

"My name's Rosie," I tell him, keeping my attention on the road. I know where I am, where we're going, so if he makes a wrong turn, I'll know. But he keeps his word, taking the road toward the bus station.

"You need to be careful, Rosie. Getting in a stranger's car could get you hurt," he warns, causing my eyes to veer his way. There's a genuine seriousness in his tone. Something I haven't heard in a long while.

"I know. But if I've already been killed inside, what difference does it make?"

My words are ominous, and he doesn't respond. Perhaps he doesn't know how, or he may never have expected me to say something like that. The rest of the drive is in utter silence.

I think about my meagre belongings as I take in his fancy car and I wonder if his kids are spoiled, or even if he has a family. The small laptop in my backpack that I managed to buy off Craigslist and the old mobile phone I got when I was living at the church are the only valuables I have.

"Here we are," stranger announces.

"Thanks," I tell him, meaning it. For the first time in my life I feel grateful for someone who did something for me without wanting something in return. Pushing the car door open, I step out.

"Hey," my savior calls to me, causing me to lean into his car once more. "Look after yourself, Rosie," he tells me.

"I'll try."

~

ABOUT THE AUTHOR

Measha Stone is an international bestselling author of erotic romance. She's had #1 top-selling books in BDSM, and suspense. She lives in the western suburbs of Chicago with her husband and children, who are just as creative and crazy as her. Her vanilla writing has been published in numerous literary magazines, but she's found her passion in erotic romance.

Contact Measha
https://www.meashawrites.com/blog

ALSO BY MEASHA STONE

Windy City Series

Hidden Heart

Secured Heart

Indebted Heart

Liberated Heart

Protecting His Pet

Protecting His Runaway

His Captive Pet

His Captive Kitten

Black Light: Valentine Roulette

Black Light: Roulette Redux

Black Light: Celebrity Roulette by Various Authors

Black Light: Roulette War by Various Authors

Black Light: Roulette Rematch by Various Authors

BEAST

Until You: Novella

GET A FREE BLACK LIGHT BOOK

Enjoy your trip to Black Light? There's a lot more sexy fun to be had. All of the books in the series can be read as standalone stories and can also be enjoyed in any reading order.

Get started with a FREE copy of **Black Light: Rocked** today. Your fun doesn't need to end yet!

BLACK COLLAR PRESS

Black Collar Press is a small publishing house started by authors Livia Grant and Jennifer Bene in late 2016. The purpose was simple - to create a place where the erotic, kinky, and exciting worlds they love to explore could thrive and be joined by other like-minded authors.

If this is something that interests you, please go to the Black Collar Press website and read through the FAQs. If your questions are not answered there, please contact us directly at: blackcollarpress@gmail.com

<small>WHERE TO FIND BLACK COLLAR PRESS:</small>

- Newsletter: http://bit.ly/2JY23Wi
- Website: http://www.blackcollarpress.com/
- Facebook: https://www.facebook.com/ blackcollarpress/
- Twitter: https://twitter.com/BlackCollarPres
- Black Light East and West may be fictitious, but you can now join our very real Facebook Group for Black Light Fans - Black Light Central

BLACK LIGHT SERIES

Did you enjoy your visit to Black Light? Have you read the other books in the series? They can all be enjoyed as standalone books read in any order.

Season One

Infamous Love, A Black Light Prequel by Livia Grant
Black Light: Rocked by Livia Grant
Black Light: Exposed by Jennifer Bene
Black Light: Valentine Roulette by Various Authors
Black Light: Suspended by Maggie Ryan
Black Light: Cuffed by Measha Stone
Black Light: Rescued by Livia Grant

Season Two
Black Light: Roulette Redux by Various Authors
Complicated Love, A Black Light Novel by Livia Grant
Black Light: Suspicion by Measha Stone
Black Light: Obsessed by Dani René
Black Light: Fearless by Maren Smith

Black Light: Possession by LK Shaw

Season Three
Black Light: Celebrity Roulette by Various Authors
Black Light: Purged by Livia Grant
Black Light: Defended by Golden Angel
Black Light: Scandalized by Livia Grant
Black Light: Charmed by Jennifer Bene

Season Four
Black Light: Roulette War by Various Authors
Black Light: Brave by Maren Smith
Black Light: Unbound by Jennifer Bene and Lesley Clark
Black Light: Branded by Kay Elle Parker

Season Five
Black Light: Roulette Rematch by Various Authors
Black Light: Bred by Shane Starrett
Black Light: Wanted by Maren Smith
Black Light: Worthy by Stella Moore
Black Light: Saved by Raisa Greywood

Season Six
Black Light: The Menagerie by Maren Smith
Infamous Trio Boxed Set by Livia Grant
Black Light: Cured by Vivian Murdock (July 2022)
Black Light: Gamble by Livia Grant (Fall 2022)
Black Light: Disciplined by Livia Grant (Fall 2022)
Black Light: Protocol by Shane Starrett (Fall 2022)
And many more planned!

Season Seven
Black Light: Roulette Finale by Various Authors (Coming Feb. 2023)